A Very Merry Manhattan Christmas

Darcie Boleyn has a huge heart and is a real softy. She never fails to cry at books and movies, whether the ending is happy or not. Darcie is in possession of an overactive imagination that often keeps her awake at night. Her childhood dream was to become a Jedi but she hasn't yet found suitable transport to take her to a galaxy far, far away. She also has reservations about how she'd look in a gold bikini, as she rather enjoys red wine, cheese and loves anything with ginger or cherries in it – especially chocolate. Darcie fell in love in New York, got married in the snow, rescues uncoordinated greyhounds and can usually be found reading or typing away on her laptop.

Also by Darcie Boleyn

Love at the Italian Lake
Love at the Northern Lights

Conwenna Cove

Summer at Conwenna Cove
Christmas at Conwenna Cove
Forever at Conwenna Cove

Cornish Hearts

The House at Greenacres
The Cottage at Plum Tree Bay The
Christmas Tea Shop

Cariad Cove Village

Coming Home to Cariad Cove
Starting Over in Cariad Cove

DARCIE BOLEYN

San Diego, California

Canelo US
An imprint of Printers Row Publishing Group
9717 Pacific Heights Blvd, San Diego, CA 92121
www.canelobooksus.com

Printers Row Publishing Group is a division of Readerlink Distribution Services, LLC. Canelo US is a registered trademark of Readerlink Distribution Services, LLC.

First published in the United Kingdom in 2016 by Canelo. This edition originally published in the United Kingdom in 2021 by Canelo.

Published in partnership with Canelo.

Correspondence regarding the content of this book should be sent to Canelo US, Editorial Department, at the above address. Author inquiries should be sent to Canelo, Unit 9, 5th Floor, Cargo Works, 1–2 Hatfields, London SE1 9PG, United Kingdom, www.canelo.co.

Publisher: Peter Norton • Associate Publisher: Ana Parker
Art Director: Charles McStravick
Senior Developmental Editor: April Graham
Editor: Angela Garcia
Production Team: Beno Chan, Julie Greene

Design: Brianna Lewis

Library of Congress Control Number: 2023930447

ISBN: 978-1-6672-0588-5

Printed in India

27 26 25 24 23   1 2 3 4 5

Chapter 1

"Don't make me do this alone! *Please*, Dale... say you'll be my plus one!"

Dale chewed his bottom lip and buried his hands deep in his pockets.

"I don't know, Lucie. I mean, Christmas in New York sounds wonderful and everything, but what about my family? Mum'll go crazy if I tell her I won't be there for the big dinner." He rubbed a large hand over his dark stubble.

"I know what Glenda's like about Christmas, but she has your brothers. Don't you think she could manage without you just this once?"

It was difficult asking Dale to put his mother's feelings to one side – after all, the Treharne Christmases were always a big affair – but the thought of going all the way to New York alone made Lucie's stomach flip. The only time she'd been abroad before was on a family holiday to France when she was ten, and she suspected that if she tried to make it to Manhattan alone, she might miss her flight or take one of those dodgy taxis and end up somewhere she didn't want to be. Besides, she knew Dale had always wanted to visit New York, and this was his chance to go all expenses paid.

"I'll think about it." Dale finished his coffee, then carefully placed the mug in the sink.

"Thank you so much!" Lucie flung her arms around his neck and kissed his stubbly cheek. "I knew I could count on my oldest friend. You're the best, Dale Treharne! Every woman should have a mate like you."

Dale cleared his throat as he gently disentangled himself from her embrace. His cheeks were flushed and he didn't meet her eyes. "I said I'd *think* about it, and I will. But it's not just Mum I need to consider: I'd have to make sure the business is taken care of too." He nodded at the sink. "That tap should be fine now. It just needed a new washer."

"Okay, thanks. The dripping's been keeping me awake, and I couldn't bear another sleepless night." The constant pings of the drops hitting the sink had even permeated her earplugs in the early hours – although she'd been tossing and turning anyway, after receiving Petra's glossy cream wedding invitation. It had been waiting on her doormat when she'd got home from work; a rectangle of card decorated with gold swirls and spidery calligraphy, pregnant with possibilities. She'd known immediately that it was linked to the mysterious text she'd received from Petra just days before.

It seemed that the past two years had seen most of Lucie's old friends get hitched or reproduce, but with many of them well into their thirties, it was hardly surprising. She knew Petra had been desperate for a proposal from Harry for years – in between their splitting up and reconciling several times – and now that he'd finally done it, Petra clearly intended to get the ring on her finger and sharpish.

"Will I see you later?"

"Would I miss the Saturday night pub quiz?" Dale raised his eyebrows.

"Meet you there at seven, then, and don't be late just because you were too nice to refuse a mug of tea from some lonely old lady!" Lucie walked him to the door of her basement flat and watched as he jogged up the stone steps. Even though it was the weekend, he was wearing his green work overalls. Dale ran his own landscape gardening business and he was doing so well that he had a team working for him now, but he still liked to oversee most projects and to give his long-term customers the personal touch. Of course, being an attractive man, he'd had to deal with his fair share of admirers over the years – from bored housewives and househusbands to teenage crushes – but he handled them all with grace and politeness. Lucie knew about them because he told her everything; after all, they were best friends, and had been since nursery school. There'd been a bit of a blip in their friendship when she'd gone off to university, but since her return to Tonbridge, they'd slipped back into their old ways and were closer than ever. There was nothing they didn't discuss, except for that time when they'd temporarily become more than just friends… And that was better left in the past.

Lucie sometimes wondered if their closeness stopped them looking for romantic relationships, but she'd never stop Dale getting involved with someone and had even tried to set him up on a few dates with women from work. She knew that he saw her as a friend and nothing more, so when she'd been out with other men – on a few rather unsuccessful occasions – he'd been happy enough for her. Still, neither had found *the one* yet, and in the meantime, they were content to keep each other company. In fact, although she'd never admitted it to Dale, she couldn't quite picture how it would work when one of them *did* get into a serious relationship, as the thought of not having Dale around as much was one that made something deep inside her ache. So she ignored it, and shut it down whenever it surfaced.

She wandered into her lounge and shivered. After weeks of rain, the November morning was at least crisp and clear, which meant Dale could finish his remaining jobs before winter set in. For Lucie the cold just reminded her that Christmas was coming – and that was never a good thing, as far as she was concerned. Although, at least this year she would hopefully be far away, avoiding all the usual festive routines that turned her cold.

–

Dale was glad he'd been able to fix that tap for Lucie before she'd decided to have a go herself. He shook his head as he pulled away from the kerb, remembering the time she'd tried to fix the toilet cistern. Luckily, he'd got there in time to put it right and stop her whole flat from being flooded. He knew women who were plumbers, electricians and carpenters, and his mother could change the oil on a car better than his father, so he knew it wasn't a female thing; it was more of a Lucie Quigley thing. For as long as he'd known Lucie, she'd been clumsy and plagued by disaster. Her first day at comprehensive school, she'd picked up the wrong rucksack by mistake and hadn't realized until she couldn't find her packed lunch. (Dale had shared his with her.) The first time she sat her driving test, she'd reversed into a parked car. It had taken her two more attempts to pass, and in the meantime, Dale had driven her wherever she'd wanted to go. Then there had been the time she'd slipped on the ice and broken her arm. She hadn't been able to wash her hair in case she got the cast wet, so Dale had done it for her over the sink.

And now...

Now she'd asked him to go to New York with her for Christmas. She was to be a bridesmaid for one of her university friends, Petra Barnsley. It wasn't that Dale didn't like Lucie's university friends, just that they lived in a different world. At sixteen, he'd gone straight from school to work at a local garden centre. A few years later, he set up his own business with his newly acquired knowledge and experience, plus a bank loan. He had lots of friends who'd been through higher education, but the circle that Lucie had become involved with were somehow different. They had the safety net of being born into money, and that gave some of them a confidence bordering on arrogance. Dale literally got his hands dirty every day, and he just felt that Petra and the people she associated with looked down on him. That, in their eyes, he was the equivalent of the hired help. Of course, he knew it could just be down to him being sensitive, but whenever he'd spent time with Lucie's university friends, he just hadn't been comfortable.

However, what Dale felt about Petra and her fiancé Harry Goldsmith was irrelevant now. He knew he'd have to go with Lucie; he just couldn't let her go alone. She'd likely miss her flight, somehow pull down the oxygen mask in the plane, flush her purse down the toilet, or do something else equally disastrous. She was easily distracted, an absolute dreamer at times. She often had her head buried in a book and her flat was bursting with dusty old paperbacks that she refused to get rid of in case she ever wanted to read them again. She read everything she could get her hands on at an amazing rate; the way she lost herself in books was something he really admired about her.

Dale felt that it was his place to look out for her. It had been that way for as long as he could remember, especially after Lucie's mum passed away and Lucie had fractured for a while. She'd come through it, though, throwing herself into her studies and achieving excellent exam results. There was no doubt about it, Lucie was strong. Dale didn't know how he'd have coped if he'd lost his own mum at thirteen, but he also knew that Lucie struggled most with her loss during the festive season. That was another reason why he'd decided to go with her.

He'd be able to ask his second in command, Jade, to keep the business ticking over for a week, so he wasn't really worried about that. He just didn't know how he was going to break the news about Christmas to his mother.

Chapter 2

"There you go… one glass of Shiraz and one bottle of IPA." Phil Coombes, a friend of Lucie and Dale's since their first days at secondary school, placed their drinks on the table.

"Cheers, Coombsey!" Dale said as he took a quick swig.

"Thank you!" Lucie smiled at Phil.

"So are we ready to win tonight or what?" Arianwen asked.

"Of course, my darling," Phil replied.

Lucie gazed at them over her wine glass. Phil had met the redheaded artist Arianwen during the final year of his accountancy degree at Cardiff University. They'd fallen head over heels in love, and Arianwen had moved to Tonbridge to live with him. The bubbly Welsh woman was always good company and never failed to make Lucie giggle. At times she said things Lucie would never dream of saying herself, but she liked Arianwen's openness and down to earth approach to life. Nothing seemed to phase her, and it was refreshing.

"I've been reading up in preparation," Arianwen explained to Lucie, her green eyes mischievous.

"For childbirth?" Lucie asked as she eyed her friend's swollen stomach. She couldn't believe that Arianwen still had a few weeks to go until her due date.

"No! I think I know enough about childbirth already." She tapped her nose. "Like shelling a pea it was last time, so third time round I'll probably sneeze and the baby'll pop out."

"I hope it *is* that easy," Phil said. "We might even be able to have that home birth you want, then, Ari."

"I'm having a home birth, Phil, come hell or high water. There's no way I'm going into hospital for this one. I want my own things around me, my own bathroom at my disposal and my own bed to sleep in afterwards."

"What's sleep?" Phil yawned.

"Something we haven't had in quite some time, I know, but at least we can *lie* in our own bed in between feeds."

Phil nodded. "I'm sure that's why I've lost all my hair." He rubbed a hand over his shiny scalp. "My mother's staying at ours tonight to give us a break. Said we can sleep through and have a lie-in tomorrow."

"He always lets me lie-in at the weekends. He's a sweetheart," Arianwen said to Lucie.

Phil's cheeks coloured at his wife's praise and his hazel eyes sparkled. "Well, you're growing our baby inside you, so you need your rest more than me."

"So what have you been reading in preparation?" Lucie asked.

"Every *Guinness Book of Records* from the past five years. Do you know it has the most amazing facts in it?"

Arianwen sipped her lemonade then shifted in her seat. "I just can't get comfortable at the moment." She rubbed her huge belly and Lucie nodded in understanding, though of course she had no idea what it must be like to be pregnant with her first child, let alone her third. "You know I have veins popping out in places I didn't even know they could."

"Really?" Lucie tried to suppress a shudder, but it was too strong.

"I know. Isn't it terrible? And as for farting!" Arianwen shook her head.

"Romance is long dead in our house; replaced by cankles, flatulence and bizarre midnight cravings."

"And that's just Phil!" Arianwen giggled.

"How are you feeling – apart from the discomfort?" Lucie asked.

"Oh, you know… exhausted, but that's what having a six year old *and* a three year old will do to you. If I'm not building Lego, I'm making healthy organic meals and sauces to conceal vegetables, or working through the mounds of washing that the kids create every day. I still haven't forgiven Phil for getting me pregnant again." She scowled at her husband but when he met her eyes, she smiled.

"You know you always wanted a large family, Ari." Phil winked.

"So I did. Masochist that I am. But I think we'll stop at three."

"Four."

"Three."

"Four?" Phil pouted at his wife.

"You'll have to be extra nice to me."

"I'm always nice to you, darling."

"Get me a bag of salt and vinegar crisps and I'll think about it."

"Your wish is my command!" Phil swept into an exaggerated bow and rushed off to the bar. He was back within minutes, carrying several bags of crisps and a bag of nuts.

"Did Lucie tell you that she's been asked to be a bridesmaid?" Dale asked.

"Have you now?" Arianwen asked. "For whom?"

"Petra Barnsley," Dale replied.

"That's your friend from London, right?" Phil asked. Lucie nodded.

"I love a good wedding," Arianwen said. "I miss getting all dressed up, having my hair and nails done, fitting into nice underwear that doesn't have to be stuffed with postnatal towels or breast pads… enjoying all that cake and champagne. But leaky boobs don't go well with a flimsy party frock, and as for varicose veins—"

"It's in New York," Dale interrupted and Lucie suspected he was keen to stop Arianwen revealing any more gory pregnancy details. "Over Christmas."

"Oooh! Even better!" Arianwen grabbed Lucie's arm. "Nothing like Manhattan at Christmas. Just think about how beautiful it will be with the lights, the parties, the Christmas trees, the snow and…"

Lucie's cheeks twitched awkwardly.

"What is it? Oh…" Arianwen's face fell. "I really am *so* sorry, Lucie. You don't like Christmas at all, do you?"

"I bet it's lovely when you have little people around." Lucie didn't want to put a dampener on things for Arianwen – and besides, it probably *was* different with children. Maybe, when… *if* … she ever had kids, she'd look forward to Christmas again.

"Yes, we'll have three by the time Santa comes," Phil said as he placed a hand on his wife's belly. "Be a fabulous one this year."

Dale finished his drink then placed the bottle carefully onto a beer mat. "I'm probably going with Lucie to New York. To the wedding."

"And how did mother Treharne take that news item?" Phil asked.

"I've yet to break it to her." Dale grimaced then picked up the beer bottle and started picking at the label.

"Rather you than me, fella!"

Lucie watched as Dale flicked bits of sticky label onto the table. She knew that his mother would give him a hard time about being away over Christmas. If he didn't come, Lucie would be nervous, but she would cope. She'd have to. Yet it would be so much better with Dale at her side. Petra worked for a private travel firm that specialized in luxury holidays, and she had managed to get discounts on everything from flights to hotel rooms. Her very rich and generous father had insisted on paying the remaining costs for the bridesmaids and their partners. Petra had sent out a letter with the invitations, to inform the select few that they wouldn't need to spend a penny. It promised to be the trip of a lifetime. Plus, in New York, Lucie could hopefully avoid the ghosts of Christmas past.

Dale caught her eye and mouthed, *It'll be fine. Don't worry.*

And she knew, in that moment, that it would.

With Dale by her side.

There was no one else she'd rather visit New York with. Christmas wedding or not, they'd be sure to have some fun.

–

"You can come with me."

Lucie turned awkwardly to face Dale. They were in the back of Arianwen's bright red Fiesta, squashed together because of the child's car seat to her left. Apparently, one car seat could be removed easily enough, and Phil had already put it in the boot, but the other one was more complicated. *Like building a Lego pirate ship*, Phil had told them apologetically, then explained that when baby number three came, they'd have to use his people carrier for all family outings.

"What do you mean?" she whispered, conscious that after three glasses of wine she didn't want to speak too loudly – she knew she got loud when she was tipsy.

"When I tell Mum."

"Nooooo." A chill filled her belly. There was nothing she wouldn't do for Dale, but facing Mrs Treharne, especially regarding something that concerned not just her middle son but also Christmas, was a terrifying prospect. "It'd be better coming just from you."

"Nope!" He patted her knee. "You're whisking me away to New York City, so you can help me break the news to her."

"I'm hardly whisking you away, Dale. You agreed to come to support me, and I'm very grateful, but you know I'd do the same for you any day, don't you?" The chill began to seep outwards, penetrating her limbs and making her stiffen.

"I do know that, Luce. But I'm not asking for that right now. I just want you to help me break the news, soften the blow or however you prefer to word it." Lucie saw a tiny muscle in his jaw twitching, which she knew from long experience meant that he was stifling laughter – at her expense.

"Can't you just tell your dad and get him to speak to her?"

"Nope."

"Oh please, Dale?"

"Nope."

Lucie sighed. Dale was right; she really should help him speak to his mum about it. Glenda had always been very kind to Lucie, ever since she'd first gone round for tea when they were in primary school. This thoughtfulness had continued through secondary school, and after Lucie's mum had passed away, Mrs Treharne had been kinder than ever, as if she sensed that Lucie was lost. With no daughters of her own, she'd seemed to enjoy Lucie's company and had taken her on frequent shopping trips during her teenage years, as well as telling her all about the facts of life. Yet Lucie still found her a bit intimidating; the woman was a fierce matriarch and extremely protective of her family. She had been a member of the PTA at St. Clotilde's while her boys attended the school, and even spent a few years as a governor there. Glenda was a woman who didn't baulk at expressing her opinion, and even though Lucie had never actually heard Dale describe a time when his mother had lost her temper, it had become the stuff of legend. Possible, yet still to be witnessed first-hand. And terrifying.

"Okay then, I'll come. When do you want to tell her?" Lucie's neck had stiffened and she moved her head from side to side in an attempt to loosen it.

"Sooner the better I figure."

"Next weekend?"

"Yeah, come round for Sunday lunch."

"Hadn't you better ask your mum first before inviting me?"

"Lucie, you know that won't be a problem. Mum abso-lutely adores you. Of course I'll ask her, but she's always telling me to bring you round."

"Next Sunday it is, then."

Lucie wriggled. Her left leg had gone numb from being pressed against the car seat, and her right was aching from trying to prevent it from brushing against Dale's. Not that the physical contact would bother either of them – they'd always been quite tactile – but it just seemed a bit strange being squashed up with him in the back of their friend's car. As if they were teenagers again, or...

"You two are like an old married couple, you know that?" Arianwen flashed them a smile in the rear-view mirror. "I'll never understand why you didn't get together at some point."

This time it was Dale who wriggled in his seat. Lucie hoped he'd look at her but he didn't, seeming instead to deliberately turn his head and stare out of the window at passing cars.

Of course, Arianwen hadn't been around before Lucie had left for university, and the thing – whatever it was – that had happened between them that summer was something that Lucie and Dale never spoke of: it was almost as if it had never happened. The very fact that Dale never raised it made Lucie certain that it was because it was something he'd rather forget.

Why else would he refrain from mentioning it?

Ever.

Chapter 3

Lucie closed the door of her car and went round to the boot. She pulled out two large carrier bags and put them on the ground, locked the car, then picked up the bags and waddled towards the school, trying to avoid bumping her shins with her awkward load.

When she reached the entrance to St. Clotilde's Primary School, Lucie ran her card through the scanner, turned around and pushed the door open with her bottom. The familiar scents of paint, cabbage and fart greeted her. The school had smelt the same ever since she'd attended it as a pupil and she suspected that it would smell that way until the day it was torn down. The thought made her heart dip; she'd imagined her own children attending the school one day. Although seeing as how she was thirty-three, had no admirers on the horizon and was still waiting to hear the ticking of her biological clock, she wondered some days whether she'd ever have kids.

There'd been men over the years, yes, but she'd never found one she could imagine living with. Something always put her off: hairy toes, hairy ears, snoring, not putting the toilet seat down... all superficial reasons to reject a man, perhaps, but how could she allow herself to fall in love with someone when she couldn't look at his feet without recoiling?

Most of the time, she didn't even get past the first date anyway: things usually went wrong. Like the last one she'd been on when the guy had paid his phone more attention than her, and when she'd caught a glance of the screen, he'd been on a dating app. *During* their date! Suffice to say, at the end of the evening she'd been relieved when they'd taken separate taxis travelling in opposite directions.

She hadn't allowed herself to really care about anyone since the Christmas after graduation, when Jamie Davenport had broken her heart. After she'd allowed herself to fall madly in love with him, the bastard had hurt her more than she could ever have imagined. She'd been like a zombie that Christmas, and her poor father and Dale had tried so hard to cheer her up, but Lucie had been inconsolable. It was after that terrible Christmas that Lucie had decided not to return to university the next year – to study for her masters in education, as she'd planned for so long – but instead to ask for more hours at the local supermarket where she'd been working to put herself through another year of higher education.

She spent the next two years at the supermarket. She didn't mind the routine and enjoyed the daily interaction with customers and the security of knowing exactly what she'd be doing on any given day. At times, she'd been convinced that she might end up working there until she reached retirement age and that retail was her destiny. Then one day she saw an advert for a teaching assistant post at St. Clotilde's. Something told her to go for it, and she'd got the job. Perhaps she could have been a teacher, had she followed up her BA in English Literature with an MA in Education, but she always reminded herself that she was happy enough in the job she did. She loved working with the children, preparing them for each term then watching with pride as they accomplished so much in their early years. She didn't get the same pay cheque as the classroom teachers, but she did get to enjoy the buzz of seeing children learn and enjoy their time at primary school.

Lucie shuffled into the staff room and put the two bags filled with recyclable materials in the corner by the pigeonholes. Dawn, the year three teacher she supported, had asked her to save up plastic bottles, toilet rolls and anything else that could be used to make Christmas decorations, so Lucie had been washing out bottles, yogurt pots and milk cartons for months. She knew the children would be delighted to start making festive decorations, and their innocent enthusiasm was so cute. She just wished that she could share their excitement in the buildup to the Christmas break.

–

Sunday morning arrived, and with it a sense of dread. The week had flown past and Lucie had barely had time to think about lunch at the Treharnes'. Today, she would help Dale break the news to Glenda, and she worried that it wasn't going to be pretty.

She showered then blow-dried her wavy, dark-blonde hair straight, before spending twenty minutes staring at the contents of her wardrobe. What did you wear in such circumstances? What was appropriate when going to tell your best friend's mother that her son would not be around for Christmas? *Because of you?* In the end, she selected a pair of indigo denim jeans and a red V-neck jumper that she paired with a navy silk scarf printed with tiny rosebuds. Smart-casual, she hoped.

At eleven o'clock, she heard the beep of a horn. She grabbed her bag and coat and went out to meet Dale. She climbed into the passenger side of his van and did a double take.

"Well, you've scrubbed up nicely!" He'd had his hair cut shorter than normal and was clean-shaven. He was wearing a grey button down shirt, which Lucie couldn't help noticing emphasized the breadth of his shoulders, along with a pair of black jeans.

"What're you trying to say, Luce? That I usually look like a sack of rotting leaves?" He stared at her, his face deadly serious.

"Of course not! Just... you know... I'm used to seeing you in your overalls or pub casuals." She watched him carefully then saw the twitching in his jaw. "You're winding me up!" She punched him playfully in the arm.

"You're too easy, Lucie."

"I'm just really nervous today."

He nodded. "Me too."

"You think your mum's going to flip?"

He shrugged. "Who knows?"

"It's like we're kids again and we're in trouble for not doing homework or something."

He nodded. "And *that* was always bad enough."

He drove them across town to the home where he had grown up. His parents owned a detached five-bedroom house that they'd renovated during the seventies. It was now worth a small fortune, but Glenda had once told Lucie that she'd never sell as it was full of memories of her boys growing up. Lucie had always thought that it would be lovely to have a home like that to return to, where there was always a warm welcome. A proper family home was like a security blanket, somewhere to run when times got tough; a place where hot chocolate and hugs were offered freely.

Lucie had never had a place like that. After her mother died, her father had moved them closer to the town, keen to escape the memories of the home he'd once shared with his wife. Following his marriage to Thelma when Lucie was at university, he'd moved again, and now they lived in a three-bedroom semi that was built in the mid-eighties. It was grey and soulless, and nothing about it felt like home to her. Luckily, she had her own flat, or she'd have been completely rootless.

Losing her mother had changed her life in so many ways, and it was now very different to the life that she'd envisaged as a child. But wasn't that just reality for many people? How many adults actually had a parental home to run to when everything overwhelmed them? Lucie would have liked to be able to go and have a cup of tea with her mum, to drop in and chat about her day, but even that was impossible. Sometimes life was so unfair.

Yet she had more than many people, and she always tried to remind herself of that when sadness crept in.

"So how should we do this today?" Dale asked her.

She chewed on her bottom lip then stared at her fingers. "Quickly?"

"Like ripping off a plaster?"

Lucie watched as an elderly man walked his ratty-haired dog along the pavement, his head nodding every time the dog stopped to sniff at something. For a moment, she wished she was the old man. Then she wished she was the dog. That way she could avoid what she was about to do. "I guess so."

"I'm not sure. I mean… Mum's always made such a big deal about Christmas. But she has said in the past that she knows things will change at some point. I think she'll be okay, especially as I'm going with you." His knuckles were white as he gripped the steering wheel.

"I hope so, Dale. I don't want to upset her but I don't want to go to New York alone either. It just wouldn't be as much fun."

Dale glanced at her quickly before turning back to the road. "So we're going to have some fun, are we?"

"As long as we can pretend it's not Christmas, yes, we will."

He shook his head. "Not sure I can oblige with that one, Lucie. If I'm going to come to New York with you in

December, it's going to be impossible to ignore Christmas. Perhaps I can even try to help you enjoy the festivities for once."

Lucie sank deeper into her seat and exhaled slowly. She wanted Dale to have a good Christmas, it wouldn't be fair to drag him all the way to New York otherwise, but as for *her* enjoying it… that might be a bit much to hope for.

Dale pulled up in front of his parents' driveway behind a brand new silver Audi. It sparkled in the morning sunshine and reminded Lucie of a small plane. All it needed was a set of wings and it could soar right off into the sky. She guessed it probably belonged to Dale's older brother, a dentist with a lucrative practice.

"Looks like Ieuan's here already," Dale said as if reading her thoughts. "Think the whole clan will be today."

Lucie's stomach flipped as she unbuckled her seatbelt. The thought of facing the whole Treharne family whilst breaking the news about Christmas was daunting. What if they all thought she was a bitch for taking Dale away? For ruining the usual festive routine. Dale and his brothers were almost as protective of their mother as she was of them, and Lucie didn't want to face their collective resentment.

"Let's do this, then," Dale said, flashing her a smile. "I think it's best if we play it by ear. See how the land lies and I'll tell her when the moment's right."

"Okay. Good plan."

They got out of the van then walked up to the front door and Dale called out as he opened it. The mouth-watering aromas of roast chicken and thyme greeted them

25

as they entered the magnolia-patterned hallway. It was warm and cosy inside.

"Hello, you two!" Glenda appeared in the kitchen doorway, an apron tied around her neck and waist, covering her usual beige trousers and pastel blouse. She hugged Dale then did the same to Lucie. "I hope you're hungry. I've made a mountain of food."

"You know me, Mum," Dale said as he rubbed his flat stomach. "Plenty of room in here."

"That's because you don't look after yourself properly at that house of yours. You need to get the kitchen in soon. Beans on toast will *not* keep you going long-term."

"It smells wonderful," Lucie said as they followed Glenda through to the kitchen.

Hank was at the central island carving a large steaming chicken. He looked far younger than his sixty years. Although his hair was greying, his skin was smooth and clear and his eyes, as he turned them to her, were as warm and lively as Dale's. Her friend had inherited his mother's dark hair and olive skin tone, and his father's eye colour and strong jaw. Hank had also passed on his height and broad shoulders, and it was one of the things that Lucie knew women admired about Dale. He didn't even have a gym membership, but good genes and an active lifestyle meant that he looked like he could play international rugby. The thickening at the bridge of his nose from a childhood break added to his charm, and had certainly provided Dale with a talking point when they were growing up. He always told people that he broke his nose play fighting with his oldest brother, but in reality it had happened when Lucie fell out of a tree and landed on him.

"Are you all right, Lucie?" Glenda placed a hand on her arm.

"Sorry?" Lucie shook herself as she realized that she'd been staring at Dale while he spoke to his father.

"You seemed far away."

"Oh yes, I'm fine thanks. Just a bit tired."

"All those hours spent preparing for the school play, no doubt," Glenda suggested as she filled the kettle with water then flicked the switch.

"Yes. It's been a busy term and the children get more and more excited by the day. Sometimes, they get so wound up they're impossible to teach. I really don't envy their parents having to deal with them during the holidays."

"That's all part of the fun, Lucie. I loved it when the boys were younger. Children are what Christmas is all about. Every parent knows that..." She bit her bottom lip. "Oh, Lucie, I'm sorry dear. Me and my big mouth. Sometimes I just prattle on and don't think. Do you forgive me?"

"Of course. I wasn't offended."

My mother didn't care about me at Christmas but normal parents do. Normal parents put their children first.

"Can I help with anything?"

Glenda glanced around the kitchen as if to check. "No, I think we're on top of it all. Why don't you and Dale

27

go and say hello to Ieuan? He's in the conservatory with Thomas, telling him all about his new Audi." Glenda rolled her eyes and Lucie giggled. Ieuan was a complete obsessive when it came to cars and Lucie was certain that he bought a new one every six months at least. But apart from brief flings with women he never brought home, he'd never settled down, and as he had such a successful private dental practice, he had plenty of money to flash around.

Lucie went through to the conservatory with Dale and they found Thomas and Ieuan deep in conversation.

"But I'm telling you, Thomas, the new model is nothing like the last one. It's a complete upgrade, to a standard that's never been seen before."

"That may well be, but they could always find faults further down the line." Thomas shook his head. "You're better off sticking with something you can trust."

"I disagree. You've had your Land Rover for what… three years now? It's ludicrous keeping a vehicle for that long."

"It's hardly lost any value at all and it won't depreciate much further. They're sturdy, built to last." Thomas thumped his knee as if to hammer the point home.

Thomas and Ieuan both looked more like their mother than their father, yet they were as tall and broad as Dale. Family photographs adorned virtually every surface in the Treharne house, evidence of how much Glenda doted on her boys. They'd matured from cute babies into awkward kids then handsome men, although Lucie thought Dale was the most attractive brother. But then she was biased.

"Hello, brothers!" Dale announced as he parked himself next to Ieuan on the sofa. "And how are you both?"

"Good, thanks. Hey, Lucie!" Thomas waved a hand; Ieuan nodded at her and offered a warm smile.

"Hi." Lucie took one of the wicker chairs. "Helen not with you?"

"Upstairs." Thomas pointed at the ceiling. "Speaking to the boys about manners."

"Oh?" Lucie raised her eyebrows.

"They were out in the garden having a farting contest and Helen caught them at it. I said it didn't matter, that at least they were doing it in the fresh air, but you know Helen…" He shrugged and Lucie gave a small nod. Thomas' wife was a stickler for propriety. She was keen on becoming mayor one day, so appearances and public profile mattered enormously to her. For years, Lucie had listened to her talking about her desire to pursue a political career – she couldn't imagine anything worse. Helen was a very driven woman and her determination had deepened with age. At thirty-eight, with a successful career in law, a slightly younger lawyer husband and two children at a private school, she certainly seemed on the way to achieving her ambitions.

"Let's hope the boys are sufficiently filled with remorse, then, or I can see them being sent to bed without any supper!" Dale flashed Lucie a grin. But Lucie knew he was joking, because while Helen was a strict parent, she also adored her children, and the idea of sending them to bed hungry would never occur to her.

Dale had taken advantage of the chance to be alone with his mother and offered to help her set the table in the dining room. As he laid another place setting, he steeled himself. He'd been trying to gauge Glenda's mood, to assess whether the time was right to bring up New York, and as she seemed in good spirits, he thought now would be as good a time as any.

"Mum…"

"Yes, darling?" Glenda turned from the sideboard, holding two crystal wine glasses.

"I have something I need to speak to you about." He inhaled slowly.

"Do you?" She smiled as she set the glasses on the table, then turned back for two more.

"Yes. It's… um… about… me and Lucie."

Please put the glasses down.

Glenda turned to him, her eyes wide and expectant. "Really?" she asked as she put the wine glasses on the table then clasped her hands together.

Dale realized that she didn't look like someone about to receive bad news. In fact, she looked extremely happy, excited even. "Yes, you see… Lucie's been my friend for a long, long time now and… you know, I care about her a lot." He thought it best to justify *why* he wouldn't be around for Christmas before breaking the news. "She means so much to me and…"

"Oh… my… goodness!" Glenda squealed.

Dale's heart leap into his mouth. *Was his mother all right?* She looked positively frantic.

"Well, the thing is—"

"It's okay, darling!" She shook her head. "I *know.*"

"You know?" Dale frowned as he tried to work out how his mother could know, and why, if she did know, she wasn't furious with him right now.

"I do. And I am so happy for you both."

"You are?"

She nodded, then walked around the table and squeezed his hands. "It's what I've wanted for… well, *forever.* We just adore Lucie, and we know how right she is for you. This is the best news you could have given me, and I can't wait to tell your father."

Dale watched his mother carefully, wondering what exactly she thought he'd meant. Then it began to dawn on him.

"Oh… uh… Mum…"

What to say? How to explain?

"What is it?" She placed a cool hand on his cheek and looked up into his face, her features etched with concern. "You and Lucie are in love, aren't you? That's good, darling. Such happy news. Well, I say *news,* but I've always known you were in love. The way you look at her, the softening in your expression when you talk about her… It's obvious, Dale. I was just waiting for you to realize. I couldn't push it, you know. Your father said to me, 'Glenda, don't force things between them. It will happen when the time is right.' But I really wanted to give

31

you both a nudge. You're not getting any younger, and it would be nice to have more grandchildren while I'm still sprightly enough to run around after them."

Dale ground his teeth together. If he told her the truth now, if he corrected his mother and ruined her belief that he was in love with Lucie and that she was in love with him, then it would really upset her. His father too, by the sound of it. That would be bad enough, but to add to this disappointment by telling them he wouldn't be around for Christmas would just be twisting the knife. He'd have to speak to Lucie and prepare her so she knew what his parents thought. After Christmas they could tell everyone that they'd split up or something, but for now, it would be better to pretend. Dale didn't like deceiving his family, but neither did he like hurting them, and he hoped that this would be the lesser of two evils.

"Look, Mum, could we keep this between us for now. It's early days, you know?" At least if she didn't tell everyone, it would make it easier to explain why they weren't acting as if they were in love.

His mother nodded then placed her forefinger over her lips before drawing a cross over her heart. She really was over the moon.

Bloody Lucie Quigley and her *I need my oldest friend with me* speech! Look at the mess he was getting into now, and all because he didn't want to let her down.

All because he didn't want her to go without him.

All because he cared too much to let her go alone.

"Lucie!"

Lucie stopped in the middle of the hallway and looked around. Someone had called her name but she couldn't see them.

"*Lucie!*"

And again. It sounded like Dale. She peered up the staircase but there was no one there.

"Over here!" The door to the downstairs cloakroom was slightly open, and she could make out an eye peering through the gap.

"Who's there?"

"Who d'you think?"

"What's wrong?"

"Quickly!"

She approached the door and gasped as Dale flung it open, pulled her inside, then locked it behind her.

"What the hell are you doing?"

"I need to talk to you."

"In here?" She frowned at the confined space. To the left was a full-length mirror, behind Dale was a small hand basin that must've been digging into his bum, then to the right was the shiny white toilet. The room smelt of orchids and vanilla, which she guessed was due to Glenda's obsession with battery-operated air fresheners that pumped out fragrance on a timer. Glenda had always bought into whatever new air freshening product had just arrived on the market, and Lucie wouldn't have been surprised if she'd owned stocks and shares in some of them.

"Now listen to me carefully." Dale's face was flushed, and she wondered if he had an upset stomach. She couldn't blame him, the idea of telling Glenda about New York was daunting, but she really didn't want to be standing this close if there was a risk he might throw up or something.

"I'm listening."

"I was trying to tell Mum about New York and Christmas, but she got the wrong end of the stick."

"What do you mean? What exactly did you say?" Lucie felt laughter bubbling in her belly. It seemed so ridiculous that she was squashed in a toilet with her best friend in his mum's house and he looked so darned serious.

"Stop smiling, Lucie! It's not funny." He snorted then rubbed a hand over his face. "Well it is kind of funny, in a terrible way, I guess."

"Dale, just tell me!" She grabbed his hands.

"Well, I was trying to break the news gently, but she just kind of assumed that we're... uh... together."

"But we are together. In the toilet."

"No, idiot! *Together* together." He tapped his fists together. "As in, a couple."

"Oh." Lucie's stomach churned and the laughter ebbed away. "Didn't you put her right?"

He shook his head. "I couldn't do it. She was thrilled and said she knew that we were right for each other. That she knew we l..." He pressed his lips together.

"That we l..." Lucie waved her arm forwards to encourage him to finish what he was about to say.

"That we... l... liked each other a lot and were such good friends. That's all. So she and dad think we're a

34

couple now. I couldn't tell her that we weren't, and that we're swanning off to New York for Christmas, because she'd have been hurt. So I say… let them believe we're together for now, then we can tell them we've split up – after Christmas."

Lucie stared at him, wondering if he'd gone mad. "We can't do that! It's deceitful, Dale. I don't want to lie to your parents or your brothers."

"Well, we're not exactly lying, just not correcting them. If we tell her both bad things at once, she'd be devastated, and I don't know if I can upset her about you and me, then tell her about Christmas. I did ask her to keep it quiet, though, just between us."

Lucie gazed into Dale's eyes and saw his love and concern for his parents. He really did mean well, and after all, he was doing this for her. Perhaps they could pretend to be a couple for a few weeks. "All right then, but we tell them the truth when we get back?"

"Of course." He nodded, then awkwardly shook her proffered hand, the ridiculousness of the situation causing them both to giggle, just as they had done so often when they were younger and about to do something they knew they shouldn't be doing.

That was the thing about being such good friends for so long. They had a shared history of good and bad times. They trusted each other to do the right thing – and some-times to do the wrong thing in the right situation. Lucie knew she'd never find another friend like Dale. If she had to pretend to be his girlfriend to make things easier on his parents, then that was what she would do. Happily.

Chapter 4

Lucie sighed as she placed her cutlery on her empty plate. "That was delicious, Glenda and Hank. Thank you so much."

Glenda smiled. "You're very welcome. But have a little breather, because there's dessert too."

Lucie rubbed her belly. "I'm about to pop."

"Nonsense. I'm sure you can squeeze some more in. We have to keep you well fed, especially now you're part of the f…" She dropped her eyes to her plate and colour flooded her cheeks.

Everyone stared at Glenda, and Lucie watched in horror as the woman's cheeks turned from pink to scarlet.

"What's all this then?" Thomas asked. "Part of the *family*?"

Glenda shook her head but she caught Hank's eye and started to smile.

Lucie suppressed a groan. *Here goes…*

"Do tell!" Helen said. "Don't keep us all in suspense here, Glenda. Lucie?" She looked from one woman to the other then to Dale. "What about you, Dale? Are you going to spill the beans?"

Dale met Lucie's eyes and she saw the panic there. *What now?*

"Actually, Mum, while we're on the topic of revelations, I have one of my own," Ieuan announced as he drained his glass of sugar-free lemonade. Lucie breathed a sigh of relief. Thankfully, the competitive nature of the Treharne brothers meant that they usually had to try to outdo one another, and Ieuan clearly didn't want to be overshadowed here.

Glenda turned to face her eldest son. "You do?"

Ieuan nodded and crossed his arms. Then uncrossed them. Then placed his palms flat on the table. "I—"

"But *I* want to know what's going on with Dale and Lucie!" It was eight-year-old Max, Thomas and Helen's eldest son.

"What have I told you about interrupting grownups?" Helen scowled at Max.

"You said it was rude unless it was something really important. And it *must* be important because they were in Granny's toilet together." Max widened his eyes to give his statement extra impact. "And my teacher says that boys and girls mustn't go into the same toilet."

All eyes turned to Dale and Lucie. Heat crawled up her throat and into her face. She knew she'd be getting all blotchy. She wished she could just disappear.

"We were uh… I couldn't find the uh… toilet paper." Dale shrugged but Max shook his head.

"Granny always has lots and lots of toilet paper, Uncle Dale. You're fibbing and Mummy says fibbing is naughty."

Helen looked from her son to Dale and nodded.

"Dale couldn't manage to turn the tap on to wash his hands, so I helped him," Lucie blurted desperately, realising it was the lamest excuse ever for being in the downstairs loo with her best friend. "He's really weak sometimes."

Max stared at her.

"And I'm really strong!" She raised her arms and curled them like a bodybuilder.

Max's mouth had fallen open.

"And I have something I *need* to say." It was Ieuan. "It doesn't involve toilets or muscles or anything like that thank goodness... well, some muscles, but that's TMI for you right now and I... uh... well... it does involve Christmas."

Lucie held her breath and glanced at Dale. How did Ieuan have news about Christmas too? She saw Dale's cheek twitch. If Ieuan was going to be away as well, then it would be worse when Dale told Glenda that he wouldn't be there, so he needed to get in first.

"I'm going to New York for Christmas!" Dale shouted, just as Ieuan exclaimed, "I'm bringing my boyfriend to Christmas dinner!"

The room fell silent.

Everyone stared at their empty plates.

The clock on the sideboard ticked.

Glenda raised her eyes and opened and closed her mouth as if gasping for air, then eyed her sons in turn as if seeking the worst offender. It was worse than that time one of the boys had emptied the chocolate advent calendar by opening the bottom and shaking all the chocolates out. Lucie had been present that December morning as Dale and his brothers had been reprimanded for being sneaky. None of them had admitted to the crime, and she didn't think they had discovered who'd done it even to this day. But there had been a grey cloud over the Treharne household for weeks. Dale had insisted that it had been one of Ieuan's friends who'd come over to play, but there was no evidence. No way of proving it to their mother. After that, Glenda only allowed the boys to have a card calendar featuring small pictures of snowmen, reindeer and puddings with holly on top. She'd said that she couldn't bear to witness the disappointment of her sons opening a calendar door and not finding a chocolate there because some greedy piggy had eaten them all.

Hank stood up suddenly, but the tablecloth was caught in his belt, where he'd tucked in his napkin, so everything flew up the table towards him, causing glasses and cutlery to fly off in all directions. Someone screamed. Someone swore. Hank gazed in shock at the lunchtime carnage, threw his napkin aside, pushed his glasses up his nose and asked, "Anyone for port?"

–

Lucie opened the door to her flat and shuffled inside, instinctively turning the thermostat up as she passed. As she hung her coat on the rail and pushed her boots under the shelf, she noticed that as Dale entered, he automatically turned the heating back down. They really were like a couple sometimes; he didn't even live there yet he was still thinking about saving her money."

"Hey, what're you doing? It's cold." She shivered as she watched him remove his coat and boots.

"You don't need it that high, Lucie. It'll cost you money and it's bad for the environment."

"Being cold is bad for me."

"Go put a jumper on." He followed her into the kitchen. "Shall I make tea?"

"Please. There are biscuits in the cupboard."

She went to her room and changed into fleecy pyjamas and a thick jumper, then headed to the bathroom. She combed out her hair and stared at her reflection in the mirror above the sink. She had terrible dark shadows under her eyes. They'd appeared this afternoon because she felt so bad about deceiving Dale's family. Following Ieuan's announcement, along with Dale's about heading to New York, there had been utter chaos. Poor Hank had pulled the tablecloth off, along with some of Glenda's best crystal wine glasses, and plates and gravy-covered cutlery had rolled off onto her thick cream carpet. Although Lucie and Dale had done their best to remove the stains, it had proved impossible to get the gravy out, so not only did she feel bad about taking Dale away at Christmas and pretending that they were dating, she also had to carry part of the responsibility for ruining Glenda's lovely home. And Glenda was house-proud. Extremely so. Even having three boys had not hindered her efforts to make her home a cosy palace.

And what about Ieuan's confession? After all the apparent philandering with women, he was gay? And he was bringing his boyfriend, who he'd later told them was called Barry, to Christmas dinner?

Lucie knew that Dale's parents were very tolerant, and that it wouldn't be the fact that Ieuan was gay that would bother them so much as the fact that they hadn't known. Glenda would no doubt blame herself for not knowing her son, and Lucie's heart went out to her. To add insult to injury, she was giving Glenda false hope, deceiving her about her relationship with Dale, and Lucie hated lying. She hated liars. Because liars caused pain; liars tore families and lives apart.

"Lucie?" Dale knocked on the door. "I'm bursting!"

"Okay. Coming!" She opened the door. "Sorry."

"No problem. Just couldn't wait any longer. You've been in here for ages. Tea's ready and I've turned the TV on."

"Thanks. Don't be long then!"

Ten minutes later, snuggled up on the sofa with a large steaming mug of tea and a packet of chocolate biscuits, Lucie gazed at the television screen. The paranormal investigators were traipsing through a cavernous cellar somewhere, their faces illuminated by night vision cameras and their eyes black holes as they wore expressions of expectant terror. Lucie loved the programme, even though Dale always claimed it was a load of rubbish – yet he always watched it with her, even jumping at some of the scarier bits.

"Are you okay about how today went, Luce?" Dale placed his mug on the side table then turned to look at her.

"Kind of."

"That was quite a dinner, eh?"

"Your mother'll never want me to come back."

"Rubbish." He shook his head. "She won't blame you for that. In fact, she's thrilled that we're finally *together*." He air quoted the last word and Lucie blushed.

"I hate deceiving them, Dale."

"Me too. But like I said, Mum just assumed that we were a couple and I didn't want to hurt her. We can tell them the truth in time. It won't be that hard to pretend to be my girlfriend will it?" He looked at her from underneath his thick, dark lashes.

"No. Of course not. It's only until we get back from New York though, right?"

He glanced away for a moment before meeting her eyes. "Of course. I mean, I could never live here with you full time anyway. It's like the Sahara!" He made a choking noise and fell backwards on the sofa, loosening his shirt and wiping his brow dramatically.

"Dale, stop it!" Lucie laughed at him. "I don't know how you can stay in that big old house of yours without central heating."

He shrugged. "I have jumpers, thick socks and a duck-down duvet."

"Even so. It must be freezing at night, Dale."

"The new boiler's going in soon, so it'll be fine. Lucky the old couple who lived there had that electric shower or I'd be really stinky by now."

"Did you know about Ieuan? At all?"

Dale sat upright and straightened his shirt. "I don't know. I mean... kind of, I guess. Now that he's admitted it, I can see that he's said and done things over the years that could have been his way of dropping clues. All those women he was seeing... we never met them. Not one. They were always models off on assignments abroad, or businesswomen travelling the country with their jobs. But now I think it was all a front. He was hiding who he really was, yet, I suspect, still trying to get us to see him properly. We just didn't read the signs."

"Like what?"

"Well the absent girlfriends, for starters. Then there were other things. Like, he FaceTimed one of his male friends a lot over Christmas last year. And on Christmas day too! And when he was in uni, he had photos of him and this guy in his room. They were all over the walls... and I mean *all* over. And he'd check out other men if we went to the pub then make out like he was joking, but now I guess I can see that he was testing my reactions to it all."

"Poor Ieuan."

"Well, at least it'll give Glenda someone else to fuss over at Christmas when I'm in NYC with you... making sure that you don't get yourself into any trouble."

"True." Lucie paused then realized what Dale had just said. "Hey! I will *not* get into any trouble."

"Not with me there you won't, but if I'd let you go alone…" He shook his head.

Lucie grabbed a cushion and whacked him over the head with it. "That's it! Pillow fight!"

And for the next ten minutes, Lucie forgot about feeling worried or guilty, forgot about Ieuan's situation, and forgot about all her other worries as she and Dale chased each other around the flat until they collapsed in laughter on her living room floor.

Exhausted.

Happy.

And more than a little bit excited about their upcoming trip.

Chapter 5

"Lucie, darling!" Petra waved from the other side of the central London bridal boutique. Lucie closed the door behind her, causing the old-fashioned bell above the door to tinkle again.

She took a deep breath, lifted her chin and plastered on what she hoped was a confident smile.

Here goes...

She strode across the shiny shop floor, acutely aware that the harsh lighting would be emphasizing her every flaw, and that the team of fluttering women surrounding Petra would no doubt be assessing her as she approached: *Age. Weight. Height. Wealth. Occupation. Worth knowing?*

Lucie had encountered some of Petra's friends before, back when they were at university together, but only for short periods of time, and she'd been younger, slimmer and angry enough at the world not to give a damn then anyway. But now... insecurity wobbled at her edges. She didn't want to be the odd one out, the short, plain bridesmaid who made the rest look good. And boy, did they look good! It was like walking into the backstage area of a catwalk show. Every single one of them was tall, slim, polished, perfect.

"Lucie!" The women parted and Petra emerged, clad in just a white basque, stockings and a scrap of lace that served as her underwear. She held out her hands and Lucie took them, relieved that her friend offered a warm welcome. "Thank you so much for coming. I know it's short notice but once Harry proposed, I thought I'd get the old ball rolling and all that! Oh darling, come here. Mwah! Mwah!" Petra kissed the air either side of Lucie's head then took a step back and smiled down at her. "Don't you just look fabulous!"

Lucie shrugged then smiled. Petra's friends were still staring at her as if she had two heads. Which today she did; a large spot had appeared on her chin overnight. Even toothpaste and concealer had done nothing to disguise the hideous protrusion. It was a greasy volcano ready to erupt at any moment. She had a brief image of aiming it at the other bridesmaids then pressing the tender flesh either side of the spot and coating them all in sticky white pus. That would show them. They wouldn't be so perfect then.

She shivered. Why was she being so defensive? These women could well be perfectly nice and she was just probably just being overly sensitive; a product of her own insecurities.

"Thank you, Petra. And you look... well..." *Too skinny. Too tanned. Too tired.* "Gorgeous as ever!"

Petra ran a hand over her platinum blonde hair and smiled broadly, flashing pearly white, perfectly straight teeth. But as she smiled, Lucie couldn't help noticing that the rest of Petra's face remained frozen. Her forehead was unlined, flawless. Her eyes had no crow's feet; not a line in sight, and her lips were full and pouty.

Oh Petra! You've succumbed…

During their time at university, Petra had always been outwardly confident and self-assured, but Lucie knew the real girl beneath the veneer. The nineteen-year-old Petra had been troubled, insecure and desperate for love and approval. She'd been the girl who'd binged on chocolate bars and pizza then gone straight for the toilet to throw it all up before she could absorb any calories. She'd exercised frantically every morning and evening in the gym, pounding away at the treadmill in her quest to remain waif-like. Lucie had worried about her; a lot.

When Petra had met Harry, she'd calculated his worth as a long-term investment, as husband material, and done everything in her power to impress him, snag him, then keep him. Lucie knew that even back then, Petra had turned a blind eye to Harry's philandering, and she could only hope that Harry had turned over a new leaf now that he was more mature and about to marry his long-suffering girlfriend. They'd had their breakups and makeups but whatever sins he committed, Petra always took him back. It wasn't exactly the recipe for a perfect relationship, but then what did Lucie know about relationship success?

"Come say hi to Mummy!" Petra took Lucie's hand in her own, her slim fingers long, cool and smooth, and guided her through the other women and over to the changing rooms. "Mummy!"

"What?" The sharp tone of Mrs Barnsley came from behind a red satin curtain. It reminded Lucie of the curtains at the theatre that hid the stage from the audience. Petra and her mother both played their parts well, Lucie knew that; she'd seen the family charade before.

"Mummy, come on out. Lucie's here."

"Lucie who?"

Petra cast Lucie an apologetic glance. "Lucie Quigley. You know… my friend from university. She's going to be one of my bridesmaids."

"Never heard of her."

Petra looked like she was holding back tears. Lucie reached out to hug her, but thought better of it. Petra had never been one for hugs, always trying to maintain that stiff upper lip that had been drilled into her since childhood.

The curtain rattled back and revealed a woman who could have been Petra's slightly older sister. Her hair was the same shade of blonde, her eyes were the same corn-flower blue and she was just as skinny as her daughter as she stood there in nothing more than an ivory slip. For a woman who had to be in her late fifties, Joanna Barnsley appeared to be very well preserved indeed. Perhaps too well preserved. A bit too angular and flawless.

"Mrs Barnsley." Lucie held out a hand. "Nice to see you again. We did meet, many years ago, so I'm not surprised you don't remember me. Congratulations, by the way!"

Joanna Barnsley's hand was papery and limp as a dishrag; and she made no effort to return Lucie's firm, solid shake. Lucie fought the urge to rub her palm on her jeans.

"Congratulations?" Joanna looked surprised.

"Well, yes… on Petra's engagement. As mother of the bride, you must be thrilled."

"Oh!" Joanna gave a small nod. "Yes, of course. Ecstatic." As her features remained frozen, it was hard to ascertain whether she was happy or not.

Lucie glanced at Petra, but her friend was wearing her own mask.

"Do you want to see the dress?" Petra tugged Lucie's hand, encouraging her to move away from her mother.

"Yes, of course!" As Lucie followed her friend to the furthest changing cubicle, she remembered this feeling. At times, Petra could be cold and aloof, hurtful even, but a lot of it was to do with concealing her own fragility. A lifetime of loneliness, neglected by her rich businessman Daddy and alcoholic high society mother, Petra had been sent away to a prestigious boarding school as a child. She'd been happy there, she'd once told Lucie, but dreaded the long lonely summers at the family home. All she'd longed for, all her life, was a family of her own and a husband who would love her. But Lucie had a terrible feeling that marrying Harry would not be her old friend's path to true happiness. Familiar feelings of protectiveness surged through Lucie. She'd experienced them during the three years at university, when she and Petra had formed an unlikely friendship through their shared enjoyment of Jane Austen and Stephen King. They'd even worked on their dissertations together, sharing ideas and proofreading each other's work. And Lucie, who had grown up with her own vulnerabilities, was able to understand Petra's. So even though they hadn't seen much of each other since graduating, their friendship still had a solid basis. It was the main reason why Lucie knew she had to accept Petra's invitation to be her bridesmaid; she couldn't risk hurting Petra by declining.

"Here…" Petra pushed the curtain out of the way to reveal a beautiful silk garment, the colour of clotted cream, that fell like a waterfall from its hanger. The top of the slim bodice was adorned with tiny seed pearls which ran diagonally from the right shoulder to the waist, then spread out like the branches of a tree down the flared skirt. It was truly breathtaking.

"Oh, Petra, you'll look absolutely stunning in that."

Petra nodded. "I know. It's from a new French designer and cost the earth, but Daddy said I could spend what I liked. This will be the society wedding of the season, so it's important that I look the part. Don't you think?" She turned sad blue eyes on Lucie.

"Yes, of course. You'll look like a princess. Absolutely. Harry will be bowled over by how lucky he is."

Petra fell silent and stared into space. Lucie followed her gaze but couldn't see anything of interest.

"Petra? Don't you think Harry will be delighted when he sees you in that dress?"

"Perhaps."

"I'm sure he will. You'll be perfection!"

"Nothing is ever perfect, Lucie. Nothing."

Lucie watched her friend carefully. She was lost for words. How should she reply to such a sad comment coming from a woman about to marry the man she loved?

Petra seemed to return from a dark corner of her mind and straightened like a puppet being hauled upwards on its strings. "And now you need to see your dress!"

Lucie battled a sudden wave of nausea at the thought. She tried to keep an eye on her weight, but although she didn't see herself as chubby, she certainly was curvy – especially compared to the gazelles surrounding her right now. Were any of them under five foot eight, or bigger than a size ten? Lucie had boobs, a bum and curvy thighs. She dressed to suit her shape and didn't bother following fashion, because a lot of the time it did nothing to flatter her figure.

"Mariella!" Petra curled a finger at a woman holding a tape measure and she approached them promptly. "This is Lucie. She's the last of my bridesmaids."

The woman eyed Lucie from top to toe. "So all eight are now present?" The woman's English was laced with an accent, possibly German, but Lucie couldn't be sure.

"Yes. Could you show her the dress?"

"Certainly. One moment."

Mariella marched off and Lucie marvelled at her perfectly styled grey hair. It was swept into an elegant chignon and not a hair was out of place. It must have taken a lot of strong hairspray to get that hold. Lucie touched her own hair. She'd been up at six to wash and dry it, but she knew that the walk from the station had destroyed her attempts at styling it, and that her hair was probably now lying flat and shapeless, with the usual kinks that stopped it looking sleek and shiny.

"Don't worry, I've arranged for us to have the best stylists for the wedding, so we'll sort your hair and your… uh… eyebrows and all that once we get to New York."

Lucie opened her mouth to reply but stopped herself. In Petra's world, women were immaculate from the hair on their heads down to the lack of hair on their nether regions. She'd deal with any fussy stylists when she had to. She'd never waxed her eyebrows and she wasn't about to start now.

She hoped.

She'd wait and see…

Well, she didn't want to be the only almost-monobrowed woman there, now did she?

"Here we are." Mariella returned with a garment draped over her arm. She pulled the tape measure from around her neck with her free hand and again eyed Lucie up and down. "I think we need to let this out. Or maybe even start from scratch."

Lucie willed herself not to blush but Mariella had just passed judgement on her weight and it was not an easy thing to ignore. She almost felt as if she should apologize to Petra and to Mariella for being bigger than a size ten but that would be ridiculous.

"That's okay though, isn't it, Mariella? I mean… you can make the dress bigger can't you?"

Mariella pursed her lips and held up the garment.

The shop fell silent and Lucie realized that everyone else was listening.

She scrunched up her toes and fought the urge to run from the room and out onto the street, to hide herself from these skinny rich people and their scorn. But she was an adult, and running away would be ridiculous. She liked her curves most of the time, so she wouldn't let these women's opinions sully her confidence.

"I can add extra material, yes. But it will cost more, obviously." Mariella raised a silver eyebrow at Petra.

"That's not a problem. Daddy will cover it, of course!" Petra waved a dismissive hand at Mariella and the shop owner turned on her heel and marched away.

"So, Lucie, are you bringing a plus one?"

"Yes."

"Might I ask who it is?"

Lucie chewed her lip. Dale and Petra had never really hit it off. They'd only met a few times, but Dale just seemed uncomfortable around Petra, and Lucie wasn't really sure what Petra thought about him.

"Dale."

"*Dale?*" Petra frowned. "Your old friend the gardener. Don't you have a significant other now, Lucie? What about that Charles… What was his name again? The one you told me about with the country house and the labradors. Wasn't he a teacher at a private school?"

"Oh, that didn't work out." Lucie shook her head. Charles had lasted for almost a month, but when he'd whispered to her, over dinner at a very nice little Italian restaurant, that he wanted to wear her bra and panties, Lucie had gone home alone. Some people enjoyed that type of thing, and they were perfectly entitled to, but it just wasn't Lucie's cup of tea. Besides, Charles was six foot four and at least eighteen stone; he'd have stretched her knickers beyond repair, and it was so difficult to find comfortable ones.

"But Dale…" Petra widened her eyes and defensiveness bubbled inside Lucie. What was wrong with Dale? He was a good guy. She had to stop Petra right now, before she said anything mean about Dale, because Lucie knew that she'd be unable to stop herself from venting if he was attacked.

"Yes." She took a deep breath. "We're together. He's my boyfriend now."

"You're together?" Petra's eyes widened, moving her eyebrows a millimetre or two up her forehead, as her surprise defied the botox.

"Yes. We are."

"How long?"

"Oh…" *How long? Dammit! Think!* "A… a few months."

"You're *with* him? He's your lover? You're bumping uglies?"

Uglies? "Why is that surprising? And Dale is gorgeous."

"Well no… I mean… he's easy on the eye, I can't deny that, and I wouldn't say no if I was after a bit of rough… but… as a potential husband?"

Lucie counted to ten. She would not bite. Petra's privileged, if lonely, upbringing had taught her to pass judgement on others without consideration for their feelings. So what if she wasn't actually dating Dale; it just seemed to be the right way to shut Petra up. And his parents thought they were together, so letting Petra believe it too wouldn't hurt. They might even look more convincing in the photographs if they had to behave like they were a couple.

"We're in love. Madly. Moving in together too."

Digging yourself deeper.

"Oh. Well, congratulations. So he'll be sharing your room in New York? Sitting with you for the wedding meal? Holding your hand?"

"Of course." *Is she testing me?*

"Wonderful!" Petra recovered quickly. "He might even propose when you're out there. How romantic would that be? A Christmas proposal in Manhattan." Petra's eyes glazed over.

"Hmmm."

"You know…" Petra sighed.

"Yes?"

"Harry didn't actually ask me like that." She glanced around conspiratorially. "He didn't make what I think of as a proper proposal."

"He didn't?"

Petra shook her head then moved closer to Lucie. "It was more of a… well… it doesn't matter. It just wasn't as romantic as I would have hoped." She blew out her cheeks, then continued as if she couldn't keep it in any longer. "Put it this way, he was drunk, he'd been misbe-having and I was annoyed. It was more of an 'I guess the time has come' than a declaration of undying love." Petra seemed to shrink as she relayed these details, and Lucie's heart ached for her.

"I'm so sorry."

Petra pulled herself upright. "It's okay." She plastered on a bright smile. "I got what I wanted, right? That is all that matters."

Lucie smiled in a way that she hoped was encouraging, but inside she was filled with pity. *Poor Petra.* For all her apparent snobbery, she had such an air of vulnerability. Not many people saw it, but Lucie did. She was probably one of the only ones who knew that Petra was not a complete spiky-edged ice-maiden, that underneath it all, she was just as lost as most people.

–

Three hours later, Lucie was slouched on a leather sofa in one of London's trendy bars. The dim lighting was a blessing, since she knew her cheeks were red, her eye makeup was smudged and her hair now sat helmet-like on her head. The dress fitting had been exhausting and somewhat humiliating as she'd been measured, prodded and talked about as if she wasn't actually there. As Petra, Joanna and Mariella had debated how best to make the curvy bridesmaid look just right for the wedding, so that she'd fit in with the rest, Lucie had allowed herself to drift away, enjoying memories of the night before at her flat with Dale. They'd shared an extra large pizza and giggled at that American TV show where the insane group of friends played pranks on one another. Of course, she now had to tell him that he was attending the wedding as her boyfriend, but seeing as she'd allowed his parents to believe it, she hoped he wouldn't mind deceiving the wedding party too.

By the time Mariella had finished with her, Lucie hadn't a clue what the dress was going to look like. She'd been lost in the comfort of her daydreams. All she knew was that it was bright, silky and floaty and that she'd liked the sensation of the material against her skin. Whether it would suit her or not, she had no idea, and she didn't really mind. It would be Petra's day, after all, and Lucie wanted to help make it a good one. So even if she ended up resembling a pavlova, she'd do it with her head held high.

They'd arrived at the bar to be greeted with a champagne spread apparently arranged by Harry, and Lucie had sunk two glasses of fizz immediately, keen to numb herself from the trauma of her dress fitting experience. It had worked nicely and now she was full of canapés – she might have had more than her fair share but the other bridesmaids hadn't eaten a thing – and she was enjoying her third glass of Veuve Clicquot. She'd only allow herself one more drink, as she had to get the train back at four and she didn't want to fall asleep and end up at the wrong station. She'd done that once before, after a night out with some people from work, and it hadn't been pretty, especially when she'd been woken up by a policeman at the station who'd thought she needed medical assistance.

She hadn't, she'd just been in a very deep sleep and what he thought was blood down her front turned out to be the chilli sauce from her kebab. She cringed at the memory. The taxi home had cost a fortune and the grease had ruined a perfectly good blouse.

"Mind if I sit?"

Lucie glanced up at the woman who'd approached her. She'd seen the pretty blonde at the boutique but hadn't recognized her.

"No, of course not. Help yourself." Lucie patted the seat next to her and the woman sat down.

"I'm Tania Fitzroy. Petra's Maid of Honour." She held out a hand and Lucie took it. Tania's handshake was businesslike but her skin was cool and smooth as marble.

"Lucie Quigley."

"Yes, I know. Lucie Quigley, Petra's giggly friend from university. AKA giggly Quigley."

"Giggly Quigley?" Lucie vaguely recalled Petra calling her this once or twice a long time ago but she hadn't thought the nickname had stuck. "Impressive that you know that. I'd quite forgotten it myself." Lucie nodded. Affecting a light-hearted air had been part of the persona she'd tried to create for herself at university. No one had known her there, it had been a fresh start and she wanted to be the girl who had fun, the girl who didn't give a damn, the girl whose mother hadn't died in a car crash.

"As Maid of Honour, I *made* – excuse the pun – it my business to know who the rest of the bridesmaids would be. I found out age, background, marital status and a few odd anecdotes to feed my speech. I needed a nickname for you all as part of the fun. It's always good to make your audience laugh, don't you agree? Especially with some rip-roaring stories from the past!" She widened her eyes as she said *past*, making Lucie think of a documentary she'd watched recently about people taking illegal drugs. They often had that half-crazed stare, and she wondered for a moment if Tania indulged or if she was just a bit loopy.

Lucie gave a small smile, although she was a bit concerned now about which anecdotes Tania would be sharing. She couldn't think of any terrible tales from her friendship with Petra, but Tania didn't seem like the type to spare anyone's dignity.

She drained her glass and shrugged inwardly. The champagne had dulled her self-consciousness to an acceptable level, and she no longer cared if she was being judged. Tania certainly wouldn't be calling her giggly Quigley if she'd known her growing up. She'd let it go, though. No sense fighting it, and it didn't really matter. Better to be known as giggly Quigley than the sad, quiet one.

"She's making a mistake, you know?" Tania raised an eyebrow as she gazed at Petra. The bride-to-be was browsing the canapé selection, her hand hovering over each one then withdrawing, no doubt after she counted the calories.

"What, eating?"

"No!" Tania frowned at Lucie. "Marrying Harry. It'll end in tears."

Lucie sat up, suddenly alert. "You think so?"

"Of course. Petra is making a *huge* mistake going through with this debacle. He doesn't love her. Not at all."

Lucie stared at Tania, taking in her shoulder length blonde hair, a shade or two lighter than her own, and shining with health and vitality. In profile, the woman was very similar to Petra, but she was about six pounds heavier, slim but not as gaunt as her friend, and slightly shorter. Her pneumatic breasts strained at a black silk vest top, and Lucie guessed that she'd probably had some form of enhancement. Harry had tried several times to convince Petra to have a boob job, but she hadn't been keen. In fact, as a frequent flier, she'd been terrified of having implants in case they exploded during a long haul flight, so she'd resisted, although it seemed that she had now had work done on her face. Lucie couldn't understand why a man would want to change the woman he loved. Wasn't true love about desiring someone just the way they were? If it *was* true love, of course.

Tania wasn't beautiful in the supermodel way that Petra was, but she was certainly attractive. Yet she had an edge to her as she stared at Petra, as if she was evaluating the bride-to-be's every move, every word, every thought. It could have been the champagne affecting Lucie's judgement, but there was something about Tania that made her uneasy, as if she was a tigress about to pounce or a snake about to bite.

"Have you spoken to Petra about this?" Lucie placed her glass on the table in front of the sofa.

"I've tried but she won't hear it. She's determined to be *Mrs* Harry Goldsmith at any cost."

"But you're her Maid of Honour. Surely you should try to get her to see sense... if that's how you feel."

Tania turned stern hazel eyes on Lucie. "It's not just how I feel, it's the truth. But she won't listen, so now she'll have to deal with the consequences." She rooted around in her designer handbag and pulled out a small brown container with a white label. Lucie caught sight of small black writing, but couldn't read it from that angle. "I've such a headache." She unscrewed the lid and shook three small white pills onto her palm. She thumbed them for a moment, before throwing them into her mouth and following up with a gulp of champagne. Lucie tried not to stare. Or to judge. This was how other people lived. Some of them.

"*You* could try talking to her, Lucie. Perhaps she'd listen to you. She always speaks so fondly of you."

Lucie looked from Tania to Petra and back again. Was this woman she'd only just met correct? Should she interfere, try to get Petra to see that things weren't right with Harry? But what evidence did she have? An old hunch and the word of a stranger?

"I don't think it's really my place. What if you're wrong? I mean... how do you know?" Lucie picked up her glass, but it was empty so she put it down again.

Tania shook her head slowly and placed a finger on her glossy lips. "Can't say. It's private. But if you won't tell her to reconsider... then it will all end in tears. Don't say I didn't warn you."

Tania stood and straightened her silky tunic before bending right over, graceful as a ballet dancer, to run a hand down each trouser leg. She sprang back up, and with a shake of her blonde mane she was gone, leaving Lucie with her empty glass and a sinking feeling in her belly. She wanted to talk to someone about what Tania had said, and about her own concerns. She wanted to speak to Dale and ask his advice but he would probably still be at work, Saturday or not, and it wasn't the sort of conversation to have over the phone.

Instead, she thought about what Dale would say. Probably tell her to stay out of it, not to interfere. She didn't see Petra and Harry that often, so she had no real basis for her concerns. Just a hunch and now the word of a woman who could well be genuine, but who could also have her own ulterior motives.

She had no right to go to Petra and ruin her happiness, however fragile it might be. No right at all. She had no evidence to present to her friend, and saying something would only cause Petra pain.

Yet as she gathered her things and walked over to her old friend to say goodbye, what Tania had said nagged at her like toothache. What if Petra *was* making a huge mistake, and Harry didn't love her as she deserved? Or, what if Petra was well aware of this and was going into the marriage with her eyes wide open? They had experienced a turbulent relationship, so Petra wasn't some naïve eighteen year old marrying her very own Prince Charming. Petra knew what she was doing, what she wanted, where she was headed. Of course she did.

The thoughts swirled around Lucie's head for the rest of the afternoon. As the train carried her past fields and trees, houses and high-rises, industrial estates and waste-land, Lucie couldn't help wondering if she should have tried to talk to Petra. Other people's lives could be so complicated, so confusing and so disturbing. She was glad to get back to her flat and settle into the comfort of her own predictable life.

Chapter 6

Lucie pulled her scarf up around her cheeks. An icy wind was howling across the park, battering the skeletal trees and stealing their remaining leaves, and she wondered at the wisdom of agreeing to a Sunday stroll with Dale.

"See!" he said, pulling his grey wool hat down over his ears. "I told you it would blow the cobwebs away."

"Dale, it's the first week of December. It'll likely *freeze* the cobwebs."

"Well, after all that champagne yesterday I thought you could do with clearing your head."

Lucie nodded. He was right. When she'd got back to the flat, she'd briefly texted him to let him know how it went. She'd been a bit tipsy and a trifle muddled by all that she'd heard. Petra's world was so complicated, and one that she didn't really know if she wanted to become involved in. Still, she didn't see the bride-to-be that often, and after the wedding, she'd probably see her even less. So if she played her role as bridesmaid, she could free herself from any future social obligations. With these thoughts swirling in her alcohol-fuddled brain, she'd crawled into bed and slept right through to nine-thirty this morning.

"You're right. It's certainly helping with that." She gazed at the black shapes of the trees with their branches reaching into the leaden sky, shuddering in the wind as if shaking in the cold, just like she was. At least it wasn't raining – but that was mainly because the clouds were being whipped along so violently. Something about the bleakness of the landscape tore at her heart but then didn't everyone feel that way? Spring was a time of optimism; winter was one of gloom.

"You okay, Luce?" Dale nudged her.

"Just thinking about how grim winter is."

Dale sniffed. His nose was pink and his eyes watered. "It can be. But I try to think of it as the season when the old is cleared away in preparation for the new."

The old family cleared away to make room for a new one? Wasn't that what some people did?

"It just reminds me of how quickly time passes. I mean, one minute it's summer, then before I know it, December's here again. You'd think I'd be over it all by now, wouldn't you?"

"Lucie, be kind to yourself. You can't help feeling like you do about Christmas. People dislike different times for different reasons. Look at how teachers hate September because it means they're going back to work after a long summer holiday, but then parents all over the country are sighing with relief that their kids are out of the way again."

Lucie laughed. "I don't mind September term. I like meeting the new pupils and looking ahead to a fresh year. But then, I'm not the class teacher with all that responsibility, so I guess I can understand how they feel." She thought of the familiar moans and groans in the staff room every year when the autumn term resumed, and the countdown to half-term that began immediately. So many times she'd heard teachers say that it was *just four weeks* or *just two weeks* until they broke up, then following it up with a comment about how they needed to stop wishing their lives away. Then someone else would chirp in with a story about someone they knew who'd dropped dead at forty-five and they'd all agree to count their blessings… until the next break time.

"Losing your mum on Christmas Eve is something you're never going to forget, Lucie. *Ever.* Talk about rubbish timing. Don't get me wrong, it would have been a tragedy whenever it happened, but for you it also means that you hate Christmas."

Even if the car hadn't crashed, I'd still have lost her anyway. My childhood would have been ruined by the one woman who should have been making it better. Who should have been there for me.

Dale knew about the accident, obviously. But there were things that Lucie had learned about her mother that she hadn't shared with anyone. Not even Dale. She just couldn't bear it, as if saying it aloud would somehow make it real. If she didn't say it, it didn't really happen that way. Her mother had loved her to the end and nothing could change that. She had been torn away from Lucie and her father by a tragic accident. *That* was bad enough.

"I know."

"And then that loser Jamie… well…" Dale shrugged. "You were always better off without him."

Lucie sighed, and watched as her breath came out white in the icy air. Dale was right. They'd spoken about these things so many times, but he never seemed irritated by her inability to let them go. He always listened patiently and reassured her. Lucie just hoped that she was as good a friend to Dale in return.

They reached the entrance to the park and Dale grinned. "Fancy another circuit?"

"Dale, I can't feel my toes and I'm sure I have frostbite in my nose. If I lose a toe or two, I'll never look the same in flip-flops again."

"You're not used to being outdoors. You're too accustomed to central heating and easy living, Quigley."

"Is that right, Bear Grylls?" She pulled a face at him.

"Careful, you'll get stuck like that."

"Whatever! Then I'll be the most interesting of Petra's bridesmaids won't I? I already look out of place compared to their perfection."

"You're perfect just the way you are." He held her gaze for a moment and a warm tingling spread through her body. Lucie took a step closer to him, as if drawn by a magnet, and she wobbled on her toes as a powerful gust of wind buffeted them. She put her hand out to steady herself and it connected with Dale's hard chest.

She looked at her hand. Then looked up at Dale.

Something flashed across his face but it disappeared quickly and Lucie wondered if she'd even seen it. Whatever it was.

"How about I buy you a hot chocolate?" he asked, breaking the spell. He held out his arm and she tucked her hand under his elbow.

"That's the best idea you've had in ages. And if we get inside immediately, I might get to keep all of my toes."

–

Lucie draped her hat and coat on the old-fashioned stand in the corner and took a seat at a table by the window. The small cafe was warm and cosy, a haven from the bitter cold of the December afternoon. Lights twinkled around the windows, bright against the dull afternoon sky, and in spite of herself she felt a flicker of joy. Whatever her feelings about Christmas, even Lucie couldn't resist the smell of cinnamon, coffee and cake.

She sat still, gazing out through the glass with its misty edges. The next few weeks would be very busy, with everything going on at school and getting ready to go away for the wedding. She needed to check her passport, although she was certain it was still valid from when she'd renewed it while considering a last minute sunshine break a few years ago. She hadn't gone, of course. Something had cropped up and before she knew it, the holidays were over and she was back at work, promising herself she'd do something next year. She'd even suggested to Dale that they go away together, but he'd frowned and said that with so much going on with the business and his house renovations, he didn't think it was the best time. But now they were getting a break, and in one of the most exciting cities in the world.

"There you go." Dale placed a large glass mug full of hot chocolate in front of her. Steam rose off the top, where whipped cream and marshmallows floated. Next to her drink, he put a small red plate with a large donut. Its freshly baked aroma filled Lucie's nostrils and she licked her lips as she imagined putting the sugar coated treat in her mouth.

"Back in a sec." Dale returned to the counter.

"Fancied a mince pie," he said, as he put his own plate on the table, along with another hot chocolate.

"I don't know how you can eat those things." Lucie shuddered. Growing up, she'd loved mince pies, with their sweet, spiced filling and crumbly pastry, but now they just reminded her of that Christmas Eve and the ensuing nausea that followed. Once something had exited through your nose, you were never going to relish it again.

"You don't know what you're missing," Dale said as he bit into his pie. Pastry crumbs tumbled from his mouth and he swept them up with a napkin. "Very fresh," he mumbled from behind his hand.

Lucie nodded and sipped her chocolate. The fluffy cream and melted marshmallows slipped silkily over her tongue. It was heavenly, as sweet and comforting as a hug and absolutely delicious.

As they sat in the warmth, defrosting after their walk, carols rang out from speakers around the cafe. The coffee machine buzzed and frothed. In spite of herself, Lucie sang along to the carols in her head: *Hark the herald angels sing…*

"What do you think about getting a tree this year, Luce?" Dale asked innocently, as if he hadn't asked her every year for the past five years.

"You know how I feel about Christmas trees."

"But look at that one. It's pretty, right?" Dale gestured at the tree in the corner. It stood around five feet tall and was decorated with twinkling white lights and multi-coloured tinsel. At the top sat a dainty angel with rosy cheeks. Fat snowmen hung around the tree, each one wearing tiny hats and scarves and holding a candy cane, a wrapped gift or a hymn book. They all wore the same gleeful expression, insisting that Christmas was a time of fun and cheer, that everyone – even those who melted in the sunshine – should celebrate the festive season.

"It's all right. I guess. If you buy into all that festive nonsense." Lucie sniffed and tucked her hair behind her ears.

Dale was not deterred.

"It would be one way of taking a positive step forwards, you know."

"I do know what you mean, and I can understand why you think this would be a good idea. But—"

Dale held up a hand. "Were you wavering there, Miss Quigley? I think you were. After all, it's not the season that's to blame for what happened, right?"

"Dale, if we get a real tree… I mean, if *I* get a real tree… it will die when we're in New York."

"So get an artificial one then." He raised his eyebrows above his big dark eyes.

73

Lucie sighed and gazed at the cafe tree. The angel seemed to be smiling right at her, encouraging her, and even the snowmen didn't look too bad, now that she was getting used to them. Their grins lifted her spirits, and she could imagine that seeing similar decorations at home might well make her feel a little bit festive.

Go on! For Dale's sake.

"Okay, here's the deal: because you spend so much time at my flat, we will get a tree this year. But… it will be small and the decorations will be tasteful. You know I don't like fussy or showy décor." She smiled.

"No, you just like books. Everywhere!"

"There's nothing wrong with my books, Dale. I have several first editions, in fact." Lucie thought of the piles of paperbacks in her flat: from the ones in the corner of her bedroom and on the bookshelf, to those on top of the two wardrobes and the pile in the rather cramped bathroom. Then she had more in the lounge, on shelves and behind the sofa, as well as in the small hallway. Of course, she did have an ereader now, and often downloaded books, but she still couldn't resist whenever she was out and about and came across a book sale.

"First editions of what?"

She looked upwards. "Um… Sweet Valley High."

"Sweet Valley High?"

"Yes, you know, those lovely stories I used to read about the high school twins."

"Right."

"I can't part with them, Dale. They have—"

"Memories. I know. Don't worry."

"My books are like old friends."

"Do you ever actually re-read them though, Luce?"

"Sometimes."

"Anyway, we're agreed about the tree?"

She held out her hand and Dale took it.

"Agreed." The smile that lit up his handsome face made Lucie glad that she'd given in on this one detail. It had been twenty years since she'd last celebrated Christmas, and with Dale spending so much time at her flat she did feel a bit guilty that he didn't get to enjoy the festive things he otherwise might have done. His own house was such a mess with the renovations, and she knew that if he wasn't always at hers being such a good friend to her, then he might have been able to finish them off sooner. Plus, he'd agreed to come to New York with her. So she owed him this, at least.

-

"Dale, I said tasteful…" Lucie stared at the monstrosity in her living room. It was huge, reaching from floor to ceiling. Dale had moved a pile of books from the corner of the room and neatly stacked them behind the sofa, with the others, to make space. It was shaking with the weight of decorations in every colour of the rainbow, and white lights flashed quickly among the branches. It made her eyes hurt. "That's going to give me a migraine." She threw her coat over the back of the sofa and pulled off her boots.

"Thought I'd surprise you." Dale smiled broadly and Lucie's brief flicker of irritation faded away. She'd come home after a particularly tiring day overseeing Christmas play practice to find that Dale had rushed out and purchased a tree – no doubt before she could change her mind – and that it was not as understated as she'd envisaged.

"Well… thanks." She sank onto the sofa and stared at it.

"Don't you like it?" Dale sat next to her and she watched as his grin faded. "I tried really hard to get it right."

"It's lovely. Honestly. Thank you." She was over-whelmed by guilt at her initial irritable reaction. Dale had tried hard to please her.

"Really?" He watched her carefully, his eyes wary.

"It's growing on me as we speak." She leaned back on the sofa and stretched out her legs. Even though she'd worn comfy boots, her feet were aching after running around all day organizing the children, dealing with minor tantrums and mopping up tears – from staff as well as pupils. Something occurred to her. "What time did you finish work today? It's only four-thirty now."

Dale blushed and toyed with a length of purple tinsel that he hadn't yet added to the tree.

"Dale Treharne? What's up?" She turned in her seat and tucked her legs underneath her. "Oh no. Did I upset you? I do like the tree. I'm just so tired and I felt a bit grumpy when I came in but I didn't want to offend you. I was being insensitive. I'm sorry. Dale?"

76

He glanced at her. "It's not about the tree."

"Oh. Well… Have you changed your mind about going away? I understand if you have. It was a big ask anyway. I don't mind… I'll manage."

His face had darkened. She was uncomfortable seeing him like this. Dale was usually so upbeat and optimistic, and it took a lot to drag him down.

He shook his head. "It's not that. It's something else." He pulled at the tinsel and a thin, shiny strand came off. He put it on his leg, then pulled out another. And another.

"What? What's happened?"

"It's kind of embarrassing."

"Does it require a cuppa?"

His blush deepened.

"Tell me!" She reached out and rubbed his arm. "Dale, you know you don't have to be embarrassed with me. You can tell me *anything*."

He raised his dark eyes to meet hers. "It's the kind of thing that another bloke would react differently to, I'm sure. I feel like such an idiot. Like I brought it on myself. I just didn't know what to do, Luce." He shook his head then lifted the pile of tinsel from his thigh and dropped it on the table.

Lucie's heart thundered and a queasy feeling rose in her stomach. Something bad had happened. Dale never finished work early. "I'm sure you didn't."

He shrugged, but his eyes were wary. "I don't want you to think badly of me."

"Hey." She stopped rubbing his arm and placed a hand over his. "I could never think badly of you. I'd defend you to the last."

He sighed. "Okay." He took a deep breath. "I did the Manning garden this morning, just some general maintenance, then went across to the Smith place. I usually have the team with me, but Brian had asked for the day off to see his kids' plays, Jade was on another job and Ruby was sick. Anyhow, there's usually no one there, as Mrs Smith is always dashing off to social engagements and her husband just about lives in the city."

"But not today?"

He pursed his lips. "No. Today Mrs Smith was there, and she called me in to talk to me about some ideas she'd had for the garden for next year. They're thinking of putting in a hot tub and a sunhouse, and she wanted me to look over some sketches she'd had done. She's not bad... some kind of art graduate, I think. I could appreciate the sketches she'd drawn. It all seemed innocuous enough, and I had no reason to suspect that she had any other ideas when she invited me in."

"Oh no. I don't like the sound of this."

He frowned. "She gave me a coffee, and while I was poring over the sketches, she disappeared." He inhaled sharply then licked his lips. "I don't think I did anything to encourage her, Luce. I was being my normal self. You know how I am with clients, very professional."

"I do know. You're an oxymoron – friendly yet aloof. So what did she do?" Lucie knew that someone who wanted to see it as something else could misconstrue Dale's friendliness. Like a lonely woman – or a horny one, perhaps.

He hung his head and rubbed a hand over his eyes, as if the memory was just too much for him to bear. "She came back into the kitchen wearing some flimsy, transparent nightie thing, with feathery slippers."

"What?" Lucie suppressed a giggle. Poor Dale. *Feathery slippers! A transparent nightie!* "That old cliché, hey?"

"Don't get me wrong... she's in good shape for a woman in her fifties, but you know, Luce... I'm not that kind of guy. A lot of men would have been up for it, but it just turned me cold. I was mortified, to be honest. I could see... well... *everything*!"

"Oh no! Did she say anything?" Lucie knew Dale was easily embarrassed if anything even remotely erotic appeared on TV, from a passionate kiss shared by characters on a soap opera to those weird adverts for lingerie and sex toys that sometimes flashed up late at night. He always made an excuse to leave the room.

He nodded. "That she'd seen me looking at her and knew that I wanted her. That today she'd ensured that we'd have time to be alone so we could f... Do stuff. Then she put on some music and—"

"What music?"

"I don't know. Does it matter? Some old-fashioned stuff, like Ella Fitzgerald or something."

"Oh."

"What'd you mean, 'Oh'?"

"Just… you know. One of *those* women."

"Luce, I don't know why that matters. Anyway, she kind of danced across the kitchen, thrusting her hips at me and licking her lips. Things were sticking out and she kept lifting the hem of the nightie suggestively and bits of the feathers kept drifting off the slippers and… I didn't know where to look and… I kept telling myself to get up and leave, but I was kind of frozen."

"You were?"

"With sheer terror. Or horror. I don't really know which, it was all so surreal. You just don't expect people to behave like that."

"What did you say?"

"Say?"

"Yes. Didn't you say anything?"

"No. I couldn't. My mind went blank. Then… When she reached me, she ran a hand over my chest, said I was a big boy and that she needed satisfying with my big, hard—"

"I get it!" Lucie held up a hand. "No need to tell me what else she said. Bloody hell, Dale!" Lucie was filled with conflicting emotions: she felt sorry for Dale, having been subjected to the attentions of this woman, and she was also absolutely furious that this Mrs Smith would dare to upset her friend. Coming on to him like that was disgusting!

"Anyway, that was enough to scare me into action, so I jumped up and left."

"Oh, Dale."

His face fell. "I didn't even say goodbye. I guess I've lost that contract now. It paid well, too."

"But it's not worth it. You don't have to go through things like that. You should... I don't know... sue for sexual harassment."

"And if I did that, I'd lose most of my clients."

"But it's not fair. Loyal people would stick by you."

"Some would, but I'm a landscape gardener, Lucie. People talk. I need to develop my customer base, not scare them off. I've been approached before, like that time the househusband asked me if I needed a soak in the jacuzzi to ease my backache, but at least he wasn't so blatant. He kept his clothes on and it was more approach by pun than chiffon and feathers. I wasn't even sure that he was serious. But with Mrs Smith... I don't know. I think she might have been drinking."

"That is *no* excuse." Lucie gazed at Dale's profile. He *was* very attractive. She could see why other women would want him. But she also had a depth of feeling for him that had nothing to do with sexual attraction. He was a good guy. He'd never set out to hurt anyone, and he worked so hard. This wasn't fair. Sometimes his innocence still surprised her, but he'd always had a strong moral code and while some men – and women – would jump into bed with anyone, Dale wasn't like that.

"Better get this tinsel finished." He snapped back into normal industrious mode and continued decorating the tree. Lucie stared at the small pile of purple tinsel on the table, her mind racing as she thought back over what he'd told her. It wasn't fair that he'd been subjected to that, and she wished it hadn't happened. But it had, and although it meant he'd probably lose that client, he'd find others. He was good at what he did.

She wanted to help him feel better, but she didn't know what to do.

Then she did.

Dale was trying hard to make her tree look good; he'd been working on it for most of the afternoon, it seemed. Even after going through that horrid experience. It was time to make him feel appreciated. She pushed her exhaustion to one side and got up off the sofa, ignoring the dull throbbing in her feet and the tension between her shoulders. "Let me help you."

"Really?" He smiled at her, his eyes crinkling at the corners. "But I wanted to get this done for you so you wouldn't have to—"

"I want to help, Dale. You've done a fantastic job, and it's so beautiful. I love it. I *really* love it! I know..." she gulped, "Let's put some carols on."

"Carols?"

"Yes. There's probably one of your old CDs around here somewhere. One that you brought over a few years back, to try to make me feel festive."

She located it on one of her shelves, wiped the dust from the cover and popped it into the CD player. As *Silent Night* rang out, she dug around in the bags of decorations that Dale had bought.

An hour later, when they flopped onto the sofa with a glass of the mulled wine that she'd run out to buy from the corner shop, she couldn't help but smile. Not only had they decorated the tree, the fireplace had its own set of lights and a branch entwined with holly and ivy; the pictures on the walls and the piles of books were draped with tinsel; there were festive throws over the sofa and chairs, and Frankincense candles burning on the coffee table. For someone who hated Christmas, Lucie had a flat surprisingly full of festive cheer.

"You know what, Dale?"

Her friend turned to her and clinked his glass against hers.

"This isn't so bad after all. Kind of like… acclimatizing myself to Christmas."

"Ready to hit the most festive city in the world."

"Exactly."

And as she relaxed into the couch, sipping her warm spiced wine as the day's tension slowly slipped away, she knew that this was a step she'd needed to take for a while. Twenty years was a long time to hate Christmas.

Chapter 7

"Hey! Go easy with the glitter!" Lucie chuckled as she gazed at the children gathered around the small table in front of her. Aged seven or eight, they were still small enough to sit in the specially sized plastic chairs that the school provided for its younger pupils, although some of them kept standing up as their card-making enthusiasm overwhelmed them. Lucie was also perched on one of the chairs, although she couldn't help being aware that there was a slight overhang of bottom on either side.

"Is my card okay?"

Lucie met Jacob McGurl's innocent green eyes. He held out his creation for her to check, and as he lifted it a mixture of purple and gold glitter drifted onto the old newspapers spread out on the table.

"Let me see." Lucie took the card and smiled. "It's beautiful, Jacob." He had drawn a picture of him standing next to a Christmas tree with his mother. They were smiling, their oversized two-dimensional heads as round as coins. They both wore wellies and glitter snow was falling from the rather sunny sky. In the top right corner of the card was another figure. It had wings and wore a long silver gown. Its one stick hand was outstretched, as if it were waving at the people below. Lucie's throat tightened as she realized the significance of the figure at the top.

"Do you think my mummy will like it?" Jacob asked, sniffing, then rubbing his nose on his sleeve.

Lucie nodded slowly. She took in his pale face, his chapped lips and his light brown hair that was in need of a cut. "I think she'll love it, sweetheart."

A smile broke out on his face.

"That's Daddy in the sky, watching over us. Mummy said he's an angel now and he'll always be watching over me. I wish he was here though. I told her I don't want him to be in the sky, I want him home again."

"Of course you do, Jacob."

"But he had the cancer and it was too strong for him and he died." Lucie tried to keep a neutral expression as Jacob told her about his father in the matter-of-fact way that children often did. He'd passed away during the summer, after a short fight against pancreatic cancer that had stolen him away from his wife and child in barely a few weeks. It was tragic in so many ways, and Lucie wished that she could make it all better for this young boy.

"I want my Mummy to have a good Christmas. She's been very sad this year because she misses my Daddy so much."

"I'm sure she does."

"Last night I heard my nanny McGurl telling Mummy that she didn't want Christmas to come, but Mummy shouted at her that we would have Christmas no matter what. I was in bed but I heard them, and I crept to the top of the stairs and listened. I know it was naughty, but I was worried."

Lucie glanced at the other children around the table, but they were all absorbed in their festive creativity, ignoring the outpouring that was happening right next to them. This happened sometimes; children would start talking about something that was going on in their lives, then it would all pour out as if the floodgates had opened. It was difficult when the subjects of their conversations were as emotional as this, but Lucie knew that Jacob needed to speak to someone and he had chosen her. So she would listen and be as reassuring as she could.

"Is Nanny McGurl your Daddy's mummy then?"

He nodded then sniffed again. "She said she doesn't want Christmas because Daddy won't be there. It will never be the same again."

Lucie gently laid his card on the table.

"But your Mummy will want you to have a good Christmas, because that's what your Daddy would want, Jacob."

"Yes, that's what she told me this morning. My Daddy loved Christmas and always bought the tree and made us cake and made it all fun." He paused, lost in his thoughts. "I miss him," he whispered as his eyes filled with tears.

"I know you do." Lucie took his hand and he stood next to her then placed his head on her shoulder and cried quietly. One of the girls briefly looked up and saw Jacob leaning on Lucie but she shrugged and went back to her glitter pot. "Your Daddy will miss you too, Jacob, but he would want you to be happy, because he loves you very much." She patted his back then slid her free hand into her cardigan pocket and pulled out a tissue. Jacob lifted his head and nodded solemnly then let Lucie wipe his eyes and nose.

"I'm being brave for my mummy."

"You are *very* brave, Jacob. But she won't mind if you cry. Don't try to hold your sadness in."

"I can tell you, Miss Quigley. Can't I?"

"Yes, you can. Anytime you need to tell me, I'm here to listen."

The class teacher caught Lucie's eye over Jacob's shoulder and mouthed *Is he okay?* Lucie gave her a quick nod to show that she was dealing with the situation.

"Well, this is a beautiful card. How about if we make some special decorations for your tree, too?"

"Yes, please." Jacob smiled and released her hand, then took his seat.

As Lucie handed him pieces of card, some small silver stars, and the non-toxic glue that smelt strangely like popcorn, she thought about what he'd said. She tried to ignore the blob of snot on her right shoulder. This young boy had lost his father just months ago. He'd overheard an argument between his mother and grandmother that he should never have had to hear. But these things happened. And, in spite of everything he'd been through, he still wanted to celebrate Christmas. So that his mother could enjoy it, and in memory of his father. Her heart ached for him, but it swelled with pride too. He was being so brave and positive – and he was only seven years old.

She watched as he carefully cut out a snowman, his tongue poking out of the side of his mouth in concentration. She thought then about Dale two evenings ago, bringing her a tree and asking her to try to enjoy some aspects of the festive season. Guilt washed over her. If this child could put some enthusiasm into celebrating Christmas for his mother's sake, and if Dale could go to such lengths to help her enjoy the festivities, then she should try too. Not just be tolerant of it, but aim for something more. She had no right to be so stubborn, so glum, when others around her were making such an effort.

"Here you are, Jacob. This will add some extra sparkle." She held out the plastic tube of gold glitter.

"Thank you, miss," he said, and as he smiled at her, his puffy red eyes crinkling at the corners, Lucie knew that the time had come to start making some big changes in her own attitude.

–

Lucie parked her car and pulled up the handbrake. As the engine ticked over, seemingly affronted by the chilly air, she tried to prepare herself for what she was about to do.

Visiting her father and stepmother was never easy. Her father had remarried ten years ago, and since then he'd changed. He was not the man Lucie knew before. It could be that he'd actually become the man he was meant to be all along, the man he would have been if her mother had survived, but that was something Lucie would never know. The main issue now was that every visit was surrounded by drama. She'd never known a woman who craved attention like her stepmother did – except for her stepsisters, perhaps.

She took a few deep breaths, then grabbed her handbag and the tote bag of gifts, from the passenger footwell, and got out of the car. She'd deliberately parked further along the street, even though there was a space in front of her father's driveway, because she wanted to gather her thoughts before they saw that she'd arrived. Thelma always seemed to pounce on her, rushing out onto the driveway and berating her for something or other before she could even get to her father, and that was something that Lucie always tried to avoid.

Today, she'd won this small victory. Next time, who knew?

She walked along the street, then turned left onto the Quigley drive and approached the front door. Sure enough, before she could even raise her hand to knock, the door swung inwards and there was Thelma, her jet black beehive hairsprayed in place, its colour only broken by the white-blonde streaks in her thick fringe. She was clad in a pink velour tracksuit with a fluffy white kitten over her left breast. The kitten was wearing a collar that sparkled with rhinestones. Because, well, Thelma loved rhinestones.

"Lucie! Wherever is your car? I've been watching out for you for the past thirty-three minutes. I thought you told your father you'd be here by eleven? That's what he said. I'd swear on it, I would. So you're late! Late! Oh deary me!" She paused, pursing her small fuchsia-coated lips in such a way that her mouth resembled a cat's bottom. Lucie fought the nervous laughter that bubbled in her belly.

A sudden yelping was followed by a screech from Thelma as something shot out from beneath her. Lucie watched as it headed straight for her then circled her ankles repeatedly like a lasso. "Mary Puppins, stop that right now!" Thelma yelled at her tiny silver Chihuahua. She turned as her husband appeared in the doorway. "I've told you not to leave the door open, Mark! A million times!"

"I think you'll find that *you* left the door open, darling." He stepped out into the cold morning.

"Hey, Dad," Lucie said as she tried to step over the tiny creature that was still racing around her, its tongue dangling from its open mouth.

"Watch it… You'll squish her!" Thelma screamed.

Lucie wobbled, one leg raised, as her stepmother dived at her, making a grab for Mary Puppins.

"Gotcha!"

The small dog was caught firmly under Thelma's elbow. Lucie regained her balance, only to find her step-mother crawling awkwardly along the floor on her hands and knees. She glanced at her father, who shrugged in resignation. Thelma was wheezing loudly.

"Let me help you up, dear." Mark leaned over and offered his hand.

"You'll all be the death of me. You and your daughter and naughty Mary Puppins," she said as she hobbled into the house with Mark supporting her by the elbow.

"You're stronger than you think, my angel," Mark said as they entered the hallway.

"But my nerves!" Thelma whined. "My poor nerves can't take it." She clung to her husband. "I need to lie down now."

"Yes, dear, of course."

Lucie stood and watched. The bottom of her stepmother's pink velour trousers was emblazoned with the words *Hot Mama*. Her instincts screamed at her, telling her to turn and run, back to her car and her quiet, calm life, but she knew she couldn't do that. She needed to visit before she headed off to New York. She owed her father that. She probably owed it to Thelma, too, if she was being magnanimous.

Inside, the house was positively tropical, and her fingers tingled as they warmed up. She hadn't realized quite how chilly it had been outside, but it was evidently cold enough to mess with her circulation. She hung her coat on the banister, then removed her shoes and tucked them onto the rack under the stairs. The house her father had bought with his wife was not one that Lucie would have chosen, but she knew he'd been able to pay for it outright with the life insurance her mother had insisted on having and the proceeds from the sale of their old family home. It was weird, that: as if her mother might have known something was going to happen to her. She'd provided for her husband through her death, but Mark Quigley hadn't touched the money until he'd become involved with Thelma and she'd wanted to know why he had so much money sitting around in a savings account.

Mark had told Lucie all this not long after he'd got together with Thelma, after consuming a few beers on his birthday. He'd actually seemed proud of his new wife for pushing him to spend the money he'd left untouched for nearly ten years. The thought that her father was surrendering his financial security and independence made Lucie nervous, because if anything went wrong with his second marriage, then Thelma would surely get at least half. But Lucie also felt that it wasn't her place to interfere, and that her father had to make his own mistakes.

If it *was* a mistake. Because for all that Thelma could be quite annoying, she really did seem to make her father happy. *Hot Mama* popped into her head and she grimaced.

Lucie made her way through to the kitchen and found her father filling the kettle.

"Cup of tea, love?"

"Please."

"Cold out today."

"Freezing."

"She'll be all right, love." He nodded towards the lounge.

"Oh... yes, I'm sure she will."

"She's putting her feet up for ten minutes. She was so excited about you coming around, you know. She got herself a bit worked up. She even bathed Mary Puppins this morning and cleaned the house. Twice."

Lucie smiled. She knew that Thelma cleaned every day, thoroughly, and that her obsession with cleaning was probably a form of OCD, but there was no point saying that to her father. What good would it do? He probably already knew it, anyway.

"There's really no need. You should see my flat, Dad. Thelma would probably have a fit."

He nodded, then dropped tea bags into a pot and poured on boiling water. Lucie watched him carefully, noting how he seemed to have put on a little weight since she'd seen him last, most of it settling around his belly. His chestnut-brown hair was still quite thick at the front, but when he turned away she could see that it was thinning over his crown and a few grey hairs shone as they caught the light. "She's the same when she goes round to Lauren and Abigail's. Hates mess, she does, of any kind. And our little Mary Puppins is the cleanest dog in Tonbridge, I don't doubt it."

His face brightened, and Lucie saw the father she'd grown up with, the dad who'd played Scrabble with her, who'd held her hand when she couldn't sleep and who'd practised French with her as preparation for her GCSE oral exam. A sudden pang of loss overwhelmed her. She missed that man. Missed the closeness they'd once shared. But he was happy now, and she couldn't begrudge him that. He deserved to be with someone he loved. A woman who'd stand by him through whatever life threw at them.

Her father carried their teas on a tray through to the lounge. Thelma was on the sofa, her flesh-coloured popsock-clad feet raised on a cushion, a hand draped across her forehead. She peered at them as they entered the room, then whimpered.

"Here you are, darling, here's some sweet tea." Mark placed the mug, featuring a fluffy kitten, on the side table next to his wife.

Lucie took a seat. Peering into her mug, she saw the tea was a deep orange, strong enough to stand a spoon in, as her mother used to say. Her father had always liked his strong, and Lucie had always managed to make it drinkable by adding plenty of milk. However, he had clearly forgotten and she didn't have the heart to remind him.

"Where's Mary Puppins?" Thelma asked.

Mark looked around him as if he suspected that the dog was hiding somewhere. "Oh. I thought she'd be with you. Perhaps she's in the hallway."

"I'll check, shall I?" Lucie put her mug on the tray then prepared to search the house. She didn't have to look far, because there was Mary Puppins, going for gold on her left shoe, the flowered pump folded right over as she humped it like it was the love of her life. "Oh, no! Mary Puppins! Cut it out!" She approached the dog but as she reached out, it growled at her then resumed its humping, pausing only to lick the shoe every so often as if it needed some affectionate encouragement to surrender in that way. "Now, come on, doggie… that's my shoe."

Lucie cautiously stretched her arm out again, but the dog froze. Its ears flicked back and its tongue poked out like a serpent's as it bared tiny white teeth.

"Come on, Puppins. Give me my shoe. Don't be a little bitch."

"Best let her wear herself out."

Lucie jumped.

"Sorry, love, didn't mean to startle you. But I find it's best to let her do whatever she needs to do. Let her finish what she started and all that."

Lucie turned to face her father. "What? Really?"

He nodded. "She gets grouchy if you stop her when she's engrossed."

"She makes a habit of this?" Lucie wrinkled her nose, imagining smelly shoes covered in dog drool and goodness knows what else.

"Unfortunately she does. She stole one of Abigail's shoes just last week – some shiny, strappy affair – and when Abi tried to get it back, Mary Puppins wouldn't let it go. It was one of those expensive designer thingies as well and Abi was furious." He shrugged. "But what can you do?"

"Put your shoes somewhere else?" Lucie stared at the open shoe rack tucked in the space beneath the stairwell. Surely the dog had easy access to all the shoes there, so putting them higher up might make more sense.

"It's an idea, love, for sure," her father replied, as if it had never occurred to him. "Let's go drink our tea, shall we?"

Lucie gave her pump one last glance, winced at the growing stain on the toe where the dog kept licking it, then followed her father back into the lounge. That was yet another thing she'd need to add to her going away list

– a new pair of shoes. Somehow she didn't think the pair she'd worn today would ever be quite the same.

-

The first hour of her visit passed with polite conversation in her father and stepmother's spotless lounge. Lucie nodded and shook her head and made all the right noises as Thelma told her all about her varicose veins – which she tried to show Lucie by peeling down her popsocks, but which didn't look all that swollen from Lucie's perspective – and about her frozen shoulder – which actually seemed pretty mobile – and about her female problems – which Lucie tried to block out, as she really had no desire to hear about her stepmother's irregular menstrual cycle, or how she suspected that she had cysts on her ovaries and might need a hysterectomy.

Lucie watched Thelma carefully as she talked, the diatribe clearly making her feel more and more sorry for herself by the moment. At fifty-five, Thelma was an attractive woman, even with her puckered mouth. Her black hair with its streaked fringe was expertly coloured, no greys on show, and her skin glowed with what must be fake tan, as they hadn't seen the sun for some time. She had large green eyes that were always emphasized with a thick flick of liquid liner. She could easily pass for someone much younger. Yet even ten years earlier, Thelma had been like this. Lucie could recall the first time she met her and how she'd been treated to a retelling of Thelma's latest doctor's visit.

Afterwards, as he drove her home, Mark had quietly explained that Thelma had suffered a bad childhood and that it left her neurotic about certain things, yet he had seemed very accepting of his new partner's ways. Thinking about it now, Lucie wondered if it was Thelma's apparent vulnerabilities that had drawn her father to his new wife; had he been afraid of being abandoned again? A woman as needy as Thelma would surely never leave him. It was more than likely that she would, in fact, *always* need him.

Lucie swallowed the dregs of her third mug of strong tea and tried not to grimace. "Thanks, Dad. That was a great cuppa."

"Anytime, love, anytime. Now, how about some lunch? After we've eaten, I've got something for you."

"You have?"

He nodded. "Not a Christmas gift, although we do have a little something here for you somewhere, but Thelma said you can have it when you come home from your trip. If that's all right?"

Lucie smiled her assent. Thelma's need to be in control, even over something as trivial as when she received her presents, didn't surprise her. Last week Lucie had informed her father that she'd be away over Christmas, and he'd actually seemed a bit relieved. Possibly because it meant one less person to worry about when trying to negotiate Christmas plans.

"That's great, thanks." Lucie flashed a smile at Thelma, but her stepmother was fanning herself with a TV guide. "So what else do you have for me?" She hoped it was books. Sometimes her father picked up books he thought she might like from the second-hand book stalls at the market, and she liked his eclectic selection. They weren't usually the kind of thing she'd have chosen herself but she enjoyed the challenge of reading something different.

"It's a box of old things that I found in the attic the other day. Bits and bobs left over from your childhood. I'd forgotten it was there, but when I showed Thelma she said I should give it to you. 'No sense in it being up there,' she said. 'It's clutter,' she said, and besides… she thought it was time you had some of your things now you're settled in your own place and not likely to move for a while."

Lucie watched her father carefully. "I am happy there, Dad. I love my flat."

"And now that you're… *involved*." Thelma sat up and swung her legs over the edge of the sofa.

"What?"

Thelma nodded. "I saw Dale's mother at the super-market. She told me *all* about it. We've been waiting for you to tell *us* too!" She clapped her hands, her fragility apparently forgotten.

"He's a good one that Dale. Always liked him." Mark looked at Lucie and her colour rose.

"What did Glenda say, exactly?" Lucie glanced from Mark to Thelma and back again.

"That you two have finally admitted that you're in love and that things look… well… You *are* going off to New York together for Christmas." Thelma made a kissing noise and winked. "Why didn't you tell us? You should have told us, Lucie. It's not nice finding out things about my step-daughter second hand you know. I was positively mortified! Wasn't I, Mark?"

He nodded. "Mortified."

"So don't do that, Lucie. Don't keep such important matters from us. *We* are your parents, you know!"

Lucie swallowed a retort. She was too old to be biting back with *you're not my mother*. It was clear that there was no point trying to deny things. It would only complicate matters. Better to let everyone believe what they wanted until after Christmas, then their fake breakup could be done for the benefit of everyone. If she admitted the truth here today, it might prove too much for the gossipy Thelma, and she could well take it all back to Glenda and Hank. And knowing they'd been deceived would be devastating for Dale's parents. "I didn't mean to keep it from you. Glenda found out accidentally. It's just early days and we were going to tell you soon. I promise. But now I don't need to."

"We're happy for you, Lucie. Really happy. Maybe you can enjoy Christmas this year, eh? Now you've got yourself a nice man to spend it with." Her father leaned over and squeezed her hand then began to clear the mugs.

Lucie opened her mouth to agree, but her attention was captured by Mary Puppins racing into the room dragging a now very battered shoe. Then, as if deliberately mocking Lucie, the dog mounted her find on the rug, and proceeded to show Lucie exactly how much damage a Chihuahua could do to a flowered ballet pump.

—

Lucie finished drying the last dinner plate then folded the tea towel and placed it on the kitchen worktop. "That was a lovely lunch, thanks Dad."

"No problem at all. I enjoy cooking now I've got more time."

"Retirement suits you." Lucie smiled at him.

"I'm glad I could retire at sixty-one. I know that the pension age for people of your generation will be much higher."

"Work til you drop, eh?" Lucie shook her head. "It's wrong, but with an aging population, things will be difficult."

"Marry a rich man and you won't have to worry."

Lucie's eyes snapped up, but her father was laughing. "Good plan! When you find one, snag him for me."

"You've got Dale now and I'm sure he'll be able to give you a good life and look after you. And it's not just about money anyway, is it love? You need to be with someone who'll love you and be true to you, someone who won't…"

They fell into a silence that lasted for a few minutes, each of them lost in their thoughts. But Lucie suspected that her father was thinking the same thing she was. *About Mum.*

"Anyway, I wanted you to have that box of things, so I'll go get it. You can make us another cuppa if you like."

He left the kitchen and Lucie filled the kettle. She dropped tea bags into the pot and splashed milk into three mugs. Whenever she visited her father, she always drank at least six mugs of tea. She was glad that Mark seemed happy with his lot. After her mother had died, he'd been understandably distraught, lost and confused for a long time. He'd gone through the stages of grief with textbook predictability; his anger and frustration often giving way to bouts of despair and depression. But he'd always been there for Lucie when she'd needed him. She'd tried to support him too, tried to be a good daughter and to help him see that there was still fun to be had, that life could still offer enjoyment. But it had been hard. They'd both been so shocked.

Lucie poured the boiling water over the teabags, appreciating the familiar sound of water hitting the bottom of the teapot. Small things like that had helped her keep going when things seemed really bleak. As had her father. And Dale. She laughed as she recalled him pulling her into Glenda's cloakroom to tell her that they had to pretend to be dating. And all because he was prepared to go to New York with her, to support her. *Again*.

"What're you chuckling about?" Mark asked as he came into the kitchen carrying a battered cardboard box. Scrawled on the side in thick black marker was written: **FOR LUCIE**.

"Oh, nothing. Just a joke I heard recently."

He nodded as if he knew what she meant, then put the box on the table.

"Don't pour one for Thelma. She's gone for a nap."

"Oh. Okay." Exactly how much napping and lying down did her stepmother do? It was a wonder she got anything done around the house.

Lucie filled two mugs with tea and took them to the table.

"Thanks, love." He stared at the surface of his tea. "You know, Thelma needs me."

"I can see that."

"And it's good for me. Can you understand that, Lucie?" He scanned her face with his blue eyes, so much like her own. "I never really felt that your mother did. It was as if she was holding something back. But Thelma… well, she is who she is. She might be a bit of," he lowered his voice, "a pain sometimes. Don't tell her I said that." He winked. "But I know that she loves me and needs me. She's not always like this… ill and so on. We do have fun. We enjoy watching TV together and going shopping and… you know… lots of things old people do."

"You're not old, Dad! But I do know you're happy together. And I know that you love each other madly. Life is short, and you have to grab happiness while you can."

"That's why I'm glad you and Dale have finally admitted your feelings for each other. He'll have your back, Lucie. He'll look after you and that's all a man can ask, for his daughter."

Lucie didn't want to lie to her father, but it was too late to tell him the truth. Besides, Dale did look after her, so it wasn't a complete lie, just bending the truth a little. "So what's in the box?"

"Things you should have had long ago. Things from your childhood, from your mum."

"I wish she'd known her own parents."

"Me too. It was something she carried with her always. That sadness from being shunted from one foster home to another… Pam was always keen to prove herself, desperate to ensure that people saw her worth."

"You think that's why she…" Lucie bit her lip, unable to voice her thoughts.

He nodded. "Quite possibly, love. When my parents were around, though, she did love them. And they completely adored her. She was just eighteen when we met – so wild and rebellious. I was bowled over by her, obsessed even. After we first met, I couldn't stop thinking about her and I went to the phone box about ten times a day to call her. I must've spent a fortune just to hear her voice. When she finally agreed to go out with me, and I took her home, Mam and Dad fell for her too. They used to treat her as if she was their own daughter… Dad was always slipping her money to get her hair done or to buy things for you."

"I miss Granny and Grandad. Even after all these years."

"Me too, love. Every day. Just like I miss your mum. When my parents died, your mum missed them too, and losing them had a lasting impact upon her. She'd never had that type of unconditional love and losing it broke something inside her. She was never the same afterwards. I tried so hard to make her happy, to be the husband she wanted me to be, but I just don't think I had what she needed."

Lucie slid her hand over his. "You can go through the box now or take it home and look through it in your own time. There's quite a bit in there. Might be a bit emotional, you know."

"Thanks, Dad. I think I'll leave it until later then. I need to get going soon anyway."

"Of course."

They finished their tea, then Lucie went to search of her shoes. Mary Puppins had fallen asleep on her soft pink bed, next to the sofa in the lounge. Her tiny ribcage rose and fell, and each time she exhaled, her tongue poked out from between her teeth and waggled. Lucie located her shoe under the coffee table then sneaked back out of the room. As she was gingerly slipping her foot into the sticky pump, her father came out into the hallway carrying the box. He handed it to her. "I'll tell Thelma you said goodbye, shall I?"

"Please, Dad."

She leaned forwards and pecked his cheek, inhaling his familiar spicy aftershave. He patted her shoulder, awkward now with his adult daughter. "Take care, Lucie, and have fun in New York. Be very careful if you go on that subway mind, as I've read that it can be dangerous at night. All sorts of undesirables travelling on it just waiting for the next naïve tourist to attack."

"I think that's scaremongering, Dad, but I promise I'll be careful. And Dale will be with me. Not many people are going to mess with him, being the size he is."

"Say hello to him for us and make sure to bring him round for dinner when you get home."

"I will."

Lucie smiled at her father then walked to her car. She was relieved that her father hadn't expected her to go through the box in front of him. It was something best done in her own home, alone. And that was what she intended to do.

–

Lucie switched on the lamps in the lounge, casting shadows across the wooden floor. The afternoon was dark and it felt much later than three-thirty. A light drizzle was falling, and it made even the inside of her flat feel cold and damp.

She was about to sit down when the tree Dale had bought caught her eye, so she went over and turned the fairy lights on. They twinkled agreeably, giving her lounge a warm glow, and she silently thanked her friend for being so considerate.

Once she'd made a mug of tea, she took it into the lounge and sat on the sofa. *For Lucie.*

What was inside the box?

She wished that someone was with her so she could ask them to look first. If Dale was here, he'd do it. But he wasn't. And her curiosity wouldn't wait until he was.

She needed to do this now.

As she reached for the lid, her hands trembled slightly. But she knew that she had to look. She absolutely had to.

She gently lifted the lid. She scooted to the edge of the sofa then peered in. It all looked innocuous enough – lots of pieces of paper, brown and white envelopes, and what appeared to be a photo album.

It couldn't hurt to look, could it?

She removed the album first and ran a hand over the bumpy green cover. It seemed to be made out of lots of narrow strips of thick paper or card all woven together. Her name was on the front, written in gold foil and covered with cellotape that was peeling up at the edges. As she opened the cover, a waft of memories flooded through her as the scent of violets emerged.

"Mum," she whispered, her throat closing over. Her mother had always worn a distinctive perfume and somehow, the fragrance was captured within the pages of this album. Then she saw why. There was a sprig of flowers taped to the inside of the front cover, tiny dried violets that were brittle with age and storage. She touched one gently and it crumbled beneath her fingers, the dark purple dust staining her skin. "Mum," she said again, as pain rose in her chest. She took a few deep breaths to calm herself, well aware now that this would not be easy.

The first page of the album showed her mother and father posing for the camera. Her mother had a Bonnie Tyler eighties haircut, permed and backcombed. Her skin glowed from time spent in the sun – no doubt without sun-cream – and her eyes were bright green against her tan. Next to her stood Lucie's father; taller and skinnier than she'd ever seen him, his face radiating happiness. Mark's hair was thick and spiky, and in his face Lucie could see her own. It was a strong resemblance, apart from the long, golden moustache which sat above his top lip, testament to the fashion at the time. One arm was wrapped around her mother's back, but his other hand rested on her mother's protruding belly, proud and protective. Lucie smiled at the hope in their faces, at how they clearly thought they had a lifetime ahead of them, starting with the imminent arrival of their first child.

Turning over the page, she found several photographs of her early days, in which her parents both had that pale, exhausted and terrified look of new parents. The shock of being responsible for another human being had evidently affected them enormously, as had the sleep deprivation. But there was also love in their expressions, deep, protective, overwhelming, terrifying love. As they cradled her in their arms, sat next to her crib, or pushed her in the big old-fashioned pram, their feelings for their new child showed in the way their bodies were turned towards her in every shot.

The next few pages charted her toddler years, featuring a potty, a ride-on car, a white and green checked high-chair with long wooden legs and a red harness, as well as moments captured with her grandparents. Some of the photographs were Polaroids, with their thick white borders. Her grandmother wore glasses that were now trendy again, with thick black frames. Seeing family members that were no longer around made Lucie feel strange, as if a dark cloud had settled over her, yet occasional rays of sunshine broke through. It was so good to look back on happy times and run her eyes over their faces, remembering little details, yet it was also painful, because it brought home how real they had once been. Her grandparents and her mother were just like her; people with hopes and dreams and futures ahead of them. Until they weren't. And one day, perhaps someone would do what Lucie was doing right now, look back at photographs of her and wonder how she used to feel, what she had wanted and what her dreams had been. It made her want to run out and grab hold of the people she knew and loved, to hug them tight and remind them how much she cared about them; that whatever happened in life, they were once there, with her, alive.

Just over halfway through the album, she found a blank page. Beneath the sticky see-through plastic were two squares that were lighter than the rest of the page. She stared at them for a moment, wondering why someone had removed the photographs. From somewhere in the deepest recesses of her mind, a whisper of a memory surfaced. At first blurry, undefined as smoke, until the scent of violets and the mustiness of the album itself, lent it shape.

The baby!

Her little brother.

Stillborn seven months into the pregnancy, when she was six.

The nights she'd lain in her small single bed listening to her mother crying, the sound muffled by the walls and the pillow that Pam had buried her face in.

But still. Lucie had heard her. Lucie had known.

There had been a second pregnancy, but there had been no second child. How devastating that must have been for her parents. Life-changing. How did people come back from that?

Perhaps they never really did.

The missing photographs were of her mother during that second pregnancy, taken from the album by Pam herself, or perhaps by Lucie's father. Who knew? It had been done to protect Lucie, to protect her parents. To save them all the pain of looking at the promises that had been made, things that had been possible, but were lost before they'd even had a chance to begin. There had been no pictures of the baby, no evidence of his existence except for those photos taken during Pam's pregnancy.

After everything Pam had suffered growing up, to think she was creating her perfect little family, then to have it taken away, must have destroyed her. And Mark. But wasn't that how life worked? Other people's lives could look perfect from the outside, yet in reality they were just as sorrowful as the next. Everyone had troubles to bear.

Lucie flicked through the rest of the album, registering her childhood, yet unable to ignore the sadness in her parents' eyes, the lack of joy in their smiles for the camera, the sense that something was missing. Some*one* was missing. Something had fractured and everything had changed.

And at that moment, she understood her mother a little better.

And her heart ached.

–

"Thanks for coming round." Lucie walked through to the lounge and Dale followed, then slumped onto the sofa next to her.

"Where else would I be? I mean, you're my girlfriend now, remember?" He squeezed her shoulder.

"My father and Thelma think so too." She tucked her legs underneath her.

"They do?"

Lucie nodded. "They bumped into your mother and she couldn't keep the joy out of her voice apparently. I bet she's told everyone, Dale!"

"Even the postman."

"She'll be wanting us to pose for a Christmas card soon."

"That's okay. I have a Christmas jumper ready."

"Dale, be serious! All this will make it harder to call off the relationship, you know?"

He watched as a tiny line appeared between her brows. He was trying to keep everything to do with their fake relationship light-hearted, but he could tell that something else was bothering Lucie. In fact, as he studied her closely, he could see that her eyes and nose were red, as if she'd been crying.

"Has something happened?"

She chewed her lip and nodded at the box on the coffee table.

"You got me an early gift?"

"Dale!"

"Sorry. What is it?"

"My father gave it to me today. It's full of old things… from my childhood."

"Oh." His stomach rolled. This didn't sound good.

"Photographs, school reports, cards – stuff like that."

"You've been through it all?"

"Yes. It was strange… kind of nice, yet also really, really sad."

"I get that. You did have some awful hairstyles back then, Luce."

"Shut up!" She scowled at him. "I don't mean like that, although my hair was quite bad in the nineties, but it was going through the photos. It was lovely to look at them, but it also hurt." She rubbed at her chest. Dale moved a bit closer to Lucie.

"You want to show me?"

"Okay."

He sat and listened as she talked him through the photographs; some she recalled being taken, but for many she'd been so young that she had no memory of them at all. She was so cute as a child, all blonde curls and dimples, with sparkling blue eyes full of mischief. But when she got to a page that was blank, with two lighter spaces where photographs had clearly been removed, she went quiet.

"What were these photos here, Luce? Did you take them out?"

She shook her head. "It was when my mother got pregnant again."

He ran a hand over his head. "God, I remember that. Vaguely. She..." He stopped. How could you describe what happened to Lucie's little brother?

"Lost him. He was stillborn. Arrived too early. Now they might have been able to save him..."

"Yes, perhaps. So sad."

Lucie leaned her head on Dale's shoulder. "I hadn't thought about him in ages. He's always been just a memory, and because he never even took a breath, I didn't know him. Not at all."

"You were really young too, Luce."

"Yes, there's that."

"I kind of remember you telling me about it in school... and I think we talked about it years later when we'd had a few beers... but..."

"It's one of those things you just forget about – deliberately, I think. Self-preservation. Until you're reminded."

He moved slightly, so he could wrap his arm around her shoulders, and she snuggled closer. They sat quietly for a while, staring at the blank spaces on the page as if they held the answers to their unspoken questions. "Did you speak to your dad about this?"

"No. I didn't open the box until I came home, so I don't know if he removed the photos or if it was my mother. I haven't seen this album in years and it ends before she... you know."

Dale flicked through a few more pages and sure enough, the photos stopped when Lucie turned twelve. The final photograph was of her twelfth birthday party.

"Is that me?" He pointed at a head in the background, but it was hard to tell, as the image was dark and fuzzy.

"I think so. I had some friends round, so you were probably there."

"Why'd she stop taking photos?" He frowned as he looked at the twelve-year-old Lucie, her face still innocent. Her life still whole. Her heart still unbroken. Her mother still there to support and comfort her.

She shrugged. "Perhaps that was when things started to change. Perhaps the camera broke, or perhaps she just didn't get the films developed. I guess we'll never know. There are a few odd pictures in the box too – that she might have taken, or they could be from someone else, but she stopped putting them in the album at this point. She must have had other priorities."

"You'd have started secondary school, she might have been a bit lost," he suggested gently.

"Maybe."

"So what else is in there?" As he'd done thousands of times before, he wished he could help Lucie, take away her pain. But he couldn't. All he could do was be there.

–

Twenty minutes later, Dale was wiping away tears of laughter.

"Oh Luce, I can't believe you were so bad at P.E."

"I was never the athletic type, Dale. It's not that funny."

"But this comment here… *Lucie could try harder in gym class. Deliberately throwing herself at the high-jump bar so she* can spend the lesson sitting on the benches talking to her friends does not qualify as making an effort."

"Well if I hit it off three times, I got to chill out. It seemed ridiculous to keep on trying when I was rubbish at it anyway."

"And this one… *Lucie must try not to throw the discus straight at her teacher's head.*"

"Well, she kept telling me to spin around before I let go. I told her and told her that I couldn't do it but she wouldn't listen. So when I did spin and release the damned thing, I couldn't help what direction it flew off in."

"Did it hit her?" Dale pictured the P.E. teacher being knocked out by a discus.

"No. But only because she had lightning-quick reactions and she ducked in time."

"Oh, Luce! You're so funny." He wiped his eyes again then looked at her.

In the late afternoon darkness, with just the lights from the tree and the two floor lamps, the lounge was cosy and festive. Lucie had pulled her hair into a messy bun, and some of it had sprung out so that tendrils hung around her cheeks and over her forehead. Dale pushed a curl away, but it bounced back into place. He tried to speak, but his voice was lodged in his throat, so he just stared at her instead.

She was beautiful.

She was perfect.

She was his soulmate.

But he had always known that.

She leaned forwards and kissed his cheek, then slid her arm over his chest and snuggled into him. And he wondered if she could feel his heart beating hard, if she suspected at all that it did so just for her.

That it had always done so.

Just for her.

–

Lucie and Dale paused in front of the stall and waited for Glenda and Hank to catch up. The trip to the Tonbridge Christmas market was an annual affair for Dale's parents, and this year Glenda had insisted that Dale and Lucie tag along. Lucie didn't mind; she was, in fact, quite enjoying the Sunday morning stroll around the pretty festive stalls with their colourful crafts. The market catered to a wide variety of needs and there was so much to see: from cakes to preserves, clothes to boots, jewellery to dog beds. The stalls were decorated with holly, ivy and mistletoe, and elaborately decorated Christmas trees were dotted around the perimeter of the long stay car park, making its mundane everyday purpose easy to forget.

The fresh winter air was fragrant with mulled wine, donuts, crepes and hog roast, and although it was only mid-morning, Lucie's stomach rumbled. She hoped that they would stop for refreshments at some point so they could savour the delights on offer.

"See anything you like, Lucie?" Glenda squeezed in next to her and eyed the pretty silver jewellery.

"I have to be honest, Glenda, it's all beautiful."

"Dale!" Glenda reached around Lucie and tapped her son's shoulder. "Perfect opportunity here, you know."

Lucie was suddenly too hot in her woollen coat and black beret. She loosened her scarf and let the cold air caress her throat.

"Yes, mother, thank you." Dale sighed as if frustrated with Glenda's interference.

"Just saying." Glenda turned to Hank. "Let's find somewhere to have a warm drink and leave these two alone for a moment so they can look at the jewellery in peace."

Lucie turned just in time to see Glenda winking at her husband.

"Yes, darling." Hank shuffled after his wife, laden with bags: Glenda was on a mission to get as much of her Christmas shopping done as possible.

"Have you seen anything you like, Luce?" Dale asked.

"It's all very pretty."

"Well, you know… you *are* my girlfriend now, so I *am* allowed to buy you things."

Lucie met his gaze and although he was smiling play-fully, there was something serious in his eyes. It made her heartbeat quicken.

"Oh, Dale, I don't know. I still feel a bit bad about all this. Your mum is so happy that we're together."

"Does it make you wonder what it would be like if we really *were*?" he asked, suddenly finding something on his shoe intensely interesting.

How to answer that?

Lucie nudged him. "How d'you fancy a hot chocolate?"

He looked up. "Or a mulled wine?"

"Dale Treharne! Isn't it a bit early for that?"

"Dad's driving."

"Oh okay, why not. It does smell delicious."

"You find Mum and Dad and I'll be there in a moment."

"Why? What're you going to do?"

"I've seen something I want to pick up." He gestured at the stall.

"What, for you?" she teased.

"No… I, uh… I think Mum might like it."

"Have you? Which one? I didn't know Glenda liked silver, she always wears that gold chain your Dad bought her. And her rings are all gold too."

"Lucie…" He widened his eyes. "Take a hint."

"Oh. Okay. Don't be long."

Lucie turned and headed in the direction she'd seen Hank and Glenda go, the thought of a mulled wine too tempting to resist. But she couldn't help wondering what it was that had caught Dale's eye, and if it was, as she suspected, actually for her.

–

Dale watched as the woman at the jewellery stall wrapped the silver pendant in purple tissue paper. As soon as he'd seen the tiny book with the opal heart on its cover, he'd known that it would be perfect for Lucie. He'd been contemplating how to purchase it discreetly when his mother had made the comment about getting

Lucie something from the stall. Typical Mum, making everything seem so black and white, when in reality, things were far more complicated.

He bought Lucie gifts every year, and always chose them carefully, but he'd never ventured as far as jewellery. It wasn't the type of thing friends bought for each other; it was too intimate. But this pendant was different. For starters, it was a book, which was appropriate. In addition, it was silver, and he'd only ever seen Lucie wear silver jewellery, so in that respect, it was perfect. Finally, it just felt like the right time to get her something this pretty, this personal and special.

"Here you go." The stallholder handed him the small parcel. "I've wrapped it in plenty of tissue so it will protect the opal. It's such a pretty piece, isn't it?"

Dale nodded.

"I think your girlfriend will love it. The opal will match her pretty eyes."

"Thank you. She does have pretty eyes." He glanced behind the woman. "Can I have two of those, too?"

"Yes, of course."

He tucked the small parcel into his jacket pocket, then went in search of Lucie and his parents.

–

Lucie waved at Dale as he walked towards them. He manoeuvred his way through the metal chairs and tables then sat next to her.

"So, what did you buy?" Glenda asked, leaning forwards eagerly.

"These." Dale held up two red Santa hats with big white pompoms on the ends. He removed his beanie then pulled one of the Santa hats on. "The other one is for you, Lucie."

She scrunched up her nose. "You want me to wear *that*?"

"This is a Christmas market and we are getting into the festive spirit. So yes, I *would* like you to wear the Santa hat."

Lucie nodded. "Okay then." She replaced her beret with the red hat, then smoothed her hair down around her cheeks.

"Suits you." Dale winked at her.

"Photo opportunity!" Glenda sang as she pulled her mobile from her bag. "Get closer, you two."

Dale shuffled his chair closer to Lucie's and wrapped his arm around her, then rested his cheek against hers. As they smiled for photographs, Lucie was acutely aware of how good he smelled and how smooth his clean-shaven cheek felt next to her skin. If she turned just a fraction, she could kiss him.

"Lucie?" It was Glenda. "You've gone bright red, dear. Whatever's wrong?"

"N… nothing. Just rather… warm, all of a sudden."

She wriggled out from under Dale's arm and fanned her cheeks with her hands.

"Now that my darling wife has finished taking the photos, shall we get some drinks and a bite to eat?" Hank asked. "I'm famished."

"Lucie and I would like a mulled wine each," Dale said. "And I think I'll have a savoury crepe."

"That sounds good." Lucie ran a finger down the menu. "There's one with brie, bacon and cranberry sauce."

"Perfect."

Hank and Dale went to the counter to order. Glenda passed Lucie her mobile. "Check out the photos. You two make a lovely couple."

Lucie flicked through the pictures. She had to agree with Glenda; she did look good with Dale at her side.

"I wonder what he bought you." Glenda wiggled her eyebrows. "Something sparkly, I hope."

Lucie chewed her cheek. She didn't want to encourage Glenda, but then it seemed that she didn't need much help seeing more in Lucie and Dale's relationship than there was in reality. Glenda had her heart set on Lucie and Dale being together. *Forever.*

"Food will be about ten minutes as they're quite busy, but here's a mulled wine to be going on with." Dale had returned with a large ceramic mug decorated with a very jolly snowman. She picked it up and cradled it between her palms. She breathed in the aromas of clove, nutmeg and ginger. Slices of orange and lemon floated in the wine, and she fought the temptation to lift them out and pop them in her mouth.

Across the car park, a band started playing and the market filled with music and cheer. "This is wonderful, isn't it? I do love it when the Salvation Army band plays carols." Glenda leaned back in her chair and crossed her ankles. She had a mug of mulled wine too, and Hank had coffee.

"While we wait for food, shall we play a game?" Dale asked.

"A game?" Lucie blew on her wine then took a tentative sip. Her mouth was filled with fruits and spices, the blackberry and cherry of the wine delicately enhanced with citrus and cinnamon.

"Yes. We all share one memory about Christmas. Good or bad." He glanced at Lucie. "But good would be better, obviously."

"Go on then."

"Mum? Do you want to go first?"

Glenda ran her tongue over her teeth. "Yes. Okay. What about the grommets story?"

"Oh, no. Not that one, Mum!"

"Dale, it was one of the most stressful times of my life."

"What's this?" Lucie asked.

"Hasn't she told you this one before, Luce?"

Lucie shook her head.

"It is quite a funny tale," Hank said.

"It wasn't funny at the time." Glenda scowled at her husband. "Well, Lucie. It was the Christmas when Dale was five. He was having terrible trouble with glue ear and the doctors recommended having grommets inserted to help drain the fluid away from the middle ear."

"Poor Dale."

"Yes. He had a bit of a rough time of it that winter. We took him to the hospital for the operation and they placed him on a ward with three other children who were all in for the same thing. I was allowed to wait with him in the anaesthetic room until he went through to theatre." Glenda took a sip of her wine. "The anaesthetist gave him the injection, then told him to relax and go to sleep."

"But I didn't."

Lucie looked at Dale. "It didn't work?"

"I lay there and closed my eyes, but nothing happened."

"So what did they do?"

"They gave him another dose. Apparently some people have a higher tolerance than others."

"But the second dose didn't work either," Dale added. "I drifted off for a bit but next thing I knew, I woke up as they were wheeling me through the doors into theatre."

"Oh my goodness! Were you scared?" Lucie asked.

"Not really."

"He just looked around him and asked, 'What's going on? Where am I?'" Glenda said.

"Then Mum started to cry and told them it wasn't working."

"So didn't you have the operation?"

"Yep. They realized that they needed to do something else, so next thing I knew, they had the anaesthetic gas on me."

"This was just weeks before Christmas, Lucie. I was a wreck that year."

"And I proved that I'm superhuman!" Dale laughed.

"But what if you ever have to have another operation?" Lucie was overwhelmed with concern. "It could be dangerous, right?"

"Well, there was that time when he was fourteen and he had to have teeth extracted so they could fit his braces," Hank said. "I went with him that time – Glenda couldn't face it."

"Didn't it work then?"

"Nope. Had to have extra then, too. More injections in my gums and the roof of my mouth."

"Dale, that's awful."

"What can you do? I just have a high tolerance to anaesthetic."

"What's your story, Hank?" Lucie asked.

"That one, I think. Same as Glenda." Hank finished his coffee. "I can't top that one."

"Dale?"

"I think one of my favourites must be the year Dad dressed up as Santa and got stuck on the roof."

"I remember that one!" Lucie giggled. "You had to get the fire brigade out, didn't you?"

Hank frowned. "It was not at all funny."

"It was afterwards, Hank. You were clinging to the chimney for dear life." Glenda patted her husband's arm.

"I don't like heights." Hank shrugged.

"Well, why did you go up there, Dad?"

"I wanted to convince you boys that Santa was real."

"But it didn't work, did it?" Dale asked.

"Nope. I climbed out of the attic window and it shut on me so I couldn't get back in. The roof tiles were frosty and I realized that I could have a nasty fall. It wasn't my best decision ever. Your poor mother was downstairs trying to keep you lot from seeing me climbing up there."

"The plan was that once he was up there, I'd take you boys into the garden and we could wave at Santa."

"But instead, Santa was clinging to the chimney and shouting for help!" Dale chuckled heartily.

"Yes, we've had some good times, haven't we?" Glenda took her husband's hand, her love for him etched on her face. "You two have plenty of these ahead too. You're going to be so happy."

A lump caught in Lucie's throat. She had no doubt that Dale would make a good husband... for someone, anyway.

"Lucie? Do you have a good story?" Glenda placed her empty mug on the table.

Lucie paused. "I'll tell you when we get back from New York. I have a feeling this is going to be a good one, and that Dale and I will have some tales to tell." She reached out and slipped her hand into Dale's, and was filled with warmth when he squeezed her fingers.

"It will be, Luce. I promise."

–

The day of the school play arrived, and with it an unexpected flurry of snow. As a result, the school telephone lines and email inboxes were jammed from seven am. It was decided that the school should remain open, dependent upon how the morning panned out. Staff members were encouraged to maintain a sense of calm and order, as apparently the weather forecast for the rest of the day was 'uncertain': forecaster-speak for 'there might be more snow but we don't have a clue how much or where it's going to fall.'

Lucie did her best to settle the pupils as they divested themselves of hats, scarves, gloves and wellington boots, but spirits were high and with Christmas just over a week away, not much was going to soothe the savage pack that is a group of year three children when Santa will soon be visiting.

By ten-thirty, the pupils had changed into costumes and were waiting to be called to the hall. Beyond the old-fashioned windows the day was dark, so all the internal lights were on. It gave the room a false golden glow, and the clear reflections in the windows made the classroom appear twice its actual size.

Lucie was fitting a cotton-wool beard onto one of the three kings when the head teacher entered the classroom. The children immediately stood up and Mrs McMahon waved at them distractedly to sit back down. She beckoned to Lucie and Mrs Hughes to follow her to the door, which they did carefully, both aware that this would have roused the suspicions of the pupils, had they not been otherwise occupied.

"Ladies, the forecast does not look good. Apparently a snowstorm is making its way down to us and will be here by early afternoon. We have enough time to get the play done, but then the children will have to go home." She looked crestfallen, as if the weather had deliberately set out to destroy the end of term for her school. She had a tendency to take things like this personally, which Lucie found a bit ridiculous, but then everyone had their foibles. "I'm not sure if we'll be back before Friday, so let's do our utmost to ensure that this morning's production runs smoothly. At least then we can send the children off for the holidays with a positive conclusion."

"Of course," Lucie agreed.

Mrs Hughes frowned. "But I need to think about my own children too. They're in school and they'll be sent home if it's that bad. I've no one there for them."

"I know that, Dawn, but I've checked and the secondary schools won't be closing until after lunch so the free school meals children still get to eat. So you have until then."

Dawn nodded but she still looked worried.

"I don't need to rush off, so you go as soon as we're done, Dawn, and I'll stay and help tidy up."

"Thank you, Lucie. That's so kind of you. It's just with Billy having had the flu recently, and my mother not being well enough to drive, I can't risk him having to walk home. Christmas will be ruined if he gets sick too."

Lucie understood Dawn's maternal concerns, but the Christmas bit rankled her. People were so strange with their festive obsessions. No one could get ill or die at Christmas otherwise it would all be ruined! Well, Christmas had been ruined for her a long time ago and she'd survived. She shook herself. *Stop being so miserable! Christmas is probably great when you have your own kids.*

They put the finishing touches to costumes, rescued a sheep who'd managed to get herself locked in the toilet and had to be calmed down with a cup of hot chocolate, then guided the children down to the main hall, all the time shushing and gesturing at them to be quiet. It was like a game of whack-a-mole, though: as soon as one child was settled, another further along started giggling and Lucie had to bite her lip to stop herself grinning, which they would likely take as encouragement.

From outside the doors to the main hall, they heard Mrs McMahon addressing the parents, giving them the usual spiel about how she'd seen a lot of plays in her twenty-plus years of teaching, but this had to be one of the best yet. She said this every year, but it still made Lucie smile. It meant so much to the children, and she loved seeing their happy expressions when they were praised by their head teacher. In their youthful innocence, they fully believed everything she said.

Then the hall fell quiet.

The only sounds were the sniffs and coughs of the children behind her.

They were like coiled springs in a mattress, lined up in pairs, ready to burst into the hall to sing and dance and repeat their lines. To celebrate life, love and the excitement of knowing that Christmas was just around the corner.

A note rang out from inside the hall.

Then another.

And another.

The hall doors opened with a creak and the children crept in.

Silent night… Holy night… All is calm…

For all that Lucie hated Christmas, hearing this song from the mouths of innocents made goosebumps rise on her arms and the tiny hairs on her neck stand on end.

She followed the children in and supervised as they took their places on the benches in front of the stage. As they sang the rest of the ancient hymn, one she'd sung herself as a child and one her mother had loved, she had to swallow hard against the emotion lodged in her throat.

The play went well. It was, Lucie admitted to herself, the best one yet. The school had decided to go with a traditional nativity this year, but elements of other religions were incorporated to reflect the multi-cultural catchment area. As always, there were wonderful moments, where the talented actors played their parts well, as well as a few hiccups, as could only be expected when so many young children were trying to remember both their lines and where to be and when. Mary – Chetana Singh – stole the show in her beautiful blue and gold sari. She was cool, calm and collected, even when Liam Waters, playing Joseph, dropped the baby Jesus. The baby happened to be one of those real life dolls that actually had a small penis – as was revealed when Joseph went to pick the doll up and only grabbed the corner of the swaddling. This caused the audience to gasp, which was followed by a ripple of laughter, making Joseph turn away in embarrassment.

Lucie sat facing the children, close enough to prompt them if they forgot their lines and to offer reassuring smiles to the nervous ones. Or, in the case of Charlie Samuels, to frown and wag a finger when he kept trying to knock the crown off one of the three kings sitting in front of him. She feigned ignorance at the usual nose-picking and waving from the infant children, and tried not to giggle at the response from the audience when the little donkey turned out to be a labrador. His mother hadn't been able to find a donkey costume, so had opted for what she thought most closely resembled one.

Lucie had to suppress a smile at one point when little Jacob's waving became particularly fervent. A woman had come into the hall late, creeping along the side of the audience until she found a seat. Jacob's eyes lit up and a grin spread across his face. Lucie turned to see what had caused his excitement and there, with his mother in the second row, was an older woman who Lucie guessed must be his nan. Perhaps she'd declined the invitation from her grandson at first but then changed her mind. Lucie was glad for Jacob; it would mean so much to him.

As she turned back to the stage, the scents, the songs, the atmosphere and the sense of magic in the air conjured a vivid memory of her own days as a pupil at St. Clotilde's. She pictured her mother sat there in the crowd, her pretty face etched with pride as she smiled and waved at Lucie. And Lucie had been proud too; proud of her attractive mother, of the woman who tucked her in at night and read her stories, who sang and danced with her to ABBA songs, who brushed and plaited her hair better than anyone else could have done. Her mother had loved Christmas. And back then, Lucie had loved it too. The emotion was so positive, so vibrant and so joyous, that she held it close and vowed to return to it later.

As the children sang their final song, *We Wish You a Merry Christmas*, Lucie turned to the windows high up in the hall walls. Snow was falling heavily now. In the corner of the hall, the large tree twinkled with lights. She could smell pine and people and sweaty feet – some of the pupils had removed their shoes to get into character – and the buzz of anticipation was palpable.

She thought of Dale's face when she'd told him she loved the tree he'd bought for her, and of the hotel they'd be staying in that overlooked Central Park, and how excited Dale had been about that fact.

Something inside her shifted.

Just a fraction.

She had to take a deep breath.

And it was okay.

Christmas was coming, and for the first time in a long time, Lucie Quigley wasn't completely filled with dread.

–

Snow fell for the next two days and school was cancelled. Then, as often happens with British weather, it stopped snowing and the pure white flakes turned to grey mush in the gutters and on pavements. From a winter wonderland, Tonbridge became a wet, sludgy mess.

Lucie and Dale were heading to see his parents before they left for New York, in order to deliver gifts and cards. With everything that had been going on, Lucie hadn't seen Glenda and Hank since they'd been to the Christmas market, and she was rather anxious. Lucie knew that maintaining her fake relationship with Dale in front of them would be increasingly difficult, especially without the distractions that the market stalls had offered.

"Stop worrying now," Dale said as they pulled up in front of his parents' house. "Just act natural."

"'Act natural?' How do I do that while creating a convincing charade? 'Natural' means us just being friends, Dale."

He turned in his seat to her and took her hand. "Lucie, it's only for an hour or so. Just make sure that when you look at me, you smile and imagine I'm someone you fancy."

"Someone I fancy?"

"Yes, you know… like Chris Hemsworth, Ryan Gosling, whoever." He grinned.

"And who will you be imagining when you look at me?"

His expression changed, the laughter left his eyes and something more serious settled there.

"Dale?"

"Come on, let's get inside." He opened his door and got out.

"Dale! Tell me now. I want to know who you'll be picturing. At least tell me that." She gave a small laugh but for some reason her stomach had knotted.

Dale leaned back into the van and held Lucie's gaze. "That's for me to know. Now come on, or my mother'll wear a hole in the carpet by the window, wondering what we're doing out here."

He slammed the door and Lucie was left alone in the silent van, watching as he walked around the front and came to open her door. As she slipped out of her seat and turned around the lift the gift bag out of the footwell, she released a deep breath. She didn't know why whoever Dale might be thinking of should matter to her. But it did. Because she knew she wouldn't be picturing Chris or Ryan – or any other celebrity, for that matter. She wouldn't need to, when she had Dale by her side.

"Hello, Lucie!" Glenda enveloped her in a hug.

"Hi, Glenda. How have you been?"

"Busy with Christmas preparations, you know. But we've missed you!" Glenda released Lucie and met her eyes. "How was the end of term?"

"Well, the last two days were called off because of the snow, but the play on Wednesday was fabulous. The children did such a good job, and it was so much fun."

"I used to love the Christmas plays. Such emotional times, watching my boys in their little costumes, fidgeting and waving when they spotted me. I do miss those times."

"Did you go to see your grandchildren's plays?"

Glenda shook her head. "The tickets were limited, so Helen's mother went. My turn next year, apparently." She paused and tucked a strand of hair behind her ear. "I need some more grandchildren now, so I have more school events to attend." She smiled to show she was teasing, but Lucie had to avert her eyes.

"Now, now, Glenda! One step at a time, eh? Lucie and Dale need some time as a couple before they add to the Treharne family. Isn't that right, son?" Hank patted Dale on the back and was rewarded with a grateful smile from his son.

"Yes, Dad. We certainly do need some time. It's way too soon for babies and all that, Mum." Dale slid an arm around Lucie's shoulders and she leant against him, grateful for the support.

"But you'll make such beautiful children when you do." Glenda clapped her hands together and stared at her son and Lucie. "*Beautiful*, with your combined genes. Right, ignore me! I'm just a sentimental old fool. I'll make some tea." She left the hall, and Hank followed her.

"This is really difficult," she whispered.

"I know. I'm sorry. She's just over the moon about us."

"But baby talk? Already?"

"I'm really sorry. I can't help how she is. I know she's a bit overbearing at times but it's only because she cares about you, Luce. She cares about you a lot."

"I know." And it was true, she thought, as she hung her coat on the banister then followed Dale into the kitchen. It almost made her wish that she and Dale actually were an item. Because then she would be feeling happy and hopeful, rather than cruel and deceitful. If she really was

Dale's girlfriend, all this would be so nice, even being teased about having children and becoming a proper part of Dale's family. They were a warm and friendly bunch and had always made Lucie feel so welcome.

In the kitchen, the aroma of freshly baked cakes greeted her and she licked her lips. Glenda had always enjoyed baking, and her husband, sons and visitors all appreciated her offerings in the kitchen. Lucie was no exception.

"Lucie, I've made mince pies but I know you hate them, so I baked some gingerbread especially for you."

"Wow! Thank you." Lucie eyed the delights cooling on a wire rack. The aromas of ginger and cinnamon permeated the air and made her mouth water.

They sat around the kitchen island. Glenda placed a pot of tea in the middle, then four small bone china plates with festive red and green napkins. As Hank poured the tea, they helped themselves to mince pies and biscuits and Lucie munched away, listening to Dale telling his parents about the garden he was planning for his renovation. It sounded incredibly complicated to Lucie, as he discussed the wood he would use for the decking and which shrubs he'd be planting to create wind-screening and privacy. He even had an area of the garden reserved for herbs, which made Glenda clap her hands, as she knew she'd have access to them too.

Lucie finished her gingerbread and dusted off her hands with her napkin. The kitchen was warm and homely. The radio was on low in the corner and a choir sang carols, their pure voices ringing out, the echoes created by the cathedral's high ceilings creating a haunting clarity. Goosebumps rose on Lucie's arms.

Outside, drizzle was falling, drifting sideways and melting what remained of the snow. The Treharnes' back garden was neat and tidy, a rectangular lawn surrounded by pruned rosebushes and hardy shrubs. At the far end of the garden stood a row of emerald green thujas, planted by Dale to provide privacy from the house behind his parents'. The garden was as familiar to Lucie as the back of her hand, because she'd spent hours and hours out there with Dale and his family. Parties, barbecues, sunbathing, snowball fights; they had all happened out there. It was even where Lucie and Dale had shared their first kiss, when she was eighteen and he was just twenty. The kiss that had led to something more. She could picture it clearly now, although it was a memory she often suppressed.

They'd been to a concert in Hyde Park with friends, out in the sunshine and the balmy breeze all day long. Their noses were sunburnt and they were hot and exhausted after a day filled with excitement. They'd drunk too much cider, danced like fools and enjoyed just being young and alive.

Dale's parents had been away on holiday in Italy. Lucie hadn't wanted the day to end, so Dale had suggested she come home with him for some more cider and music. The friends they'd been with had left them at the station, but Lucie and Dale hadn't minded. They'd been high on life, and were still singing the songs they'd enjoyed that day.

Outside, as they'd opened cans of Strongbow and lain on the grass, staring up the orange and plum streaked sky, something had changed between them. The years of friendship had fallen away, and as their eyes had met they'd kissed; furiously, excitedly, drunkenly. But passionately. Their discovery of each other hadn't been hindered by awkwardness or fear of parental interruption. Dale's younger brother Thomas had been away with friends, his older brother Ieuan long ago moved out.

When Lucie had suggested that they go inside and continue what they'd started, Dale hadn't paused for a moment. But he'd then asked her if she was 'sure' about thirty times before they'd made it to his bedroom, so Lucie had given up telling him she was, and resorted to kissing him instead.

"Lucie?"

She blinked hard, warmth flooding her cheeks as she realized where her thoughts had strayed.

"Oh… uh, yes?"

"I just asked if you'd like to open your presents now, or wait until after Christmas."

Lucie met Glenda's curious eyes and nodded. "Whatever Dale wants is fine with me."

She tried to force the images of what had happened over the next two weeks from her mind. They'd been hungry for each other, their appetite for what they'd started insatiable. Unfettered by responsibility or concerns about the future and crazy with young lust, they had devoured each other, only parting when Dale had to go to work at the garden centre.

"I say we wait until we're back from New York, then we can have a second Christmas. What do you think, Mum?"

"That would be wonderful, Dale! Shall I get another turkey in?"

Hank groaned. "Now you've given your mother an excuse to cook another Christmas dinner with all the trimmings."

Glenda laughed. "Hank, don't pretend you're not thrilled."

"Well, my love, the thought of eating two of your amazing dinners is certainly something to look forward to. It's just that I'm getting so fat."

"Nonsense, darling. You're as fit and handsome as the day we met." Glenda got up and took the plates to the sink. "I'll have to write another list now. This is so exciting. *Two* Christmas days. You know, when you told me you were going to be away, I was a bit upset about it, although I'd never have let on. But you made it better by sharing your fabulous news… and now you've made it all even better by giving me the chance to celebrate twice."

Dale caught Lucie's eye and winked. She smiled but inside everything had turned jittery. They'd agreed to end their relationship after Christmas, to pretend that it hadn't worked out, but now they would have to maintain the façade for a bit longer as Lucie sat amongst Dale's family and opened the gifts they'd chosen for her, then ate the food that Glenda had prepared with love in her heart and a smile on her face.

"Lucie." Dale reached over the island and patted her hand. "You okay? You seemed far away for a while there."

"I'm fine. Just overwhelmed by memories. Must be the time of year."

"Probably is." He nodded. "Let's put their presents under the tree."

Lucie went out into the hallway and picked up the large gift bag she'd brought with her. She'd ordered the presents online after her last visit to the Treharne house. She'd suspected she probably wouldn't get much time to go shopping, and she'd been right.

In the lounge, Dale was on his knees arranging his gifts under the six-foot synthetic spruce that Glenda had bought to replace the old tree she'd had for about ten years.

"Like the real tree scent, Luce?" He wiggled his eyebrows.

"*That's* what the smell is?"

"It came with a spray that makes the tree smell like a real one."

"I'm not convinced. It's a bit like…" She bit her lip as Hank entered the room.

"Toilet cleaner?" He laughed. "I've been telling her that for a week. I said it smelled like something you'd pour down the lavatory, but she won't have it and she keeps spritzing more on."

Dale stood up. "I've placed all your pressies under there."

"I've got more here," Lucie said as she held out the bag.

"You two should've pooled together this year," Hank said. "You're a couple now. Save money by just buying one gift between you. Absolute madness otherwise." He stared at them and Lucie had to turn to the tree to hide her rising blush. Did he see through them? Had he guessed that they were acting? But why would he?

"Let me help," Dale said as he took the gifts from Lucie then tucked them under the tree with the ones he'd bought. Lucie kept her back to Hank, pretending to be focused on what Dale was doing to avoid having to make eye contact with the man she'd grown up knowing. She hadn't been as close to Hank as to Glenda, but he'd still been there throughout her teenage years, giving her and Dale lifts, handing them cash when he knew they'd already spent their pocket money and telling Lucie to take care when she went off to university. Granted, she had her own father, but Hank had been there too, and she'd known she could ask him for anything.

When all the gifts were under the tree and they'd enjoyed another mug of tea, Dale looked at his watch. "I guess we'd better be going, then."

"You can stay for lunch if you like." Glenda gestured at the fridge. "I've got an enormous ham in there. I can easily make some sandwiches."

"Thanks, Mum, but I know you've got visiting of your own to do."

"Yes, Glenda. There's no getting out of visiting my cousin and his lovely wife." Hank shook his head.

"Are you going to see Ted and Alice?" Lucie asked, recalling Hank's cousins from Birmingham.

"We are indeed. And staying overnight, too." Hank winked at Lucie.

"Family, eh?" Glenda sighed. "We have to take the rough with the smooth."

Hank laughed. "That's no way to speak about my side of the family. Ted can't help being a bit rough around the edges. He means well."

"It's the jokes, though." Glenda shuddered. "The terribly obscene jokes."

"They are a bit rude, but we should be used to them by now."

"How Alice has put up with them all these years, I'll never know." Glenda tutted then led the way into the hall. "Oh! Would you look at that." She pointed above Lucie and Dale's heads.

They both looked up.

And Lucie sighed inwardly.

"Oh! Mistletoe. How nice!" Dale exposed his neat white teeth in an exaggerated grin.

"Now you have to kiss," Glenda said.

"It's true," Hank added. "'Tis the rule of Christmas."

"I'm not sure that's true, Dad."

"It is, son. If you don't kiss under the mistletoe, it's bad luck."

Lucie looked at Glenda and Hank then at Dale. They really weren't being given much choice here. If they declined, it would seem strange.

Dale obviously realized it too.

"Come here then, Quigley."

He held out his arms and she walked into them. His hands were warm on her shoulders and as he moved them up to her cheeks, her heart began to pound. She couldn't believe he was going to do this; to kiss her, right in front of his parents.

He held her gaze for a moment then leaned towards her.

His scent washed over her; citrus, ginger, warm delicious male. It roused a hundred butterflies in her stomach.

She closed her eyes.

And melted as his warm lips met hers in the softest of kisses.

The hallway spun as she breathed him in.

Then…

It was over as quickly as it had begun, and as Dale released her, she stumbled backwards and landed on her bottom on the stairs.

"Luce! Sorry!" Dale took her hands and helped her up.

"Dale! You dropped her," Glenda scolded.

"No I didn't. She stumbled." Dale pulled Lucie to his side and wrapped an arm around her shoulder.

"Well, just you mind you look after her in New York." Glenda kissed her son on the cheek then did the same to Lucie.

"Yes, take care, kids. It's a big old city and you need to keep yourselves safe."

"Dad, we're both grown ups now, you know." Dale rolled his eyes.

"You'll always be my little boy." Glenda patted his cheek and Lucie smiled. The fact that her six foot tall, thirty-four year old friend would always be Glenda's little boy was just too amusing.

"And you'll always be our little Lucie," Glenda added, bringing a lump to Lucie's throat. "So take care and keep in touch. I want to know where you go, what you do and what it's like. Enjoy the wedding and, of course, have fun!"

Dale led Lucie to the door and they stepped out into the cold drizzle.

"See you soon." Dale nodded at his parents then walked to the van. Lucie was conscious of the fact that he still had his heavy arm draped around her.

"Bye, darlings!" Glenda called to them.

Lucie turned back to wave, and as Glenda closed the door, Lucie was certain she'd had tears in her eyes.

"That went well," Dale said.

"Yes."

Dale opened the door for her then went around to the driver's side, and as Lucie climbed into her seat, she pressed her fingers over her mouth where Dale's kiss still tingled.

"Yes, it did," she whispered to herself.

–

"How are you feeling?" Lucie asked as she took a seat on a big squishy red sofa in the Coombes' lounge.

"Oh, I'm okay. A bit tired, I guess." Phil yawned loudly.

"Not *you*! Arianwen," Lucie said, shaking her head. "I can't believe the baby came early."

"Only six days early, so not too bad. It can go two weeks either way." Arianwen adjusted her position on the sofa and grimaced.

"Good timing, I think," Dale said as he sat next to Lucie. "At least we get to meet baby number three before we head off to Manhattan."

"What I wouldn't give to fly away for a week of glamour." Phil rubbed his eyes. "Instead, I'm in for another two years of sleepless nights and early starts."

Arianwen frowned. "At least you don't feel like your groin is on fire. I tell you… every single time I move, it stings."

"That sounds awful!" Lucie winced in sympathy. "Do you need anything from the pharmacy?"

"It's okay." Arianwen shook her head. "I've got these special salts to put in the bath water, and as long as I pour a jug of water over myself when I pee, it doesn't burn too badly."

Lucie glanced at Dale and was shocked at how pale he'd gone. "You okay?" she whispered.

"Just all this talk of pain. Not my cup of tea."

She squeezed his arm. "Be strong."

"She needs to drink lots of water and to rest." Phil got up and went to the door. "I'll put the kettle on."

"So was the labour tough, then?" Lucie asked. "You said something last time we saw you… that it would be easy the third time around?"

"Not this one. He's huge!" Arianwen gestured at the crib in the corner of the room. "I didn't even get a chance to fill the birthing pool. He came right out after twenty minutes of contractions, but in his hurry one arm was above his head."

"Like Superman?"

"Yes, Dale, if that helps. It didn't help me though… if you know what I mean."

Phil entered the room carrying what looked like a rubber ring. He handed it to his wife and she lifted herself a bit then slipped the ring underneath her.

"Oh, that's better."

"But the baby's all right?" Lucie asked.

"Yes. Strong as an ox."

"Takes after me." Phil grinned as he peered into the crib. "You want to hold him?"

"Wha… me?" Lucie glanced at Dale.

"Yes, you." Phil lifted a bundle from the crib then brought it over to Lucie. She stared at him, her stomach tightening.

"I'm not that good with tiny babies."

"Well then, you'll be fine with Sid. He's not tiny." Phil placed the bundle in her arms and Lucie gazed down into a scrunched up red face. She looked up again, intending to ask Phil to take the baby back but he'd gone. She couldn't ask Arianwen to get up and take the baby when she'd just got settled, so instead, she had to sit tight.

Dale asked after the other two boys and Arianwen said Phil's mother had taken them out for lunch, to give them a few hours alone with the baby. It was crucial that their other sons feel as important as ever, and this was one way of doing that. Hopefully, when they returned, their parents would be able to give them some quality time while Phil's mother helped out with baby Sid.

"Dammit! Now I need the loo again. Won't be long." Arianwen got up and waddled out of the room, leaving Dale and Lucie literally holding the baby.

Lucie gently pushed open the blanket around the baby to have a better look at him. His face moved in sleep, his ruby mouth pursing and his downy eyebrows moving up and down. He had a full head of black hair and tiny, dark pink ears that were flat against his head. As Lucie ran a finger over his hand, he grabbed hold of it instinctively and she gasped.

"He seems to like you." Dale spoke softly. He'd moved closer to Lucie and was leaning into her to get a closer look at the baby.

"He's asleep."

"Yes, but look how tightly he's holding you, Luce."

"In his sleep."

"So you want one now?"

"What?"

"Does it make you broody?"

Lucie gazed at the small person in her arms. He fit there perfectly. She lowered her head and inhaled. He smelt warm and clean, and like something she didn't recognize; a scent that must be inherent to babies. Was this what she wanted? Did she yearn to be a mother? To create her own tiny being; to bring a life into the world for which she would be responsible.

"I don't know."

"You don't know?"

"Well… he's cute and everything, and he smells quite good, but I've never really had that deep maternal craving that I hear other women talking about. Maybe one day, if things are right, if the situation is right, then I'll feel differently."

"I can understand that."

"What about you?"

He smiled. "I don't think men get that whole craving for a baby thing, do they?"

"Really?"

"Well… it's different, isn't it?"

"I bet some men do. There must be men who want to be fathers, like *really* want to. Look at Phil."

"I guess so. But personally, I've never had an over-whelming desire. I mean… if it happens one day, then I guess I'll be happy. If it doesn't, I'm not sure that I'll feel like I've missed out."

They sat there staring at the baby in silence.

"Is there something wrong with us, Dale?"

"How so?"

"Well we're both thirty-something, both single and we spend all our time together. Does that make us odd?"

"Hey, Luce. What's brought all this on?" He was so close to her that she could feel the heat of his breath on her cheek as he spoke.

"Oh, I don't know. Just with my childhood being so… irregular, I wonder if it's ruined me. If I can't have a normal life."

"What's normal to one person is not normal to another. We're all different. Not everyone needs to be a wife or husband, a mother or a father."

"Glenda will be disappointed."

"In me or in us?" He shrugged. "She has two perfectly nice grandsons. She doesn't need more."

"I don't think *she* sees it that way."

"Well, I think that whatever's going to be will be. My mother will be fine whether she has more grandchildren or not. And anyway, this isn't about her, it's about you and me and what we want from life. You can't do things just to make other people happy, you know. If you did, then you'd make yourself unhappy in the process."

Lucie nodded.

"I think he's waking up!" She froze as the baby started to wriggle in her arms. "Dale, help!"

He moved in front of her and deftly took the baby from her arms. He lifted Sid as if the baby were made of feathers, then rocked him in one arm as naturally as if he'd fathered twenty children and brought them all up singlehandedly.

"How do you know how to do that?" Lucie asked.

"I have two nephews, remember."

"Where have Phil and Arianwen got to?" Lucie asked as she stood. "I thought we were having tea."

"Go take a look. I'll watch this one."

Lucie went out into the kitchen and sighed as she saw the chaos. In front of the log burner was an empty birthing pool, a hosepipe hanging over the edge and stretching towards the taps. Dirty dishes were piled up next to the sink, and a heap of washing lay on the floor in front of the machine, while inside was a load that had clearly finished its cycle but been forgotten. "So this is what happens when you have a baby." She rolled up her sleeves. "Time to help out."

Forty minutes later, she'd filled the dishwasher and put it on a hot cycle, folded up the birthing pool and tuck it behind the bench in the corner near the window, emptied the washing machine and sorted through the clothes so that some now aired on downstairs radiators, while others tumbled around in the drier next to the washing machine. As she was putting another load of bibs and babygrows on to boil, she heard footsteps.

"Oh, Lucie, I'm so sorry. I don't know what happened." Phil traipsed into the kitchen, his eyes red and puffy, his face pale. "Ari went upstairs to use the loo and I went up to check on her. You know... she's a bit under the weather... and she'd already gone and sat on the bed. I sat next to her for a moment and before I knew it, I was waking up. I've left her there, sleeping. She's out cold." He glanced around the kitchen. "Wow! You shouldn't have done this, but thank you. It looks amazing."

"Don't be daft, Phil. It was no trouble at all. You've had a new arrival and you have enough to do."

"My mother tried to tackle it when she got here this morning, but I wouldn't let her. I told her I'd sort it when she took the boys out, but then Ari needed a bath and I had to help her while watching Sid. Then you came and..." He smiled. "Sorry. I'm just sleep deprived. No one ever tells you how badly the loss of sleep will affect you. But it's like torture. You can't think straight, you get emotional over ridiculous things like TV adverts and you walk around with your head full of cotton wool. I've been through it twice already and should have been more prepared this time, but even so... I did forget exactly how tough it is in the first few days."

"It's fine. Why don't you go back to bed and we'll watch Sid for an hour."

Phil's face lit up at the suggestion, then it fell again. "Ari's feeding him herself and he'll be due a feed soon. Uh... where is he?"

"Dale has him."

"Dale?" Phil's eyebrows lifted.

"He's a natural. Who knew, eh?"

They went through to the lounge and found Dale in the rocking chair by the fireplace, moving his feet from toe to heel in a regular movement. Safely tucked in his arms was the baby, fast asleep.

"Looks like you've got everything under control. I might just grab a nap then. If that's okay?" Phil asked Lucie.

She waved him away. "Go on. I'll wake you when the baby wakes."

"Again... thank you." Phil smiled then disappeared into the hallway.

"Looks like you've got that covered," Lucie whispered.

"Where've you been?"

"Cleaning up. The kitchen was in a bit of a mess so I did what I could."

"This little one hasn't stirred."

"He must feel safe in your arms."

Dale smiled as he gazed at the baby. "I guess I have that effect on some people."

"I guess you do." Lucie watched him as he moved back and forth, the slow steady rhythm making her start to relax. "I'll make us a cup of tea, shall I?"

Lucie returned to the kitchen and clicked the switch on the kettle then leaned against the unit as she waited for it to boil.

She would never to cease to be surprised by her best friend. Just when she thought she knew him, he pulled out something she didn't know he could do. In the past, it had included cooking up a delicious lasagne, singing like Sinatra at karaoke, buying her the perfect pair of boots for her birthday, and just yesterday, he'd kissed her under the mistletoe in a way that had made her toes curl with desire. Now he was showing off how great he was with kids.

Dale Treharne was everything a woman could ask for.

The perfect man.

A sudden wave of fear washed over her.

What if he turned out to be another woman's perfect man?

She had no idea how she would deal with that. None at all.

Chapter 8

"Do you think it will snow in New York?" Lucie asked Dale as they fastened their seatbelts.

He leaned over and checked that she'd done hers properly.

"Who knows? They do get snow in December, and sometimes there are dreadful blizzards. Why, are you hopeful?"

Lucie nodded. She really was. She'd seen cards of famous New York landmarks in the snow and spent the days before their departure browsing similar images online. "I'd like to walk through Central Park as the snow falls. It's just one of those things I've always wanted to do, you know?"

Dale smiled, his brown eyes warm with anticipation. "I do. I'd like that too. I packed my hat, scarf and gloves just in case. And we can go ice skating in Central Park or at the Rockefeller Centre."

"I'd like to see the Statue of Liberty."

"And the Museum of Natural History."

"And Macy's."

"Thank you, Dale."

He frowned. "Why're you thanking me, Luce?"

"Oh you know... for coming away with me. For always supporting me. For being my best friend my whole life."

He shook his head. "That's always been a pleasure. No need for thanks. Besides, I couldn't let you go alone, could I? I doubt you'd even have got on the flight in time."

Lucie playfully punched him in the shoulder. "I'm not that much of an idiot."

He leaned over her to peer out of the window. "Can't see much right now."

Lucie followed his gaze. "Just clouds. Hope it's clearer when we're above the USA."

"Me too. But then if I'm right, we won't see much except for a bit of New England."

The flight passed quickly, the time broken up with two meals, inflight movies and Dale's frequent interruptions to deliver facts about New York. Lucie couldn't help feeling excited. Her stomach fizzed with the thought that in just a few hours she would be in one of the most exciting cities in the world, a city she'd seen numerous times on television and in films, yet never had the chance to visit before. She might not have been able to afford to go there for a few years yet, had it not been for this opportunity. Petra's parents had covered the flights and accommodation, insisting that none of the bridesmaids would be inconvenienced in any way. Of course, the Christmas Eve wedding meant that many of the guests and wedding party would be away from their own homes and families for Christmas, so the Barnsleys' generosity was, in some way, Lucie suspected, also a form of compensation.

As the plane began to descend, Lucie slipped her hand into Dale's. She didn't mind flying, but takeoff and landing always filled her with a sense of unease. Dale squeezed her hand tight.

"You know, I'm really looking forward to spending Christmas in New York with you. Even though we've had to fib to my family about our relationship being something more than it is. The idea of a luxury hotel suite all to myself, with a view of Central Park and room service. Well, who wouldn't be happy at the thought of that?"

Lucie met his eyes. "Me too. I mean, being in Manhattan will be great. And again, I am sorry about your parents. But... uh... Dale. There's something I haven't told you yet, and I'm hoping you're going to be okay with it." She chewed her bottom lip.

"Don't tell me you've lost your passport already, Luce?" He rolled his eyes.

"No. It's not that. It's more to do with fibs. I should have told you sooner but we've been so busy."

"Right..." He sat up straighter, adjusting his position as if to prepare for bad news. "Go on then."

"You won't actually have a room to yourself."

A tiny line appeared between his eyebrows. "I'm not sharing with someone I don't know, Luce."

"It's someone you know very well."

"Not Harry?"

"You don't know Harry well, idiot."

Understanding dawned on his face. "You?"

She nodded.

"That's a bit… unconventional, isn't it? So Petra's daddy isn't so generous as to pay for two rooms, eh?"

"I said he didn't need to."

"But why?"

"Dale, don't you get it?"

His eyes widened. "They think we're a couple too, don't they?"

"Yes."

"You told them that we're together."

"Yes." She didn't plan on explaining that she'd been defending him to Petra. She wouldn't want to hurt him like that. Lucie knew that Dale wasn't exactly Petra's number one fan, but she couldn't bear the thought of him feeling even more out of place than he already would. She wanted him to have a good time, to enjoy New York. It was his Christmas too and he deserved to have a good one.

"Fair enough." He shrugged.

"Are you all right with that?"

"Why wouldn't I be? Everyone else we know thinks we're together."

Just then the plane bounced and Lucie yelped.

"It's okay. Just a spot of turbulence," Dale soothed.

She inclined her head. "Of course." She could cope with turbulence in the air, as long as Dale was there to hold her hand. In fact, she could cope with turbulence over the next week – because no doubt there would be some bumps along the way, if what Tania had told her about Petra and Harry was true – because she'd have her best friend by her side. As always.

–

"Wow!" Dale stood in front of the floor-to-ceiling window, gazing out at the incredible view.

"Dale!" Lucie squealed, jumping up and down. "It's amazing!" She flung herself into his arms and squeezed.

"I know. I've never seen anything like it."

A throat clearing from the door alerted them to the fact that the porter was still in the room.

"Sorry." Dale crossed the room and tucked a note into the young man's hand then closed the door behind him. "I keep forgetting about the tipping thing."

"How much did you give him?"

Dale tapped his nose. "That's for me to deal with. You sorted the taxi."

"But you gave the doorman something as well."

"Don't worry about it."

"Well, we'll have to share the tipping or you'll end up broke."

He smiled.

"Dale, this is just the best. Even without snow."

He watched her turn back to the window and stare out at the Manhattan skyline. It really was incredible. They'd had a good flight and made it through JFK smoothly, even locating their baggage immediately. They'd both been silent as their cab made its way towards Manhattan. Dale had to keep reminding himself to close his mouth; he didn't want to look like a fool and embarrass Lucie. She was so upbeat right now, even though the anniversary of her mother's death was just days away. It had always been a difficult time for her, and some years she'd descended into a state of despair, but this year he was hoping that a change of scenery would break the pattern and help her to heal.

"Shall we check out the rest of the suite?"

"Sure!" She bounced over to him, her cheeks slightly flushed, and grabbed his hand again. She'd been doing that a lot lately, taking his hand, tucking hers into the crook of his arm, hugging him. She was tactile, he'd known her for long enough not to be surprised when she touched him, but something seemed different now. Perhaps it was just him. After all, they'd told his parents they were a couple, and his mother had been so pleased. It could just be in his head. They'd been on a long flight, there was a time difference to take into account and they were both thrilled to be in Manhattan. It was probably just that, and nothing more. He'd sworn to himself years ago that he'd buried any romantic feelings for Lucie after that summer before she went to university. It had been intense, something he'd thought he'd never get over, but he had, and he knew he didn't ever want to feel like that again. Losing her had been a mountain to climb, one he'd managed, but only just.

How good it had been to know that Lucie was his, even though they'd been so young and innocent back then. Dale couldn't risk losing her again. Being her friend was the safest way for them to be together. He couldn't be with Lucie if she didn't want him as much as he would her.

Chapter 9

"Right, I've had a text from Petra. She said she doesn't need me until Friday, when all the bridesmaids will go through a hair and makeup trial at The Plaza salon. So that gives us this evening and one whole day of freedom in Manhattan."

They were relaxing on the plush sofa in the lounge of their suite. They'd taken it in turns to use the ensuite bathroom to wash away the long flight and now wore fluffy white hotel-issue robes. Lucie stretched out her legs and wiggled her toes in the thick pile of the carpet.

Dale nodded. "So I can begin my mission."

"Your mission?"

"To show you that Christmas can be fun."

Lucie took a deep breath then released it slowly. "I'm trying to stay open minded."

"You do that. I'm taking you somewhere special tonight."

"Where?" Her stomach fluttered.

"You'll know when we get there. Dress warmly and wear comfortable shoes."

"Okay… I brought mostly flats with me. Everything I read said that coming here involves a lot of walking so I wasn't going to get caught out."

"You can take the bedroom to dress, but don't be too long."

"Yes, sir."

"All I'm saying is that you don't need to fuss over your clothing, because it's cold out and you'll be covered up in your hat and coat."

Lucie headed into the bedroom and closed the white double doors behind her. As she turned around, she stared at the king-size bed. It was the biggest bed she'd ever seen, and it was made up with bright white, high thread count sheets embroidered with gold thread. Gold and silver scatter cushions adorned the surface and there was even a golden bolster pillow. It was pure luxury, and Lucie knew that Petra's parents must be paying out a fortune per night.

Even so, as big as the bed was, Lucie hadn't yet worked out how she and Dale were going to play things. Would she take the bed, or would he? Would they try to share? She wouldn't mind sharing with him, as there was certainly enough room, yet the thought made her flutter. She'd fallen asleep on Dale a thousand times as they watched movies at her flat, and growing up they'd shared a tent in the garden many times after begging their parents to let them camp out, but being here in this expensive room with its elaborate décor and magnificent bed seemed to be casting a different light on things. It seemed almost criminal to have such a lovely bed and not to share it with a lover.

She shook her head. The long flight, arriving in Manhattan, and the promise of an exciting few days were probably playing havoc with her emotions. Dale was her best friend, her platonic soulmate and nothing more. They could sort out the sleeping arrangements later. Dale would have it all worked out.

–

Lucie marched along next to Dale, glancing at him every so often. The tip of his nose was red from the fresh evening wind and his eyes were watering.

"Will you tell me now?"

"Nope."

"But why not?"

"I want you to try to guess."

Lucie thought back to the hours they'd spent looking at images of New York on her laptop, but they'd talked about so many places that it could be any one of them.

"Give me a clue."

"Okay." He stopped and she turned to him. "It's on 49th Street."

"Ummmm…" She tried to remember. What was on 49th Street? Was it Macy's?

"It's between Fifth and Sixth Avenues."

"Ummmmm…"

"No idea? Come on, we're nearly there!"

"I'm trying to remember. Come on brain, work!" She tapped the side of her head, as if trying to dislodge the name of their destination.

Dale took her arm and carried on walking, but soon they were caught up in a crowd of people. Lucie felt Dale's fingers tighten around her and she moved closer to him, suddenly terrified of losing him in the throng of people.

"Stay close, Luce," he said as he pulled her to his side. They shuffled along and Lucie tried to see where they were going, but the crowd was thick, and being quite petite she couldn't see above the people in front of her.

"I can't see a thing," she said, panic bubbling to the surface. Would it be like this all the time in Manhattan? It was all right for Dale, he was much taller.

"Over there." Dale pointed. He stepped out of the flow of bodies and pulled Lucie in front of him.

"Wow!"

"The Rockefeller Christmas tree. Oh Dale, it's incredible!"

They stood before the enormous tree, taking in its festive magnificence.

"It's about seventy-eight feet tall. Can you believe that?" Dale asked her. "And there's around forty-five thousand lights on it."

"It's breathtaking." Lucie's heart pounded beneath her warm coat and she realized that she was trembling – but she didn't know if it was because of the cold, or emotion and awe.

"Now, I know you don't like Christmas trees, Luce, but even you can't say you're not impressed with this one."

Lucie glanced at Dale. He was staring at the tree and the twinkling lights were reflected in his eyes. He worked hard, he enjoyed simple things like a delicious meal, a walk in the park or a funny movie. He was an eternal optimist and usually saw the best in everything and everyone. He cheered Lucie up when she was low and always looked out for her. And even now, when she'd come all the way to New York, it was Dale who was with her.

Holding my hand.

She lowered her gaze to their joined hands, separated only by their gloves.

"Hey!" Dale placed a finger under her chin and gently lifted it. "You okay? You thinking about your mum?" His eyes were warm and dark.

Lucie shook her head. "I wasn't, no. I was thinking about us… this… how amazing this is. How much I care about you."

Dale opened his mouth then closed it and turned back to the tree. He blinked rapidly a few times and adjusted his warm woollen hat.

"Dale?"

He shook his head.

"Dale, what is it?"

"Come on, let's check out the ice rink. It's pretty impressive, but I thought we could go to the one in Central Park if you prefer. Unless you want to skate on this one. It's up to you, really. Whatever you want to do." He was speaking quickly, as if his thoughts were racing the way Lucie's were.

"I don't mind," she replied softly, following him. She was being an idiot, getting carried away with being in this magical place. She was tired, and probably a bit jetlagged. Dale had made it clear a long time ago that he wanted nothing more from Lucie than her friendship, and she'd just embarrassed them both with her soppy outburst.

Well, no more. No more.

Lucie would pull herself together and ensure that she didn't get all mushy on Dale again. It clearly made him very uncomfortable.

–

As Dale led Lucie to the balcony overlooking the ice rink, he had to fight the urge to release her hand and run away. Perhaps this had been a mistake, coming out here, with her, at this time of year. Dale liked Christmas but he'd always reined in his enthusiasm for it around Lucie because he knew how she felt about it. He never wanted to make it harder for her than it had to be. But this year he'd hoped to make it better, to help her to move on, and he'd been convinced that Manhattan would be the best place to try to have a very merry Christmas.

But the problem was that he was getting all mixed up in the process. The way he'd just caught Lucie looking at him made something inside him shift, something that had been lodged there for a long time. It was an emotional shield, a barrier he'd erected when he was younger and had realized that Lucie only wanted him as a friend. Sure, at the time he'd been badly hurt, but he was a grown man now, with years of experience in suppressing his emotions – wasn't that what all sensible men did? But Lucie got to him like no other woman ever had. It was because he felt protective of her and because he cared about her. Because she was the most beautiful woman he'd ever seen and because she had the tenderest heart, the warmest smile. When Lucie entered a room, the world came alive for Dale, and he knew that he'd probably never find that with another woman.

Which was why he hadn't bothered trying to find it. He'd had odd flings over the years, but none of the women he dated were ever right. They didn't have Lucie's smile or tinkly laugh, they didn't smell right or know how to tease him like she did. In his eyes she was perfect, and he knew it was idiotic, but unless he stopped caring so much about her he'd never allow himself to get into anything serious with someone else.

But Lucie was vulnerable, and there was no way that Dale was going to take advantage of that. She was probably just getting caught up in the festive excitement of Manhattan and trying to work through her grief over her mum. Twenty years might be a long time, but Dale knew from what he'd read on the subject that there was no time limit on grief. There was no clear beginning and end; it could ebb and flow, burn with acidic intensity or dull to a distant ache. And there was no telling when, or if, it would resurface and put someone on their behind again, like a powerful blow to the jaw.

It was what it was.

He had made his decision.

Whatever happened out here in New York, there would be no regrets. Not for Lucie. Not for him. This was all about getting Lucie through Christmas unscathed. This was not about what Dale wanted or needed; it was about her.

"What do you think, Luce? Up for a spot of ice skating tomorrow? Or do you want to try something else?" he asked as they stood watching the skaters circling the ice, some of them wobbly and nervous, some of them gliding gracefully.

Lucie gave what he recognized as her nervous laugh. "Maybe. Let's see how the day goes." She shivered. "But shall we go and get a warm drink now? I'm frozen."

"Of course." He hugged her to his side and they went off in search of refreshments. He had every intention of taking care of his best friend this week, but he hoped that he'd be able to look after his own heart in the process. Which meant being sensible and not letting his deeper feelings for Lucie get in the way of common sense.

–

Lucie and Dale stood in front of the bed, staring at it as if it were covered in spikes or hot coals. Lucie thought that spikes might be preferable to the nerves she was suddenly feeling. This was ridiculous! There was nothing to worry about here.

So why am I so worried?

"Why don't I take the couch in the lounge?" Dale asked. "It's certainly big enough."

Lucie met his eyes. "Don't be silly. There's plenty of room here for both of us."

"Really?"

"Really." Lucie marched to the bed and started removing the throw pillows, placing them on the chaise at the base of the bed. She was about to move the bolster pillow, but then she had an idea. "If we stick that in the middle, then there'll be no danger of me turning over and head-butting you in the night." She smiled, hoping to lighten the atmosphere.

"Do you make a habit of head-butting men in your sleep?" Dale asked, his lips twitching. "No *wonder* your relationships never last." He muttered the last sentence, but Lucie heard him.

"What did you say?"

"No-othing!" He held up his hands and shook his head.

"You did! You said my relationships never last. Right, that's it!" She scowled at him then lifted a pillow and jumped onto the bed. "Arm yourself, Treharne."

"What?"

"I said, choose a weapon. I won't take down an unarmed man."

Dale grabbed a cushion and held it up. "Oh, please don't hurt me, Miss Quigley!"

Lucie growled then flew at Dale with her cushion raised. She brought it down with a thump, and Dale gasped as the cushion met his face. Suddenly, Lucie was falling through the air. She landed on her back on the bed and realized that Dale had swiped at the backs of her knees so she would lose her balance. She squealed and tried to turn, but he was there before she could move, pinning her arms above her head while he trapped her wriggling legs with his own. "What're you doing?" She squirmed, trying to free herself, but Dale was right above her, and he was so much bigger than she was.

"Stopping you before you can ruin my good looks."

"With a cushion?" She giggled.

"Yes. I have sensitive skin." Dale rubbed his free hand over his stubble. "And you're out of control."

Lucie stared into his eyes. Her heart was pounding and she was breathless with exertion. And something else was surging through her body, something she thought she recognized. But she wasn't sure. Couldn't quite put a name on it. It felt good.

"How do I know I can trust you to let me sleep, Luce? Am I going to be woken up by you pounding me with pillows?"

She watched as his chest rose and fell quickly. Was he feeling it too?

"No, of course not. I promise that you will be safe while you sleep."

"So you're telling me I'm free from danger if I release you?" His pupils dilated.

"Yes." She'd stopped wriggling now and was conscious of the heat emanating from his body, warming her right through.

"Promise?"

"Yes."

For a moment he hovered there, his brown eyes reflecting her face like a distorted mirror. She could hear his short, sharp breaths, in and out; smell his fresh ginger-citrus scent and the clean washing powder fragrance of his clothes; feel the strength in his hands and his legs as he held her in place.

It was arousing, emotional and confusing.

So confusing.

Then Dale let go of her wrists and lifted himself from her, and Lucie allowed him to pull her to a sitting position at the edge of the bed.

"Let's get some rest," he said, avoiding eye contact. "Busy day tomorrow."

She nodded, then went into the bathroom to brush her teeth.

She stared at her reflection in the large gilt-edged mirror above the double sinks. Her cheeks were flushed, her eyes shone and her hair was a wild tangle. The way she felt about Dale sometimes baffled her, because she knew nothing could ever happen between them. Nothing like *that*, anyway. Yet just then, in the bedroom, she had wanted it to. And that scared her.

When she came back into the bedroom, hoping to speak to Dale about anything, everything; just to confirm that things were okay between them, that they were friends as they had always been and always would be, she found that he'd already fallen asleep. She gazed at him for a moment, lying on his side, facing away from her, his chest rising and falling slowly, his broad shoulders outlined by a fitted grey T-shirt.

Something in her deflated, as if she'd been filled with excitement and longing, then left too long in the sun.

She sighed, then climbed into bed next to him and switched off the bedside lamp, thinking it would take a long time to drop off, but within minutes she was drifting, her thoughts swirling around just like the snowflakes that had begun to fall outside.

Chapter 10

"Dale?" Lucie turned over in bed but her friend wasn't there. The room was dark, with thick curtains blocking out the morning light, but the door to the lounge was open a crack, and through it she could see that it was bright outside. "*Dale?*"

She pulled on her robe then headed out into the lounge. Dale was stood before the enormous window, staring out at the view.

"Dale!" She hurried to his side.

"Hey Luce, what's wrong?"

"Oh… I don't know. For a moment there I panicked. I thought…"

"You thought what?" A tiny line appeared between his eyebrows.

"Nothing. Just the remnants of a bad dream." She swallowed hard, trying to push away the nightmare. She'd been wandering the streets of Manhattan calling out Dale's name, terrified that she'd lost him forever.

"Come here." He opened his arms and she walked into his embrace, pressing her face into his T-shirt, breathing him in.

"It's okay." He squeezed her tight. "Now look at the view, Lucie." He gently released her.

"Wow!"

"Pretty amazing, huh?" he asked.

"It's incredible!"

Everything was white. During the night, there had been snow. Lots and lots of lovely snow, and now Central Park resembled a scene from a Christmas card. "It's so pretty."

"I ordered it especially for you."

Lucie stared at him.

"The snow." He grinned. "To ensure that this Christmas was perfect."

"Of course you did." Lucie nodded. "Had a word with the big guy upstairs, no doubt."

"In the penthouse?" Dale frowned.

"Ha! Oh, Dale, it is perfect. Exactly how I always imagined it would look in December. How long have you been up?"

He rubbed a hand over his eyes. His dark hair was sticking up on one side and he had creases on his cheek from the pillow. He was wearing his grey T-shirt and striped pyjama bottoms made of a soft jersey material. "A while. Getting used to the change in time zones, I think."

Lucie glanced at the sofa and just as she'd suspected, saw a pillow and blanket there.

"Oh, I uh, came out here because I was so restless. Didn't want to disturb you with my tossing and turning."

"You wouldn't have. Apart from the bad dream just before I woke up, I slept like a log."

"Didn't want to risk it anyway. We've got a busy day ahead."

"I'm really hungry." She rubbed her belly. "I feel like I haven't eaten in days."

"Me too. I ordered room service. A variety of things because I wasn't sure what you'd fancy. I thought we could eat then hit the streets."

"Sounds wonderful."

A knock at the door brought their breakfast. Dale tipped the porter then came to sit at the table.

It must be the tiredness giving her a sense of unreality, as well as the strange light from the heavy snowfall, but Lucie really did feel as if they were on a film set. As if at any moment someone would yell *CUT!* and they'd all head off to their trailers.

"This doesn't feel real, does it?" she asked Dale as he flicked out his large white napkin.

He shook his head. "I know what you mean. Yesterday we were at home in Tonbridge, and today we're in a luxurious hotel in Manhattan, about to tuck into a gourmet breakfast. I want to take pictures of everything so it lasts longer."

"Me too!" Lucie giggled. "I'm so glad you feel the same."

They feasted on fruit salad, crunchy oat granola and the thickest pancakes Lucie had ever seen, which Dale doused in golden maple syrup, and they washed it all down with freshly brewed coffee.

"Time for a day of New York fun?" Dale asked.

"Definitely!" Lucie agreed, taking one more look out of the window before she went to get ready. The combination of good food, good company and the prospect of a fun-filled day, along with the snow falling just outside the glass, was incredibly uplifting.

"You know, Dale. I think your plan might just be working."

He smiled and she was glad that she'd told him, glad that she was able to tell him truthfully that she was enjoying herself. As she padded off to the bedroom, she was filled with a warm glow. She loved a lot of things in life, but top of the list was making Dale happy.

–

The kerbs of Fifth Avenue were basically clear of snow thanks to the thick crowds of shoppers, but the fat white flakes were still falling, and Lucie had to keep brushing them off her shoulders and hat.

The window displays were like nothing she'd ever seen before. From wintery family scenes made of Swarovski crystal, to giant teddy bears and snowmen with red and green hats and scarves, to thousands of colourful twinkling lights; everything screamed decadence, festivity and elegance. Dale was clearly bursting with excitement, because he kept grabbing Lucie's hand and pulling her to the next window.

When they reached Macy's, there was a romantic tableau of a couple staring into a shop window looking at rings. Dale and Lucie paused there for a moment, and

Lucie wondered what it would be like to shop for an engagement ring with him. If they hadn't split up after that summer when they'd become lovers, but had stayed together all this time. They might even have been married with children by now...

"Lucie!" She jumped as she heard a familiar voice calling her name. "Lucie! Dale! Woo hoo, you two! Caught in the act, no less."

Petra arrived at her side, her cheeks flushed and eyes shining from the cold.

"Oh, hi Petra." Lucie took in Petra's impractical leather stiletto boots, short denim skirt – revealing very tanned, toned legs – and faux fur jacket complete with matching Russian-style hat.

"Hello, lovebirds! So which one will it be?" Petra looked from Lucie to Dale and back again.

"What?" Dale asked.

"Which *ring*, silly!"

Lucie slipped her hand into Dale's and squeezed. "Oh, it's a bit soon for that really."

"Nonsense! Now don't tell me that Dale hasn't proposed, or that he isn't planning to?" Petra placed her hands on her hips and frowned. "You can't come to New York at Christmas and not propose, Dale! You two are having me on, aren't you?"

Lucie was about to explain that they weren't when Dale took over. "Look Petra, it's something we're thinking about... if you know what I mean. But I haven't exactly popped the question yet."

"Oh!" Petra widened her heavily made-up eyes and nodded. "I get you… Sorry, darlings! I'm jumping the gun, eh? Well how about a glass of bubbly to get us all into the festive spirit? I've been Christmas shopping, but my feet are killing me and I could do with a rest."

Lucie glanced at Dale and found that he was looking at her. "What do you want to do, darling?" She hid her smile at the term of endearment he'd used.

A snowflake landed on her nose so she blew it off. "Up to you, really, *darling*."

"Well, I insist that you accompany us to the champagne bar at The Plaza," said a deep male voice behind them. They turned to find Harry Goldsmith. "My treat! To thank you both for coming all this way for our wedding."

"That would be wonderful," Dale replied.

Lucie squeezed Dale's hand again in silent thanks, then they followed Harry and Petra through the crowds.

–

"It's The Plaza!" Lucie whispered to Dale as they entered the hotel lobby. "*The Plaza*."

"I know." He grinned at her. "Champagne in The Plaza."

Harry and Petra strode through to the bar as if they did it every day, and Lucie made an effort to appear as nonchalant as she could manage, although inside she was ready to burst. She wanted to pull out her phone and take pictures of everything: from the ornate displays, to the doormen, to the chandeliers, to the champagne bar itself.

A waitress led them to a corner table where they sat in cream satin-covered chairs with golden backs. As the waitress took their order – a bottle of something Lucie couldn't even pronounce – Lucie allowed Dale to help her with her coat. She stared around the room. Golden drapes hung from the enormous windows, and dotted around the room were large plants in golden pots, giving it a somewhat Grecian feel. The edges of the room were carpeted but the centre was tiled, with an elaborate mosaic at its core. As the waitress returned from the L-shaped bar across the room that was complete with shelves bearing different types of champagne, her heels clicked on the tiles. The haunting notes of carols, sung by a church choir, tinkled from discreet speakers and gave the whole place a soothing atmosphere.

"Does anyone want anything to eat?" Harry asked as the waitress filled everyone's glasses.

"I couldn't, really," Lucie said. "I'm still full from breakfast."

Dale paused for a moment then shook his head. "Probably better not."

"Dale always has room for more food. Hollow legs, right!" She laughed but noticed that while Harry was smiling, Petra was gazing across the room.

"Petra? Everything okay?"

Petra met her gaze and suddenly sat upright as if someone had just flicked on a switch. "Yes. Fabulous, darling! Just a little tired from all the planning and preparation."

"Oh! Excuse me a moment." Harry gestured at his mobile. "I have to take this."

He dashed from the room and Petra lifted her glass and drank it down in one go.

"Work?" Dale asked.

"Probably," Petra replied. "They know we're out here to get married but even so, they give him no peace. He's answering calls morning, noon and night. You know, I hoped that by heading so far away that we'd get some time away from it all, but apparently not." She chewed her bottom lip then refilled her glass.

Lucie sipped her champagne, savouring the sophistic-ated finish. Drinking at this time of the morning seemed so decadent, but the experience was somewhat marred by a nagging at the back of her mind. She recalled what Tania had told her about Petra and Harry, and it made her uneasy. What if Tania had been right? After all, Harry could surely have told work to leave him alone for the week of his wedding, couldn't he? Yet Lucie had to admit that she didn't know much about how things worked in the City, and she suspected that high-paid bankers like Harry probably did work through their evenings, week-ends and holidays.

"Let's order another bottle!" Petra announced then summoned the waitress.

"So we're meeting again tomorrow morning, Petra?" Lucie asked, keen to distract her friend from her worries.

"Yes, darling." Petra filled their glasses from the fresh bottle of champagne. "Just to practise hair and makeup and to try the dresses on in case they need any final adjustments."

"Ooh! Makeup, eh?" Dale asked. "So you don't trust Lucie to do her own."

"Ha! Ha!" Petra flicked her long platinum blonde hair over her shoulders. "Much as Lucie does a grand old job on herself, we're going for something a bit special. I was thinking, Lucie, that we could get some highlights in your hair. Brighten it up a bit. What do you think?"

Lucie swallowed more champagne. So she wasn't just going to have to wear a dress of Petra's choosing, but she'd be caked in makeup and have her hair played about with too. "Whatever you think is best, Petra. It's your wedding."

"Wonderful!" Petra placed her empty glass on the table and watched as Harry approached.

"Sorry about that. Bloody subordinate can't make a decision without checking first. No idea how he's going to manage when he's out there on his own. Probably won't, if I'm brutally honest." He snorted and shook his head.

Petra pursed her lips in disapproval. "Well, I hope they leave you alone on Christmas Eve, because I don't think it's appropriate to answer the phone as you say your vows, Harry."

Lucie shifted uncomfortably in her seat and noticed Dale doing the same. The last thing they wanted was to get caught up in a domestic.

"That won't happen, Pets. I promise. Phone will be switched off... at least until the reception."

Petra jerked in her chair and her eyes widened, but Harry held up his hands. "Joking! Joking! It will be switched off until after Boxing Day, I promise. Now let's make a toast to friendships, to marriage and to having a very merry Christmas!" Harry announced as he refilled all the glasses.

"Cheers!"

They clinked glasses, but as Lucie eyed the couple over the bubbles, she wondered exactly how enjoyable it was going to be for Petra, and came to the conclusion that for her friend at least, it might not be very merry at all.

–

Lucie and Dale said their goodbyes to Petra and Harry then headed back out into the snow. They'd left the soon-to-be-married couple finishing off their champagne as Petra glowered at Harry over her glass.

"Okay, out with it!" Dale took hold of Lucie's upper arms.

"Out with what?"

"Whatever's bothering you. I know you, Lucie, and something's wrong."

"Oh Dale, it's just that being there with Petra and Harry… it didn't feel right."

"In what way?" He let go of her and tucked his hands into his coat pockets.

"I feel that it's not my place to analyse their relationship, but at the same time I can't help it."

"Well, it's okay to tell *me* isn't it? That won't cause any damage; you can just sound it out. But it would be a different matter if you were telling Petra all this just days before her wedding. That could kind of spoil things for her."

Lucie nodded. "Do they seem happy to you?"

Dale blinked hard. "Happy? I don't know. The thing is, I don't know them very well and I don't see them regularly, so for all I know, that could be as happy as they ever get."

"What I mean is, do they seem like a couple about to get married? They should be ultra-loved-up right now, seeing as how Harry only recently proposed and they *are* getting married in one of the most exciting cities in the world at Christmas."

"I'm honestly not sure. Weddings are supposed to be extremely stressful to plan, so perhaps it's just the pressure getting to them."

"Ever the pragmatist, Dale. So you think this is just me being overly sensitive, right?"

"No. No." He shook his head. "I would never presume to suggest that. All I'm saying is that it's difficult to judge how happy someone else's relationship is, let alone the relationship of a friend you rarely see."

Lucie watched as a snowflake melted on his cheek, leaving a crystal droplet of water. She instinctively reached out and gently wiped it away with her thumb. "I know. You are right. I don't know how they are together usually. They've been together a long time too, so it's not as if

181

they're in the first flush of love. I just believe that you should be head over heels in love in order to marry someone. Otherwise, what's the point?" She pushed a lock of hair under her hat.

"I'm sure Petra knows what she's doing. She always seemed to know exactly what she wanted." Dale shrugged. "As much as you care about her, though, you can't interfere in her life. Imagine if you did and things went wrong then she blamed you for it."

"I know." And Lucie did understand how awful that would be, but at the same time, she knew she would struggle to leave things unsaid. She vowed to only raise her concerns if she *really* had to. After all, Lucie knew how it was to be hurt by a man she loved. To find out that he wasn't who she'd thought he was. The humiliation had been devastating, and coming at Christmas time it had further compounded her loathing of the festive season.

"Come on, let's get to Central Park. There's something I want us to do and we need to make the most of today."

Lucie smiled. He was right. They were in New York, in the snow and away from everything that had hurt her in the past. As much as she cared about Petra, she also cared about Dale. And right now, it was time to focus on him.

Chapter 11

"So we'll see you in just over two hours?"

The driver nodded at Dale then handed him a receipt. Dale walked back to where Lucie was standing as she gazed at the incredible view.

"All sorted."

"You managed to book us a ride?"

"Of course."

"But how did you do that at such short notice? I thought the carriages would all have been busy at this time of year."

"Oh, I have my ways." Dale tapped the side of his nose.

"Yeah, yeah." Lucie giggled. "Bet he had a cancellation didn't he?"

"Something like that. Right, come on, time for our walk in Central Park."

Lucie rearranged her scarf so that the back of her neck was completely covered, then followed Dale through the opening on West 72nd street into the park. Everything seemed dreamlike. The snowflakes drifted lazily from the leaden sky and sounds were muffled, as if the heavens had dropped cotton wool onto everything. They crunched along the path through the freshly fallen snow, and Lucie breathed deeply of the fresh, icy air.

"Here we have Strawberry Fields." Dale gestured to their left. "In case you don't know, it's the area of the park dedicated to John Lennon. It's in the shape of a teardrop."

They stopped in front of a large mosaic on the ground. It was partially covered but it looked as though someone had already wiped some of the snow away. At the centre of the circle was a word. Lucie moved closer. "*Imagine*."

"Gosh, yes, *imagine*. It's hard to, I know, but just across the road from where we came into the park is where Lennon was shot."

Lucie covered her mouth, her eyes suddenly stinging. "Really?"

Dale nodded. "It's so sad, even all these years later."

"When did it happen?"

"December nineteen-eighty."

Lucie shook her head. "Such a long time, yet still no time at all."

"Before you were born."

"Before *you* were born, too."

"True. It's a cool vision though, right?"

"Living in harmony and all that?"

Dale nodded.

"This is beautiful, Dale, and I'm glad we started here. I like to imagine how good life could be. I mean… life is good anyway, but what I mean is… well, we all need dreams, right? Things to aspire to."

"We do. I wanted to show you the spot because it's iconic, and you can't come to Manhattan without seeing Strawberry Fields."

She tucked her hand into the crook of his arm then said, "I'm freezing!", as if she needed to explain why she wanted to get closer to him.

Next they approached a large fountain. "And this is Cherry Hill Fountain." They paused in front of the impressive landmark. "It was originally created as a watering trough for horses."

Lucie gazed at the ornamental Victorian structure with its granite dome and tiled basin. At the top of the central tower were eight frosted glass lamps and a golden spire, all now dusted with soft white snow. "It's beautiful. I can just picture horses stopping here to drink."

"Wait until you see what's next," Dale said.

"Oh, Dale!" Lucie squealed as they approached a bridge. "I know this one."

"It's Bow Bridge." He smiled. "It's uh... Hold on." He turned away and pulled his mobile from his pocket, scrolled down the screen, then tucked it away again.

"Message from home?" Lucie asked, feeling a bit disgruntled as she realized that she wanted his full attention. She didn't want anyone else interrupting this day that they'd planned to spend together.

"Something like that." His cheeks flushed. "Anyway... as I was saying... this is Bow Bridge. It's made of cast iron and spans sixty feet. The walkway, which we can't really see right now because of the snow, is made of a type of

185

hardwood that apparently turns a rich deep red when it's wet."

Lucie frowned. "You sound like a tour guide, Dale. Have you worked here in a former life perhaps?"

He laughed.

"I know you read up on some places to visit before we came, but how did you remember so much?"

His blush deepened. "I just wanted to be able to provide you with enough detail. You know... impress you a bit, I guess. So I was checking the tourist information on my phone."

"But why'd you need to impress *me*? We're relaxed together, right?"

Dale paused halfway across the bridge and gazed out across the water. "Of course we are." Lucie watched as his breath emerged from between his full lips like puffs of smoke. "I want you to enjoy this trip, Luce. It's really important to me."

"I am enjoying it, Dale. It's such a fabulous place to be."

"Isn't there someone else you'd rather be here with, though?"

Lucie paused for a moment, picturing the men she'd been with in her life, the ones she'd cast aside quickly and the ones who'd been allowed to get closer, like Jamie, who in the early days of their relationship had seemed perfect. Her stomach lurched at the memory. Then she looked back at Dale; tall, broad, dark-eyed, warm-hearted, familiar. Dale was patient and kind. He was everything that Jamie hadn't been, indeed that *no* other man had ever been for her.

"No, Dale." As she inhaled, the icy air was cleansing, renewing. *Like a fresh start. The beginning of a whole new dream.* "There is no one I would rather be here with than you."

He smiled at her then, so openly that it lit up his face and it filled her heart.

Suddenly she knew without any doubt at all.

And she was terrified.

–

"Quick! Look at the time!" Dale tapped his watch. "We need to get back for our carriage ride."

They retraced their steps across the park, back to West 72nd street. Lucie giggled as they slipped and skidded along on the snow-covered ground. Her heart was racing, her breaths coming short and sharp and her fingers were tingling where Dale was gripping them as he tried to keep her upright.

"Stop laughing, Luce! It's not funny. I had to pay extra to reserve that carriage."

"Sorry! It's just we took such a leisurely stroll and now we're having to run back. If we're not careful, one of us will break something – and if it's me, Petra will be furious. I don't think I could pull off a cast on my arm with my bridesmaid dress and, well, if it's my leg, crutches would make her absolutely furious."

They reached the edge of the park. "There he is!" Dale pointed at the large red and white carriage.

They marched over to it and the driver jumped down. "Hey there! You enjoy your walk?"

"Beautiful!" Lucie announced.

"Fascinating," Dale replied. "But we got carried away and I was worried we were going to miss you."

"I'd have waited for a bit. You made it worth my while, remember." He winked at Dale, and Lucie watched her friend's face carefully, wondering exactly how much he'd paid the driver to reserve the carriage.

Dale helped her into the cab then climbed up next to her and the driver handed them a fluffy red blanket.

"Champagne you wanted, wasn't it?" he asked as he opened a cooler box and produced a bottle and two glasses.

"Absolutely!" Dale took the glasses and handed them to Lucie then popped the cork.

"*More* champagne?" Lucie held the glasses out for Dale to fill them.

"We can't do an afternoon carriage ride around Central Park without something special to drink, now, can we?" Dale clinked his glass against hers. "Cheers, Luce! Here's to being best friends and to having a good Christmas."

"Cheers!" Lucie sipped her champagne. She wanted to say more, to make a toast to friendship and to Manhattan, but her throat was so tight that she knew she'd be unable to squeeze any words out. So instead, she snuggled under the blanket, moved a bit closer to Dale and his comforting warmth, and settled in to enjoy the ride.

Dale felt as though they'd stepped back in time as the driver clicked his tongue and the horse set off. The carriage was immaculate, with its velvet-covered seats and leather canopy. The horse even had a plume in its harness to match the deep red colour scheme.

The driver called out when they reached the first attraction on the tour. "There's the Wollman Rink. It opened in 1949 with funds donated by Kate Wollman. She donated the grand sum of six hundred thousand dollars, to commemorate her family from Kansas. Her brother William operated a stock exchange firm."

"That's a lot of money to donate," Dale replied.

"Probably not to them." The driver turned and flashed them a crooked smile. "Next up is the Carousel."

Dale was warm and comfortable and the soft rocking of the carriage combined with the cosy warmth of the blanket made him incredibly relaxed. He sipped his champagne and listened to the driver's New York twang as the knowledgeable man relayed more details about the Chess and Checkers House, the Sheep Meadow and the Central Park Zoo.

"How're you doing there?" Dale eyed Lucie's glass. "Need a top up?"

"Please." She held out her flute and waited for him to refill it.

"Have you stopped worrying now?"

"About?"

"Petra and Harry."

"Oh. Yes."

"You shouldn't worry. They're both adults and whatever they decide to do is on them."

"I know." She ran a finger around the rim of her glass.

The combination of the bubbly and the cold had made her cheeks pink, which Dale thought made her look irresistibly cute. He wondered if he'd be able to taste the champagne on her lips if he kissed her. If her lips would be warm. If she would slide her hand around his neck and pull him close.

"What?" Lucie met his eyes and heat flooded through him. "You're staring at me funny."

"Am I?"

"Yes. Like you want my champagne or something."

Or something...

"I'm a bit cold, Dale."

"Come here." He held out his arm and Lucie snuggled under it. He tucked the blanket around her and leaned slightly to clink his glass against hers. "That better?"

"Yes. You always make it better." She lifted her chin and their mouths were almost touching. Her breath was sweet and warm and he was overwhelmed by the urge to taste her.

"Lucie." His voice came out ragged. "I—"

"And here's The Plaza!" the driver announced, making Dale jump and spill the remains of his drink down the front of his coat. He pulled his arm back and rummaged in his pocket for a tissue.

When he looked up, Lucie had shuffled over on the seat, and he knew that the moment they'd just shared, when he could have told her exactly how much she meant to him, had passed.

–

Straight after breakfast the next morning, Lucie left Dale at their hotel and made her way to The Plaza. After the previous day's events, she was reluctant to leave him but she had to attend the hair and makeup trial then have a final dress fitting.

The receptionist directed her to the salon, and when she entered, she was greeted by delighted squeals and coos. Petra and her other bridesmaids had already arrived. The salon was spacious and bright, with large mirrors hanging on the walls and lots of shiny surfaces. Spotlights dropped from the ceiling, positioned precisely to create optimal illumination for the stylists. On the walls between the mirrors were small lamps with sheer pink shades.

"Lucie!" Petra bestowed her customary air kisses. "So good to see you, darling! If you take a seat, Lauren will take care of you in a moment. She's just finishing off Giana's eyebrows."

Lucie looked across to Giana and had to bite her lip. The beautiful Anglo-Italian woman was in a debate with the stylist about whether one eyebrow was thicker than the other. The stylist was being very apologetic, but even so, it didn't look like Giana was going to let the girl off easily.

"Sorry about the little tiff you and Dale witnessed over champers yesterday. It's just the pressure building, I'm sure, and I do wish Harry would turn his damned phone off just for two minutes, you know?" She paused, chewing her lower lip, and Lucie nodded, uncertain what to say – unless she told her what Tania had said, but that was a no. Dale had agreed on that one. "You and Dale seem very happy though. Did you sneak back later and look at some more rings?"

Lucie shook her head. "We went for a walk then a carriage ride. It was beautiful."

"And…" Petra raised her perfect brows as much as her frozen forehead would allow.

"And what?"

"Did he?"

"Did he what?"

"Oh Lucie, do you not have a romantic bone in that gorgeous curvaceous body of yours? Get what I'm asking." At that moment, someone turned on a hairdryer and Lucie shrugged to show that she couldn't hear her friend. "I said…" Petra pointed at her lips. "Did Dale… PROPOSE?" She shouted the last word just as the hairdryer went silent.

One of the stylists dropped a plastic hair-colour dish and it clattered to the floor, spinning in circles before coming to a shuddering stop.

Someone snorted.

Heat crawled over Lucie's chest, up her neck then into her cheeks. Everyone in the salon was staring at her and she wanted to sink into her boots and disappear.

But of course that didn't happen.

She was still stood there.

The centre of attention.

And the more time that passed, the worse it got.

"Answer her for goodness sake!" Tania shouted from her reclined position at the sinks.

"Uh…" *What do I say? What do I say?*

"Of course he did! No one takes a carriage ride around Central Park with their partner and doesn't get a proposal, do they?" It was Petra's mother, Joanna. She marched over to Lucie and stood next to her. "Congratulations! This calls for champagne." She snapped her fingers at a passing junior stylist and sent the girl in search of bubbly. "Lots of it!" Joanna called after her retreating back.

"Fabulous news, Lucie." Petra hugged her. "So happy for you."

"Thanks." Lucie stood with her friend's collarbone jutting into her cheek and patted her back. There was no point denying her engagement; it would be easier to 'call it off' at a later date, although she doubted that she'd ever see most of the women again. But even so… when she'd asked Dale to come to New York with her, they'd just been friends. Since then, they'd become a fake-couple and now they were fake-engaged. She'd have to tell him later and she wondered how he'd take it. It was a good job that he knew her so well; another man might think he was being coerced into something, the way their situation was snowballing.

"Heidi!" Joanna called the stylist over. "Now Giana's done, I want you to give this one the full works." Heidi nodded and smiled at Lucie. "Be thorough and don't spare the horses. *She needs a complete makeover.*" Joanna stage whispered as she headed towards the junior stylist, who had returned with a waiter from the bar, each of them carrying a tray of champagne and sparkling crystal glasses.

–

Two hours later, Lucie almost didn't recognize her reflection. The woman in front of her had a flaw-less complexion, perfectly arched brows and killer cheekbones. It was an incredible transformation, as if her fairy godmother had flown in and waved a magic wand. Although she wasn't convinced that the pain she'd had to endure was worth it, even to look this good. Underneath her brows, the skin throbbed where the hairs had been ripped out and her upper lip tingled unpleasantly. Her scalp ached from where her hair had been brushed and pulled and painted then washed and blow-dried. But the result was an attractive long bob that had been tinted with foils so that whenever she moved, the golden and caramel tones shone through. Somehow, the makeup artist had given her plump lips and smoky eyeshadow that emphas-ized her blue eyes. She was thrilled, if she was honest with herself.

"All done!" Heidi removed the black cape that had protected Lucie's blouse, then stood behind her. "What do you think?"

"It's amazing, what you've achieved."

"If you hadn't already had a proposal, you'd certainly get one now," Joanna said from the next chair.

Lucie smiled at her but the comment stung. Would she really need to alter her appearance so dramatically to get Dale to propose to her? She'd never thought about whether or not he was physically attracted to her – well, not for quite some time anyway. But he was Dale. She took it for granted that it didn't matter with him; that he cared about her just as she was. But now... she wondered if he actually *did* find her attractive. And after yesterday's undeniably charming and romantic carriage ride, she had good reason to wonder. He'd been about to kiss her and to tell her something – she was convinced of it – but the driver had announced their arrival at The Plaza and the moment had been lost. She'd ached all evening to ask him what he was going to say, but had been too afraid. Because how would she respond?

Petra clapped her hands, snapping Lucie out of her musings.

"Come along, ladies, time to try the dresses on one last time before you wear them for real tomorrow. I hope none of you have put on any weight, because it'll really make things difficult." Petra added an odd little laugh, but Lucie suspected that she wasn't joking and she gulped.

She hadn't been looking forward to this part at all.

–

Lucie entered the hotel suite and closed the door behind her then leant heavily against it. After a morning of being primped and pampered, she was quite sleepy.

"Dale?" Her voice echoed around the empty suite. She plodded across to the bedroom but he wasn't there, nor was he in the bathroom. Then she spotted a folded piece of paper on the pillow with her name on it.

She picked up the piece of high-quality notepaper branded with the hotel's name.

Luce,

Gone for a wander. Didn't know what time you'd return, and know you've probably forgotten to check your mobile, so thought I'd better leave you a note. Should be back around four.

D X

Lucie checked her watch. One thirty-five. She could just grab half an hour's sleep. They had the wedding rehearsal dinner later, and she didn't want to yawn her way through it. A nap would be a good plan.

She kicked off her shoes, crawled into bed and pulled up the covers.

–

"Luce? Hey, sleepy-head."

Lucie was dragged up through the layers of sleep until she opened her eyes and found Dale looking at her.

"Oh!" Her heart flipped. "What time is it?" She sat up and pushed her hair out of her eyes.

"Four-thirty. Sorry I'm a bit late, I got carried away."

"Doing what?" Lucie clicked her tongue against the roof of her mouth. It was dry, and tasted like she'd been eating almonds.

"A bit of shopping." He smiled then sat on the edge of the bed. "It's fantastic out there, Luce. I wish you could have seen it. It started snowing again and there are Christmas songs playing in all the shops. The lights everywhere are amazing. I know we saw some of them yesterday, but it's like it gets better and better the closer to Christmas we get."

Lucie watched him as he spoke and goosebumps rose on her arms. He was animated with excitement, his brown eyes twinkling. He must have missed a shave this morning because he had a shadow of dark stubble over his chin. She had a sudden urge to run her hand over it.

"You okay?" Dale peered at her, his head on one side.

"Yes, of course. Absolutely fine. I just had a busy morning."

"Your hair looks great. Really glamorous and profes-sional."

"Professional?"

"You know… like it's been done by an expensive stylist. I expect the makeup was good, too."

"*Was?*" Lucie pushed the coverlet back and swung her legs over the edge of the bed.

"Well… it's a bit smudged now."

"Oh no!" Lucie hurried over to the mirror on the wall by the door to the lounge. "I was hoping to avoid having to do it again for this evening." She stared at her reflection and sighed. She had panda eyes and a dribble streak up one cheek that had cut through the foundation. But her hair still looked good, just a bit more 'surf-babe' than 'manicured movie-star'.

"It's fixable, right?" Dale chuckled and she glared at him.

"It's not funny. I just felt exhausted and thought I'd grab a quick nap. I'd better wash this all off and start again."

"I could always do it for you." He shrugged off his coat and hung it over the back of a chair in the corner of the room.

"Ha! Funny. I still remember when you painted my toenails for me after I'd broken my arm, Dale."

"Well, how was I supposed to know that you don't paint the whole toe?" He grinned and held out his hands. Lucie shook her head as she walked over to the bathroom.

"I'll grab a shower then. We need to be at The Plaza by seven." She grabbed a clip and twirled her hair, then pinned it up.

"No problem."

Lucie closed the bathroom door and turned the shower on. As the hot water ran and she stepped under the spray, she couldn't help smiling. Dale hadn't been kidding about painting her whole toe. He really was that innocent concerning things like makeup and beauty routines. It was as if he didn't see appearances as being that important.

Of course, he looked good effortlessly, with his dark hair and eyes and his deliciously olive skin. It was harder for women, especially women like Lucie who hadn't been first in the queue when long legs and flawless complexions were being given out. Not that she usually spent much time on her looks. She was happy as long as she looked presentable, and she knew she'd never be Miss World, so what was the point in trying to be something she wasn't? She had better things to do with her time, like eating good food, discovering new authors and having fun with Dale.

–

Dale waited until he heard the shower running, then dashed back into the lounge. Time to put his plan into action.

He rummaged in the bags he'd carried around Manhattan that day and pulled out his purchases. He opened the largest box and pulled out the mini pre-lit tree he'd bought in a particularly festive department store. He straightened out the branches, draped two long swathes of silver tinsel on it then located a socket and plugged it in. Next, he grabbed the fairy he'd found in Macy's and placed it at the top of the tree. It looked just like Lucie, with its blue eyes, rosebud mouth and wavy blonde hair. Of course, Lucie's hair was a bit different now she'd had it styled – he preferred it natural, when she looked as if she'd been on a windy beach all day, but her new look wasn't bad. It would just take a bit of getting used to.

Once the tree was just right, he placed the colourfully wrapped gifts beneath it, arranging them in size order. He suspected Lucie would tease him about that, his touch of OCD, as she called it. He did like things neat and well organized, but he was convinced that it made him good at his job, so he didn't mind.

"One more thing," he said as he took his mobile over to the docking station on a sideboard near the door. He scanned through his iTunes, found the Christmas songs he'd downloaded before they left for New York and hit play. The afternoon light was fading fast and with the lights on the tree, the snow falling outside and the festive music, the room was perfect. He just hoped Lucie would think so too.

When he heard the bathroom door open, he flung himself onto the sofa and waited. Lucie wandered through into the lounge in one of the fluffy white hotel robes, drying the back of her neck with a small towel. Her hair was still twirled into a loose chignon and tiny damp curls stuck to her cheeks and forehead. "Dale, I was thinking… Oh!"

"What were you thinking?"

"Dale, it's beautiful."

He got up and crossed the room to her side. "You sure, Luce? I know I did this at your flat but I thought we should make an effort here too, seeing as how we'll be here on Christmas Day."

She placed a warm hand on his arm and smiled at him. "I'm sure. Thank you. I can't…" She paused and bit her lip.

"Luce? The last thing I wanted to do was to upset you."

"No, it's not that I'm sad. It's just that you keep doing such lovely things for me and I've got something else I need to tell you." She raised watery eyes to meet his.

"What is it?" He placed his hands on her shoulders but the heat of her skin rising through the robe made him want to pull her closer, so he removed his hands quickly and stuffed them in his pockets.

"We're… uh… kind of engaged."

"What?" He took a step backwards.

"Oh, today they were all pestering me and nagging at me in the salon, and I just wanted to shut them up."

"Hell of a way to silence them, Luce."

She pouted, something that usually worked a treat when she wanted to watch a particular movie or to order the pizza toppings of her choice. Dale just couldn't resist her when she wanted something. In fact, as he gazed at her now – so close that he could feel the heat coming off her, fresh from the shower in her fluffy white robe – he was finding her pretty hard to resist full stop. He curled his hands into fists in his pockets and dug his nails into his palms.

Damn she looked good. He could take a step towards her right now and grab hold of the belt of her robe and undo the knot. He could slide the material apart, slip his hands over her warm skin, then scoop her in his arms and take her to bed.

"Dale, are you listening?"

"What? Yes. Of course I am." He pulled his hands out of his pockets and shook them as if they were trying to mislead him.

"As I was saying, I let slip about the carriage ride in the snow with champagne and they just assumed that you'd proposed."

"Like my parents misunderstood, huh?"

She nodded. "It was so awkward and there didn't seem to be a good way of telling them it wasn't true."

"So I proposed in the carriage, did I?"

"You did."

"Sounds reasonable to me. What about a ring?"

She waved a hand over her shoulder. "I said we'd agreed to buy one in the new year."

"Right. Of course." He rubbed a hand over his face. "Was it a romantic proposal?"

Lucie smiled. "I didn't go into detail. But I guess so."

"Good. I wouldn't want to be disappointing."

"You weren't." Her eyes filled with mischief.

"Did we… did we kiss when I proposed?"

"What?"

"Well, you know. After you said yes. Did we kiss?"

"Yes, I think we did."

"Was it good?"

"Dale…"

He grabbed her hand and whisked her towards him. She gasped but didn't pull away.

He slipped his left hand around her waist and pulled her tight against him then gently raised her chin with his free hand. He ran his thumb over her lips and they parted. Then her hands were around his neck and she moved onto her toes.

And their lips met.

–

He gently released her, stepped backwards and then sank onto the sofa. He buried his face in his hands, knowing that he really should stay in control. To at least think with his head *and* his heart.

His mind skipped to *When Harry Met Sally…* and how he and Lucie had scoffed at the assertion that men and women couldn't be *just* friends. Had they been wrong? At home, when they were in their own routines, it was easier to remember who they were and how their dynamic worked, but here in Manhattan, it was proving to be more of a challenge.

"It's okay, Dale." Lucie knelt in front of him.

"No. It's not. I shouldn't have done that."

She placed a cool hand over his and caressed his fingers. "I know why you did."

He lifted his head and met her gaze. He found understanding there. It was okay. It would be okay. But for now, at least, he had to try and show some self-restraint.

"Are there presents over there?" She left his side and crouched down next to the Christmas tree, the lights brightening her whole face in the gathering twilight. "Are these for me?"

"No one else here, and I don't know the maid well enough to guess what she'd like."

"But I haven't… I haven't got you anything. Well, not much anyway."

"I don't want anything, Luce. I saw a few things today and they kind of fell off the shelves into my hands. Plus, there's one there that I picked up at the Tonbridge Christmas market."

"I thought you only bought Santa hats that day! Dale, I hope you didn't spend much!"

He shook his head but didn't meet her eyes. "Not at all. Right, I'm going to take a shower." *A very cold shower.* "And I need to shave."

"Okay. See you in a bit."

As he left the room, Dale glanced back. Lucie was sat cross-legged on the carpet next to the tree, swaying in time to a Sinatra Christmas classic, completely lost in her thoughts.

It was the most beautiful sight he'd ever seen.

–

When Dale emerged from the bathroom, Lucie was ready. She'd fluffed up her hair, done her makeup – although it wasn't as dramatic as it had been before her nap, she thought she'd done quite a good job – and was wearing the designer black lace and chiffon dress she'd picked up in a sale in London when she'd gone to be measured for her bridesmaid's gown. The dress had short lace sleeves, a round neckline that showed a hint of cleavage and was gathered just below her bust so that it floated down to just below her knees. It was very flattering, as it hid her lumps and bumps and made her feel smart and attractive.

She'd paired it with a pair of Mary-Jane wedges and silver jewellery.

"Wow!" Dale said when he saw her.

Lucie grinned. "Thank you."

"That dress must've been expensive."

"It was a bit… but I got it in the sale."

He nodded. "It's lovely."

Lucie tried not to stare at him but her eyes kept landing on his naked torso. It glistened with water under the light from the chandelier and the towel he wore was tucked in just below his navel. He was, she could no longer deny it, physically perfect. With his generous nature and ability to make her laugh, he had the whole package.

Her eyes dropped further and she flushed as they landed on another kind of package.

Stop it!

She shook herself.

This is ridiculous! Pull yourself together.

"Fancy a drink?" she asked as she walked to the door. "I'll make one while you dress."

"Great."

"G&T?"

"Please." She stole one last glance at him before leaving the bedroom and caught him towelling his hair, which made the muscles on his arms stand out and showed off his rippling abs. If she didn't know better, she might think he was posing on purpose.

Once Dale had dressed, they sat in front of the window with their drinks. Everything below them had a thick white coating and the snow was still falling. Dale had switched on a lamp and with the lights on the little tree twinkling, the room had a cosy, homely feel. Their reflections were just visible in the window and Lucie was making a conscious effort not to meet Dale's eyes. They were too dark, superimposed upon the night sky, and too full of things that Lucie could not even begin to fathom. The intensity of the kiss they'd shared had left her a bit wobbly. Though gentle and fleeting, she'd wanted it, and she'd wanted him.

She sipped her drink and savoured the strong juniper of the gin contrasting with the sweetness of the fancy elderflower tonic she'd found in the minibar. Her senses were on high alert. The lace of her sleeves caressed her shoulders, the satin of the skirt floated over her legs and even though Dale wasn't sat right next to her, she could smell his aftershave and the clean soap scent of his skin. Manhattan was certainly working its Christmas magic, and it was having a heady effect upon Lucie. And she suspected it was doing the same to Dale.

"Penny for them?" he said, making her start, and as she did so, some of her drink slopped out over the edge. Dale placed his glass on the table and came to her aid with a tissue. "It's clean, I promise," he said as he dabbed it at her skirt. As he attempted to soak the gin and tonic out of her clothing, Lucie could only feel the weight of his hand on her knee and the warmth of his breath through her floaty skirt.

"It's all right!" she snapped, pushing him away and getting up before she did something that would make them late for dinner. "Wow! Is it hot in here?" She made a show of fanning her face then quickly downed what was left in her glass. "We should be going soon."

Dale gazed up at her from his position in front of her chair, his expression unreadable. After what seemed like an eternity, he got to his feet and nodded. "I guess so."

–

On the way to The Plaza, Lucie chattered on about nothing important, telling Dale all about the other bridesmaids and how much Petra's mother liked champagne. Dale nodded and laughed at the right times, but Lucie wasn't sure that he was one hundred percent present. Perhaps he was regretting kissing her. Or, perhaps he was regretting coming and he was missing his family. The night before Christmas Eve was always a busy one at the Treharne household and by now, eggnog would be poured as the family gathered together to celebrate. The festivities always lasted for at least five days and Lucie had often dipped in and out of them, only able to manage the family happiness for short periods of time. She had enjoyed being with Dale's family but it also made her miss her mother more, as well as making Lucie angry at her for what had happened. The school counsellor she'd seen for two years afterwards had told her that anger was a by-product of grief, and that she could expect it to ebb and flow along with the pain, but Lucie's anger was more complicated than even Dale knew.

Some things were best left in the past, buried away where they couldn't rise up and hurt you. It was the time of year conjuring old demons, and she just needed to focus on the here and now and push her sadness away. This was a different type of Christmas, although with things happening between her and Dale as they were, it seemed that her emotions were beginning to simmer.

They entered the hotel and were directed to a cavernous room where the rehearsal dinner was being held for a select number of wedding guests. Petra had told her that it was be an intimate gathering, to catch up before the wedding day. But as Lucie and Dale entered the Grand Ballroom, she had to force her mouth shut. There were at least a hundred people milling about, some standing in groups and talking as they sipped from gold-rimmed champagne flutes, while others sat at their tables and picked at canapés delivered by smart waiting staff. On every table was a small golden Christmas tree decked out with LED lights. The tablecloths were gold and cream and the chairs were draped with gold and cream covers.

"Mr and Mrs Barnsley haven't spared any expense, have they?" Dale asked as he accepted two flutes of bubbly from a waiter, handing one to Lucie.

"They certainly haven't." Lucie was scanning the room, taking in the elaborate ceiling with its enormous chandeliers, the small balconies between heavy gold drapes that lined the one side of the ballroom and the pink-lit stage that sat behind what appeared to be the top table.

"A wedding of this size must take some planning, Dale."

"You want a smaller affair, hey?" he asked, winking at her. She was warmed by his tone and the little wink, his way of letting her know that all was well between them. He used to do it when they were at school, if they'd had a falling out over a mutual friend, or when one of them had been reprimanded by a teacher for not completing work or chewing gum in class. Their school had been so strict when they were younger, and Lucie had been terrified of getting into trouble. Dale had been more confident, indifferent almost to the authority of the teachers, especially when it came to standing up for Lucie. One time he even spat his gum out on the classroom floor because Lucie'd had been admonished for eating a cough sweet. Of course, he'd been disciplined for that one, but it had shifted the heat away from Lucie. Another instance of just how much he looked out for her.

"This is too much. Don't you think so?"

Dale sipped from his glass, holding his pinky at a right angle. "Oh I don't know. I'm sure mummy and daddy Treharne would see this as a paltry affair. We'll have something much bigger and better, you mark my words, Quigley."

She giggled, imagining how Glenda and Hank would react to that news. She knew her own father would have little to contribute and anyway, it was so old-fashioned now to expect the bride or groom's parents to pay for their children's weddings. Petra's family were quite traditional in that way but for regular working class and middle class people, money would be tighter, weddings less ostentatious – unless they'd won the cost of their wedding on some reality TV show, of course. And *that* thought made Lucie shudder. She'd hate to be on display for all the world to see.

Lucie couldn't see Petra anywhere. Perhaps she was in an ante-room greeting guests, or off somewhere with Harry, fine-tuning last-minute details.

Someone must have directed guests to take their seats because suddenly Lucie and Dale were the only ones left standing. "There must be a seating plan, Luce," Dale whispered from between clenched teeth.

They hurried off to the corner near the entrance where there was a giant board with a plan stuck to it. "How did we miss this?" Lucie asked.

"Too shell-shocked I guess," Dale replied as they scanned the board. "There we are." He pointed at a table. "Right next to the top table."

"Come on then!" Lucie didn't even check the plan properly, she just followed Dale, keen to sit down before they attracted too much attention.

They took their seats quickly. A noise from the doorway next to the stage made all heads turn. Petra, Harry and their parents entered the room.

"They're like royalty," Dale whispered, stifling laughter.

"They practically are."

Lucie watched Petra and Harry as they walked to the top table hand-in-hand. They stood there, flanked by their respective parents, as the guests applauded.

"Imagine getting a round of applause just for entering a room, Luce."

"Dale, be quiet." Lucie said behind her hand. "We're amongst their family and friends."

He shrugged. "It's just funny, that's all. I can't imagine going through something like this myself."

Lucie glanced at him, wondering if he meant the whole elaborate display, but the room fell silent and there was a tinkling from the top table as Petra's father tapped a spoon against his whisky glass.

"Thank you. Thank you!" Petra's father, Jackson Barnsley, raised his glass to the room. "We're extremely grateful to you all for joining us at this joyous − yet very short-notice − union of our daughter Petra with Harry. This has, I'm afraid, been a long time coming." He cleared his throat as Petra and Harry shifted in their seats, clearly uncomfortable. "But, at last, the day of their union is almost upon us and we are all very, very, *very* happy that these two are about to join themselves together." He ran fat fingers over his grey goatee beard and a thick gold signet ring glinted on his pinkie. Next to him, Joanna snorted then guzzled more champagne. No wonder Petra had issues if her father could manage to work negativity into his pre-wedding speech. And, if what Tania had told her was correct, and Harry was not as in love with his bride as he should be, then perhaps Petra was clinging to her fiancé for entirely the wrong reasons.

She turned back to the top table to find Jackson raising his glass high. The amber liquid in the crystal tumbler swished against the sides. "Congratulations to you both! May you be blessed with happiness and many, many children." He slugged his whisky then took his seat.

Next up was Harry's father. Phillip Goldsmith was quieter than Jackson and he held a champagne flute not a whisky glass, but his speech was much warmer. He spoke briefly about his love for his only son and of how he hoped they would soon hear the patter of tiny feet.

"Seems Petra and Harry have their itinerary for the foreseeable future," Dale said, shaking his head. "It's madness being forced into childbearing like that."

"What, like being forced into a fake relationship and a fake engagement? Are we really any better?" Lucie asked.

"Touché." Dale held up his hands. "But we *are* aiming to tell the truth when we go home. Aren't we?"

Lucie was about to reply when she became aware that someone was peering around the Christmas tree in the middle of their table. She tried not to look directly at the person, suspecting he or she was just looking at the top table, but curiosity overpowered her and when she met the familiar grey eyes, she started.

"What is it?" Dale's hand tightened around hers and he made a funny sound, a bit like a growl, deep within his chest.

"I didn't know *he'd* be here."

"Neither did I." Lucie went cold and weak, and if it hadn't been for Dale's firm grip, she might have floated off towards the ceiling like a helium balloon that hadn't been anchored.

Jamie Davenport waved and mouthed *Hello* at her.

She looked away.

What do I do? Shit! Shit! Shit!

It felt like a lifetime since she'd last seen him, and now here he was, in Manhattan. The physical manifestation of something she'd rather forget.

She turned away quickly.

Ignore him. Pretend he's not there.

She was relieved that Harry had got up and was talking about his new alliance with the Barnsleys – although it sounded more like a business arrangement than a romantic union – because otherwise she might have had to speak to Jamie. She eyed the room, checking out the nearest exits. She could wait until the end of the speeches then slip out when dinner was being served. That way she wouldn't have to speak to him; she could escape.

Escape the shame. The old pain. The memories. The sadness.

"Ignore him." Dale leant closer to her. "He's nothing to you now. You're *my* fiancée remember. He can't hurt you any more."

Oh Dale, you don't understand because I never told you everything.

She met Dale's eyes and sank gratefully into their depths. His hands were warm on her arms and he communicated a thousand words in his gaze. "I've got you. It's okay, Luce. I promise."

She wriggled on her chair to get closer to him and he wrapped his arm around her shoulders. His proximity made her feel safer. He was her friend; he had her back. Jamie was in her past and he couldn't hurt her anymore. She was with Dale.

I'm with Dale.

She leant over and kissed Dale's cheek softly, enjoying the sting of his aftershave on her lips, the warmth of his skin up close.

"Thank you," she whispered, as he squeezed her and handed her a glass.

But even though she knew that Dale wouldn't let anything happen to her, she still felt a black terror sweep through her that she hadn't felt in some time.

No one knew exactly how Jamie had let her down. She'd never told anyone. Not even Dale. *Especially not Dale.* She didn't think she ever would. But she was also sensible enough to know why she blamed herself just as much as she blamed him. And while he was still around, while she was still carrying this shame, she knew she'd struggle to relax.

Or to let go.

Or to move on.

Chapter 12

When the speeches were finished, Lucie tapped Dale's arm.

"I need to go."

Dale flashed a glance at Jamie, who was talking to the man at his side.

"Because of him?"

"No. Yes. No. Well sort of. I didn't know he'd be here. I can't sit opposite him and eat. I'll say I've got a migraine or something if anyone asks. You stay and have your dinner if you want."

"Absolutely not! I'm coming with you." Dale stood and took Lucie's hand then they crossed the floor towards the exit. The guests were talking and drinking as starters were served and everyone seemed immersed in their enjoyment of the pre-wedding gathering.

As they left the room, Lucie released the breath she'd been holding.

"Lucie!" She turned to find Petra hurrying towards them. "Where are you going? Oh goodness! You look awful!" She covered her mouth. "I mean... you don't look well, you've gone green."

"She's got a migraine. She needs to lie down." Dale slid his strong arm around Lucie's shoulders. "I'll take her back to the hotel."

"Oh, Lucie, no. Do you need a doctor? I can get one to come to you. Will you be all right for tomorrow?" Her eyes were wide and her mouth trembled as if she too was overcome with conflicting emotions.

"No need for a doctor. I just need a lie down."

"And that's all that's wrong?"

"Petra…" Lucie considered whether to say anything.

"What is it? Have I done something wrong? Has someone else done something?" Petra looked as if she might burst into tears.

"Look… I didn't know that Jamie would be here. Stupid really, as he's Harry's friend, but you hadn't mentioned him and I guess I hoped he just wouldn't appear."

"I'm so sorry, Lucie. I thought that with you and Dale being together now that you wouldn't mind. And with poor Jamie being as he is now, I guess I hoped you wouldn't mind so much. We didn't know if he'd actually make it out here in all honesty, but his brother brought him. Jamie's one of Harry's old university friends and Harry wanted him here. I did say that it might be awkward after you two used to date, especially when you were seated at the same table, but it was some time ago now and then I got distracted by something else and…" She wrung her hands together. "All I can say is sorry."

His brother brought him? Poor Jamie? What was poor about him?

"Can I persuade you to stay?" Petra cut into her thoughts. "We could quickly rearrange a few seats and put you, or him, at another table."

Lucie shook her head. "No. No. Thank you. Then he would think he'd upset me, and I don't want that. I'll see you tomorrow, I promise."

She kissed Petra's cheeks gently then allowed Dale to take her back to their hotel.

Once they'd closed the door to their suite, Lucie felt as if she could breathe again. Her pulse slowed and her hands stopped trembling. But the butterflies in her stomach remained, stirred into wild fluttering every time she remembered that Jamie was in New York and that he'd be at the wedding.

Dale removed his jacket and shoes and took them into the bedroom. "You want me to order something from room service?"

Lucie's stomach growled in response.

"I guess that's a yes, then? What do you fancy?"

"Anything. Surprise me. I'm going to change." She padded into the bedroom and pushed the door shut then sank onto the bed. She didn't want Dale to see exactly how bad she felt but she suspected that this was how she'd feel if she'd been hit by a bus. She'd once loved Jamie so much, thought he was everything she could ever want in a man. She'd trusted him, believed in him. But she hadn't really known him at all and her shame at that still had the power to sicken her. How could she have been so stupid? So wrong. So naïve.

She unzipped her dress, took it off, then hung it in the wardrobe. She was safe here with Dale. They would eat then sleep and everything would seem better in the morning.

It always did.

–

"That was amazing! I'm honestly glad we came back and ordered food here. Plus, I got to eat in my pyjamas." Lucie tucked her feet underneath her and snuggled into the corner of the sofa. She cradled a large mug of tea.

Dale came to sit next to her. "It was delicious." He eyed her over the steam rising from his mug. "Are you sure you're okay now?" Lucie's reaction to seeing Jamie had been dramatic. He'd known that Jamie had hurt her a few years back and that it had taken her a while to get over it, but when she saw him earlier, it looked as if she'd seen a ghost. He was worried enough anyway with tomorrow being the anniversary of her mother's death. The whole point of this trip had been to help Lucie enjoy Christmas and he'd been making progress, but now that scumbag had shown up, and Dale didn't know if it would cause a massive setback.

"I am, Dale. I was just surprised. Now I know he's here, I can deal with it and get on with being a good bridesmaid for Petra."

"He was never good enough for you, Luce." He drained his tea then placed his mug on the table. As he leaned forwards, he grimaced.

"What's wrong?"

"My neck. Must be tension. It's really stiff."

"Well, we can't have that!" Lucie placed her mug on the table then pushed Dale forwards. "Let me get behind you so I can massage your shoulders. I bet it's tension coming up from there."

Dale paused. This probably wasn't a good idea, taking into account how he'd been feeling recently. Having Lucie's hands on him, feeling them wandering over his flesh and kneading his muscles could be a recipe for disaster.

"Come on! We can't have you looking like the hunchback of Notre Dame at the wedding, can we? They'll think I don't look after my fiancé."

Dale shrugged. He couldn't argue with that.

He shifted forwards on the sofa and Lucie slipped in behind him.

"Take your T-shirt off. It'll make it easier to massage you properly." She helped him pull it over his head.

Her thighs brushed against him as she began working her thumbs into his back. She squeezed and rubbed, and soon his skin was warm and he could feel the tension draining away. But something else was happening too, and in just his baggy lounge pants it was going to be difficult to hide.

It's just a side effect of the relaxation. That's all. Relax and forget about it and it will go away.

But as Lucie continued, she ran her hands over the front of his neck, then brushed her palms over his chest and down his arms. As she leant forwards and her breasts squashed against his head and shoulders, her scent overwhelmed him – coconuts mingling with honey. He should stop this. He should get up and move away, but he was in a trance.

He cared about this woman.

He loved this woman.

And he wanted this woman more than he had ever wanted anyone.

He turned slowly, then took her in his arms and she wrapped her hands around his neck.

"Lucie," he murmured. "Are you sure we should be doing this?"

"I'm not, but I want to."

He lifted her and carried her into the bedroom then laid her down on the bed. He moved over her, holding her eyes with his, caressing her face and neck, running his hands down her curves, over her hips, drawing invisible circles on her thighs. He wanted her so badly, yet he was afraid of breaking the spell.

Suddenly, she sat up and pulled her vest top over her head. Dale's mouth went dry. She was so beautiful, more perfect than he could ever have imagined.

More perfect than he'd allowed himself to remember.

She took his hands and placed them on her, then he lowered his head and kissed her neck, her shoulders and her collar bones. He breathed her in.

This is happening.

Something he'd thought about many times, yet pushed away because Lucie was too precious to lose. Because she'd hurt him all those years ago with her rejection, and because he sensed that she needed him there. Always. As a friend.

Too much to risk in case it all went wrong.

She'd been through so much and he couldn't risk hurting her. But he wouldn't hurt her. He loved her.

He cupped her face then kissed her mouth. Delving into her with his tongue. Needing her. Taking her.

Mine.

Then he paused.

Met her eyes.

Took a deep breath.

"I love you, Luce. So, so much. I should have told you before. I wanted to tell you in the carriage, and so many other times."

He waited.

But something in her eyes changed and she sat up.

She reached for her top and covered herself, hanging her head and avoiding looking at him.

"Luce?" He reached for her but she stood up and moved away. "Lucie, please don't do this. I didn't mean to upset you. What is it? Tell me!"

But she shook her head. "It's not you. It's me."

He ran his hands over his face and pushed the heels of his palms into his eyes.

Not that line! Anything but that cheap bullshit line.

"You owe me more than that, Luce. If you don't want me, fine, but why the hell did you take things so far? I mean... Was it because of him? Seeing him tonight made

221

you think… what, that you needed to make love to me?" His voice cracked. "To escape how you feel for him?" He stood up. White-hot rage burned through him. How could this be happening?

"I need some air." He had to leave before he said something mean, hurtful, devastating. Something he could never take back.

He grabbed his jeans and shirt, then stomped into the bathroom and dressed hurriedly. He felt drunk but he'd hardly had any alcohol that evening. His stomach churned and he cringed as he washed his face in cold water, trying to break the heady fog of desire that had enveloped him.

He should never have succumbed to his emotions. Never have let things change between them. Lucie was his friend. She needed his protection, not his advances. But he was human, and she'd come onto him and made him lower the barriers he'd erected around his desire for so long. He'd never have got half-naked if it wasn't for her kissing him like that and taking off her top, and now look what had happened. All because he'd been so damned weak. He opened the bathroom door and sat on the edge of the bed to lace up his trainers.

"Will you be okay here alone?"

Lucie lifted her eyes to meet his. She was pale, and had wrapped her arms around her knees. There were traces of tears on her cheeks and it made him long to wipe them away.

But she didn't want that.

She clearly didn't want him, and had just got confused about their relationship.

As had he.

He'd give her some space now and leave her in peace, though he doubted he'd find any peace himself for quite some time.

–

As the door closed behind Dale, Lucie fell onto the bed and let the tears fall. Her chest heaved as she sobbed and curled up in a ball, wishing she could block out the sadness yet knowing such thoughts were in vain. How on earth had she allowed things to go so badly with Dale? She'd wanted him tonight. She had wanted to lose herself in making love to him, to join with him and be filled by him, completed by him; made whole again. Because Dale did that for her; he kept the blackness away, banished the chasm of loneliness that she teetered on daily and he gave her hope that future happiness was possible.

She'd been carried away with how good she felt in his arms, how sweet and tender his kisses were and how her skin had tingled as he caressed her. But then… he'd told her he loved her and she'd realized what she was doing. And it was wrong.

Lucie loved Dale, but didn't want to make love to him for the wrong reasons. She loved him too much to allow that to happen. When… if… she made love to him it would be for the right reasons. She wasn't certain that her need for him tonight didn't stem from seeing Jamie, from a need to make love to someone who cared about her, someone she knew would never hurt her as Jamie had.

Dale deserved to be loved for himself, for who he was. He deserved to be treasured by the woman he took into his arms and into his life.

But now she'd screwed things up between them. He'd even mentioned Jamie, suspecting that Lucie had stopped things going further between them because she had feelings for her ex. But nothing could be further from the truth. Lucie had no sentimental residue in her heart for Jamie. He was part of her past. A part she'd forget in an instant if she could.

Dale was her life now. And, if she could find a way to make him understand, a way to explain things to him, then perhaps he would be part of her future as well.

She got up and went into the bathroom then turned on the large tap over the bath. She could head out into the night and try to track Dale down, but she was so weary and Manhattan was so big. She would be as likely to find him as she would a needle in a haystack. Besides, he'd come back eventually.

So she would wait.

Then she would explain.

Because she couldn't bear to know that Dale was hurting, especially not because of her.

Chapter 13

Lucie woke with a jolt.

It was light in the bedroom.

Light?

She swung her legs over the edge of the bed then paused. Her heart was hammering against her ribcage and a wave of nausea swept over her. Had she fallen asleep after her bath? Had Dale returned?

But he wasn't in bed with her.

He could be in the lounge.

She pulled on the hotel robe and padded over to the door.

Please let him be here.

And he was. Stood in front of the window drinking coffee. He was dressed in the suit he'd bought to wear to the wedding, his hair still damp from the shower.

"Dale?"

He turned to her, his face unreadable, as if he'd built a wall to shut her out.

"Morning. I was going to wake you if you didn't get up soon. It's gone nine."

"Shit! I have to get to The Plaza."

"I know. There's some breakfast here if you want it. I ordered fruit salad and some croissants and there's plenty of coffee."

"Thank you."

She approached him. "Dale, we need to talk."

"Do we?" His brown eyes seemed dull in the morning light. His face thinner. As if the pain had aged him in just hours.

"I'm so sorry about what happened. I wanted to speak to you. I tried to wait up but you were gone so long."

"I walked around for a while. I needed to clear my head."

"Dale, I need to explain—"

He shook his head. "It's okay, Luce. No explanations necessary. I think we've both been a bit affected by the romance of Manhattan." He smiled briefly. "You're a bridesmaid today at your friend's wedding, then it's Christmas day tomorrow. No need to dwell on anything negative."

Lucie covered her mouth. With everything that had happened and her concerns about Dale, she'd forgotten the date. Dale caught her as she crumpled and carried her to the sofa. "I was afraid this might happen today. You've been coping well." He smoothed her hair back from her face.

"For the first time ever, I wasn't conscious from the second I woke that it was my mother's anniversary. Dale, I forgot about her."

"Not really." He took her hand and ran his thumb over her manicured nails, courtesy of the pre-wedding makeover. "You'll never forget your mum in here." He pointed at her heart. "But it's okay not to dwell on it, too. She wouldn't have wanted that for you. Besides, you're in a different place and we've been busy. It's all right not to keep going over and over it in your mind all the time."

I wasn't on her mind that day when she died…

Lucie bit back the comment. What good would it do to vocalize it now? It would just confuse Dale and make her seem bitter. Which she was; a bit. But she still grieved for the woman who'd brought her into the world, who'd passed on her wavy hair and stubby toes. But Dale was right, there were other things to deal with here and now, things that required the attention of the living. She couldn't crawl back under the duvet and hide, because she had to be Petra's bridesmaid today. This was a good thing, a positive thing. As much as she felt like hiding away, she couldn't.

"Why don't you jump in the shower, then we'll eat and head over to The Plaza."

"What will you do while I'm being done up in the salon?"

"I'll be around." He shrugged. "I'll take a walk or read a newspaper or sip champagne with some trendy New Yorkers."

"Okay. But Dale, we need to talk later. Agreed?"

He nodded.

Lucie glanced past him, out of the window. The snow had stopped but the landscape was covered with a bright, white blanket that sparkled as if covered in glitter. It made Lucie's eyes water just looking at it.

At least, that's what she told herself as she headed for the shower. She wasn't crying over how she'd had to leave things with Dale. She wasn't fighting the tears that had sprung into her eyes, as she thought about how much she had hurt him.

–

The morning flew past in a whirl of powder and mascara, blow-drying and hairspray. Before she knew it, Lucie looked like an extra from a TV show and was afraid to move her face in case she cracked the layers of foundation.

The salon in The Plaza was buzzing with women's laughter, ringing mobiles, the monotone of hairdryers and the clinking of glasses. When Lucie was done, she sauntered over to Petra, who was having thick black lashes glued to her eyelids as another stylist completed her bridal manicure.

"How're you feeling?" Lucie asked her friend.

Petra waited until her eyelashes were completed before replying. "A bit nervous. But also excited. I mean… this is what I've wanted for, like… forever, right?" Petra's blue eyes shone in her tanned face, her razor-sharp cheekbones heavily accentuated with rouge. She reminded Lucie of Ursula Andress in her heyday, all pouty lips and breath-taking beauty. Yet in spite of the makeup and perfectly coiffured platinum blonde hair, there was an air of sadness around Petra today that Lucie had not expected to see. Perhaps it was because of the speeches last night – her father had not been kind towards his daughter – or perhaps she just had pre-wedding jitters.

"You have always said that you wanted to be Mrs Harry Goldsmith. Ever since the first date you went on with him, if I remember correctly." Lucie placed a hand on Petra's shoulder, which felt thin even through the fluffy hotel robe she'd worn down to the salon.

"And I do. At least I think I do. But what if I've just been clinging on to an idea and I'm wrong, Luce?"

Lucie took a deep breath. She glanced around the salon, searching for the right words, as if they'd materialize out of the hairspray-tainted air, when she spotted Tania staring right at her. Nodding and smiling, as if she knew exactly what Petra was saying to Lucie.

"Honey…" Lucie turned her back on Tania. "You are about to make a massive commitment. And you need to do what is right for you. Not for Harry or your parents or for his parents or for anyone else. This is about your happiness and your future."

Petra opened her mouth then closed it again and pressed her lips together until they turned white. "You're right, I know that. And this *is* what I want. I'm just letting the nerves get to me!" She shook herself then took a deep breath and released it slowly. "In just a few hours I will be a happily married woman. This is my destiny." She pouted at her reflection and waved at the hairstylist. "I need you to secure this bit here at the front. I don't want it flopping when I get warm or when I have my first kiss as a newlywed."

Lucie left them to it. Petra was a grown woman and only she knew her own mind. No one had the right to try to make someone's decisions for them. She wondered if her mother had experienced comparable moments of clarity, if it had been a similar realization that had led her to get in the car that Christmas Eve and to drive away from her husband and child. Had she felt that she'd given too much of herself away? That she'd been making her decisions for other people for too long?

Lucie would never know for certain.

But she felt that she might have just developed a better understanding of her mother's motivations. People often acted in what they believed were the best interests of those they loved and cared for. But sometimes, when pressure mounted or doubts overwhelmed, something internal could snap, and when that happened, they often did things that others would describe as out of character. But perhaps, in reality, they'd been acting out of character all along, and at that point they were actually – finally – being true to themselves.

–

As the opening notes of an instrumental version of Christina Perri's *A Thousand Years* rang out, goosebumps rose on Lucie's arms. The song was truly beautiful and the combination of the piano and the cello were perfect.

She was stood in line with the other bridesmaids, her small cream rose posy held in front of her, as they waited to enter the Terrace Room, where the ceremony would take place. She was glad they'd had a glass of champagne before lining up, because she needed the courage to wear the bridesmaid gown confidently. Part of her longed to hunch over and cover her boobs, but another part was telling her she looked good, that she should embrace her curves today and hold her head up high.

She'd had a professional makeover: her gold and caramel hair was coiled into a loose chignon with strands artfully curling at her temples and at the nape of her neck. Her face glowed, her eyes were smoky blue pools and the dress, made of cream silk, caressed her curves as it fell from thin straps, outlining her bust then tumbling waterfall-like to the floor, where it brushed against her French-manicured toenails. It was the most glamorous she had ever felt. Even if Joanna *had* insisted on telling everyone that Lucie had to have a bigger dress made to accommodate her voluptuousness.

"Ready?" The tall, broad-shouldered woman who'd asked the bridesmaids this had popped up several times in the salon and looked like she belonged in a court of law, with her tight black bun and stern expression. She was, Lucie had found out, the wedding planner.

They all nodded then she tapped the first two bridesmaids on the back, sending them off into the room. She counted to five then sent the next two. She'd arranged for some of the bridesmaids to enter in pairs and for some, like Lucie, to go alone, depending on age and how they were linked to Petra.

Then it was Lucie's turn, and as she entered the room, her stomach fizzed with nerves. The Terrace Room was just as grand as the ballroom, with its high red and gold ceiling decorated with paintings in the style of the Italian renaissance, its crystal chandeliers and golden chairs. The chairs were separated from the aisle with small round tables that held tiers of candles, and at the centre of each one was a round bouquet of cream-coloured roses attached to a dozen heart-shaped helium balloons which bobbed in the warm air.

She tried to take each step carefully in order to avoid tripping on the hem of her gown, and to avoid making eye contact with the guests, but she couldn't help searching for Dale. When she found him, he flashed her a smile. She was almost halfway along when she met another pair of familiar eyes and she couldn't look away.

Jamie!

A thousand emotions flooded through her as she took him in, from his expensive haircut, to his piercing grey eyes, to his tanned skin to his...

Wheelchair?

But before she could even begin to process what she was seeing, she was falling forwards, her high-heeled sandals caught up in her gown. There was a loud ripping sound at the same time as her forehead met the floor. Her head bounced off the plush carpet that had been rolled out to create a walkway for the bridal party and her front teeth closed hard on her tongue.

The music stopped.

A silence fell over the room.

Then there was a collective intake of breath from the guests, released with as much horror as a bloodcurdling scream, as they stood to peer at the bridesmaid who'd fallen as she walked along the aisle.

Lucie lay there for a moment, too stunned to move. She could taste blood and her tongue was stinging. Strong hands suddenly landed on her shoulders and pulled her upright, eliciting another gasp from the crowd.

Lucie realized that her front was very, very cold. And very, very exposed.

Then Dale was wrapping his jacket around her and covering her with his own body, as he ushered her out of a side door.

–

"Here. Drink this." A waitress handed Lucie a tumbler. She sniffed it and shivered. "Brandy for the shock," the young woman explained.

"I think the wedding guests were probably more shocked than you were, Lucie." Dale tried to smile, to lighten the mood. He rubbed her back, the material of the fluffy robe that a receptionist had quickly found for her, soft under his fingers.

A stylist fluttered near them, trying to repair Lucie's bridesmaid gown. Dale had been admiring her as she moved along the aisle, marvelling at how beautiful she was and at how she glowed in the gorgeous silk dress that caressed her curves like a second skin. Then she'd spotted Jamie. Her face had fallen as she'd taken in the fact that he was in a wheelchair and that he was watching her too. She'd stumbled as her shoes got caught up in her dress and as she'd fallen, the thin straps had torn. When Dale had helped her up, the dress had fallen to her waist, giving everyone in the room an eyeful of her flesh-coloured petal-shaped nipple covers. Dale was mortified *for* her. Furious that people were looking at her. And he'd covered her up as quickly as he could, knocking over his chair and stepping on a few toes in his haste to reach her.

"Here you are. All done. The hem is fine, it was just the straps that took the brunt of your fall."

"I guess I stuffed up royally that time, eh?" Lucie shook her head, her cheeks scarlet. "Why is it always me, Dale? In the schoolyard, it was always *me* the ball hit when a game of football was going on. It was always *me* who dropped the test tubes in science or got the copy of *Macbeth* with the crusty old boogers in. The universe must hate me." The brandy was loosening her tongue. Dale had heard these things before, but only when Lucie'd been joking around. Now she seemed genuinely upset about them.

"Don't worry about it, lovely!" The chief stylist said as he passed. "Those lot in there have seen far more shocking things than your titty-boos. Once the reception gets under way, and they're all on their second bottle of Krug, they'll all forget about it anyway."

"I doubt it, but thanks." Lucie drained her brandy. "So what do we do now?"

"Well, it's up to you, whether you want to go into the reception or not."

"I can't believe I missed the ceremony."

"You can always watch the video," Dale suggested.

"The video?" Her eyes widened. "My boobs will be on the wedding video!" She buried her head in her hands. "It'll appear on the video camera TV shows with all the other wedding mishaps. Oh my god, Dale! I'll never live this down."

He shook his head. "I'll have a word with Harry later. They'll edit it out. I'll sort it, I promise." The thought of Lucie's fall, as well as her being indecently exposed on TV for millions to watch, made a fire burn low in his gut and his fists clenched automatically. He was never going to let that happen.

"You will?"

"Of course. Now, Luce… Do you want to talk about it?"

"What?" Her blue eyes widened.

"About *why* you fell." He took her hands.

She hung her head and a strand of hair fell over her forehead. He brushed it gently behind her ear. "I didn't know that Jamie was in a wheelchair."

"Why would you? You haven't had any contact with him since you split up, have you?"

She shook her head.

"We didn't notice last night because he was sat at the table… behind the Christmas tree."

"How is he… in a wheelchair?"

"I don't know. I only saw him when I took my seat, and by then it was too late to come and find you to warn you. I just hoped you wouldn't see him until later but they placed him right next to the aisle."

235

"It's so strange. All this time I've been thinking of him as some sort of monster, demonizing him, I guess…" She bit her lip.

"Demonizing him? Monster?" He knew Jamie had hurt her, broken her heart she'd said, but demon meant evil, horrendous, cruel. Was there more to what had gone wrong between Lucie and Jamie than she'd told him?

Lucie shook her head. "Not now," she said. "It's too busy here."

"Later then?"

"Yes. Later." The colour drained from her face. There was something bad that she hadn't told him. Something he hadn't known all these years, and that cut him deep. They told each other everything. Or so he'd thought.

"I'll get changed then we can go and get some food. In spite of everything, I'm actually quite hungry." She squeezed his shoulder as she got up. "And thank you for saving me once again."

"Anytime."

Dale watched as Lucie walked away. He was beginning to worry that he didn't know her as well as he'd thought, and he didn't like it at all.

Chapter 14

The reception was well underway when Dale and Lucie entered the Grand Ballroom. As they walked in there was a temporary lull in conversation and all eyes turned Lucie's way, but people were obviously enjoying themselves too much to waste time on the bridesmaid who'd flashed them, and their attention was soon elsewhere.

Dale guided her to their table, and once again she was thankful he was there. She probably would have travelled out for the wedding anyway, even if he hadn't been able to make it, but then she'd be going through all this alone. Even after all that had happened over the past few days, Dale still had her back, and she was indebted to him for it.

Not long afterwards, Petra and Harry entered the room to applause, evidently having finished with the formal wedding photographs.

The food was delicious, and as the champagne flowed and the string quartet played love songs, Lucie began to relax. She chatted to Dale and to the people at their table, most of whom she knew vaguely, as friends of Harry or relatives of Petra. She tried not to look around the room in case she saw Jamie again. If she couldn't see him, she could pretend he wasn't there. *Almost.* And every time she experienced a flutter of anxiety, Dale seemed to know; he'd place his hand over hers, on the small of her back, or he'd offer his familiar cheeky wink.

The speeches were loud and rowdy. Harry's best man made a particularly crude one about their teenage years and how experienced Harry was with both sexes – something Petra didn't flinch over, but which had steam coming out of Joanna's ears. Then Tania, as maid of honour, made a brief toast to Harry and Petra. She wished them all the happiness in the world, but it seemed somewhat disingenuous. Tania's body language gave her away – she didn't look at Petra at all, just Harry, then when she went to kiss them both, it was a quick air kiss for the bride and a lingering kiss on Harry's cheek as she slid her hand over his chest. Lucie wasn't certain that anyone else even noticed, but she did. The way Tania allowed her hand to linger as she kissed Harry, then moved it lower, made Lucie want to shout at her to stop. There was something wrong, and she felt sure there was more to it than just the alcohol-induced high jinx of the upper classes.

The plates were cleared away, then the cake arrived, wheeled in on a wide trolley. It was enormous. There were five square tiers, covered in scalloped white buttercream. On the top tier stood a bride and groom, arm in arm. Gold and cream-coloured fondant roses cascaded down the front, intertwined with silver ivy. The theme continued on the cake stand, with rose petals and ivy scattered around. The waitress who'd brought the cake in raised her hands to request silence. "This cake has many layers, including dark chocolate mousse, vanilla mousse and cherry mousse. Our congratulations to the bride and groom! Enjoy!"

As Petra and Harry cut the cake and posed for more photographs, gold champagne was served; something Lucie had not seen before. One woman told her that it was infused with 24-karat gold flakes and rumoured to help the drinker live a long and prosperous life. As it fizzed in her crystal glass, Lucie thought it resembled a golden snowstorm.

"You think they're trying to tell us how rich they are?" Dale asked as he peered into his glass. "All this gold everywhere... from the trees, to the glasses, to the cake, to the champagne. I've never seen so much gold. Can you imagine what my mother would say?"

Lucie smiled. Glenda would probably comment on the extravagance, but secretly enjoy the sense of luxury. She suddenly wished Dale's mother and father were here too. It would be nice to see them enjoying the good food and wine, to speak to them in the familiar comfortable way that she could.

Was that a pang of homesickness for Dale's parents?

Imagine how he must be feeling!

"Have you spoken to your mum today?"

He nodded. "Only for five minutes, though, when you were having your hair done. It was chaos back there... the boys were screaming as they got more and more wound up. My father was offering everyone eggnog or sherry, loudly, as he'd clearly been indulging in it already. Mum did say that Ieaun's boyfriend had arrived, though, and that he seemed very nice. So that's got to be a good thing."

"Do you wish you were there now? Tonight?"

He shook his head. "I'm having a good time, Luce... Mostly. Besides, someone has to look after you!"

She nudged him and laughed. "For that, I'm going to make you dance with me."

"I'll need a few more of these before I shake my booty." He raised an eyebrow at her.

The cake was served and Lucie worked her way through the different layers. The sponge was light; the mousse mouthwateringly fluffy. It made a perfect partner to the champagne, and she had to remind herself to take her time; she could already feel the warm buzz of two glasses, and she wanted to keep a clear head. She didn't fancy falling again and giving the guests another chance to capture her boobs on camera.

When everyone had finished, the plates were cleared again, then the lights dimmed and Harry and Petra made their way to the dance floor. On the stage, a full band had replaced the string quartet, and a woman clad in a figure-hugging black gown and stiletto heels picked up the microphone. As Harry took Petra into his arms, the singer began to croon, her sequins sparkling under the lights...

At last...

After a few moments, other guests took to the floor. Lucie watched them, mesmerized by their slow movements, at how they moved in time with their partners as if joined by invisible string.

A hand on her arm made her jump.

It was Dale. Standing at her side. Asking her to dance.

She took his hand and walked to the dance floor.

They paused for a moment, gazing into each other's eyes, and she wondered what he was thinking, what he was feeling. After last night, he had every right to be hurt, angry, confused. She'd not yet had the chance to explain. She opened her mouth to speak, but he shook his head. "Let's just have tonight. Everything else can wait for tomorrow."

Dale pulled her close and they moved together, in time, their knowledge of each other so perfect that they didn't need to think. The song changed once, twice, three times... Their breath became one, their warmth melded them together, and when Dale finally stood still and tilted her chin up so he could meet her eyes, it took Lucie a few seconds to emerge from the spell she'd been under.

"I have an idea."

"You don't want to dance any more?" It was hard to keep the disappointment out of her tone.

"We will... later. Come with me."

He released her then led her over to one of the tables at the edge of the room. He untied a large red heart balloon from the flower display.

"What are you doing? You can't do that!" Lucie giggled and glanced around, worried someone would catch them.

"Of course I can."

He stuffed the balloon under his suit jacket. "Now no one can see it anyway!"

"No, but you look really fat. Like Santa Claus."

"Ho ho ho! Come on, Miss Quigley, there's something we need to do."

He led her through the hotel to the lobby, then out through the front doors. A gust of ice-cold air hit them as they descended the steps' red carpet, and Lucie shivered in her thin dress. Dale noticed. He removed his jacket and wrapped it around her shoulders, then pulled it together at the front.

"It's a bit slippery, so be careful."

Lucie took his hand as they walked to the edge of the pavement and giggled at the sharpness of the Manhattan night air. "It's freezing out here! I could lose my toes." She wiggled them in her sandals to stop the snow sticking.

"We won't be long. It's just that I thought... it's been such a busy day and I thought you might want to do something... something for your mum. You know?" He stared deep into her eyes and Lucie knew that he was worrying he'd done the wrong thing.

"It's a lovely idea, Dale. Really. That's what the balloon is for?"

He nodded. "You can release it for her. Let her know you're thinking of her even though you're in New York.

I didn't want to bring it all back, Luce, I just didn't want you waking up tomorrow and feeling guilty that you hadn't done anything to mark the anniversary. I know that normally we take flowers to the grave. But this is something, right?"

She slipped her hand from his and placed it against his cheek. His skin was cool, his jaw strong to the touch. "It's perfect, Dale."

He wrapped his arm around her and pulled her around to stand in front of him. He was shivering against her. "You need your jacket back."

"It's fine. I've got you to keep me warm."

She held the balloon out.

"Merry Christmas, Mum. Wherever you are…" Her throat tightened, as it always did whenever she tried to speak to her mother. It was a combination of grief, confusion and anger. She knew that. But she would do this now. Dale had been so thoughtful, and he was right. It was twenty years since her mother had gone. She needed to do something.

Something to finally set her heart free.

"I hope you're happy and that you have found peace."

She pressed a kiss to the shiny surface of the heart then gently released it. It sailed up into the sky, towards the tiny stars that twinkled high above the city; the city that thrummed with excitement, love, sadness, anger and pain. But most importantly, with life.

Lucie was alive. She felt it more than ever. Dale held her for a few minutes as they watched, until the balloon disappeared, swallowed by the Manhattan night, then she turned in his arms.

"You're a special guy, Dale."

"You're a special lady. But we'll freeze if we stay out here any longer. I think I have frostbite in my toes already."

Lucie nodded. "You should try wearing sandals. Let's get back inside and warm up."

As they headed back inside, Lucie rubbed her hands together to try to warm them. She was so focused on this that she didn't initially notice the silence in the room.

All the guests were staring at the doorway next to the stage, as if waiting for something.

Then there was a long, piercing scream.

"What was that?" Lucie grabbed Dale's arm.

Harry came flying through the door, closely followed by Petra. She was screaming and pounding on Harry's back. Pursuing him. Her hair was now a bird's nest, her mascara was running down her cheeks and one of her false eyelashes clung to her upper lip like a wonky moustache.

Harry turned and held his arms out, trying to fend off Petra's blows, but she was clearly hysterical.

Why isn't anyone doing anything?

To their side, off in the shadows, Lucie spotted Tania. She was sporting a sly grin on her flawless, aristocratic face.

Joanna and Jackson stood nearby, apparently engaged in their own argument, and Harry's parents had retreated to stand with their family, as if involvement in this display was too far beneath them.

"I have to go to her," Lucie said to Dale, not wanting to leave him but knowing she had to help.

"Of course."

Lucie rushed over to Petra, and when she said her name, approaching cautiously to avoid being punched, her distraught friend flung herself into her arms and sobbed with the fervour of the brokenhearted.

–

Lucie ushered Petra out of the Grand Ballroom and into a smaller room along a corridor. It seemed to be some sort of parlour, with two small sofas and a fireplace. From nearby she could hear the sounds of a busy kitchen, which must have been where the wedding banquet was prepared.

"Here." Lucie helped her trembling friend to sit, then scanned the room, hoping there would be some water, but she couldn't see any. "Are you thirsty?"

Petra nodded.

"Stay here and I'll get something to drink. I'll be back quickly."

Lucie pulled the door behind her then hurried back to the reception. She located a waitress and requested water, then looked around for Dale but she couldn't see him. She didn't want to go looking for him, because she needed to get back to Petra as soon as possible. The waitress returned with the water. Lucie glanced at Harry as she left the room, and was horrified to see him leaving through a different door with Tania in his wake.

So Tania had been right all along about Harry and Petra. But she'd clearly had her own motives for trying to keep them apart. What on earth was wrong with them? If he didn't love Petra enough to be faithful to her, why did he propose?

Lucie pushed open the door to the room in which she'd left Petra, and almost dropped the glass of water when she saw who was trying to comfort her distraught friend.

"Jamie." His name was like sawdust in her mouth. Her survival instinct kicked in, telling her to run, but she couldn't exactly leave Petra right now, so she took a few steadying breaths and closed the door behind her. Besides, what could he do to her? It wasn't as if they were alone. And he was in a wheelchair. She knew people could move quickly in them – she'd watched the paralympics, after all – but suspected that the bulky furniture might hinder his speed, as he'd have to negotiate the chair around it all.

You're safe. Be calm. He can't hurt you now.

"Hi, Lucie."

"What're you doing in here?"

"What does it look like? I'm trying to comfort Petra."

"I'd have thought you were the last man to have the capacity to offer a woman comfort." The coldness in Lucie's voice surprised her, and Jamie winced.

Petra was sobbing into a napkin, oblivious to the tension in the room.

"People change, Lucie."

"Do they?"

He nodded. "Look at me." He gestured at his chair then smacked his hands against the wheels. "I've changed a lot."

"Just because you're… you're… I don't even know what's happened to you, but it doesn't change what you did."

"I know, and I've wanted to speak to you about that for years. But you never took my calls and I don't know if the letters and emails I sent even got to you? Did they, Lu?"

"Don't call me that. *Ever!*" she spat. She suddenly remembered the glass of water she was holding, and took it to Petra before she became tempted to throw it over her ex. "Here, lovely. Drink this."

Petra raised red eyes to the glass. She had snot smeared over her face and the strip of fake eyelashes had moved from her chin to her cleavage, where it now perched like a spiky slug. "Thank you." She sipped from the glass and Lucie tried not to notice as Petra's snot drifted onto the surface of the water.

Lucie perched next to Petra, trying not to glance at Jamie. But her eyes had a mind of their own, and they crept up to look at him. Outwardly, he was still the same Jamie; his face tanned, his hair well cut, his clothes smart and trendy. But his eyes were different. They were still grey, but now the grey of a stormy sky rather than the silver grey that used to remind her of the sky at dawn. She had loved to gaze into Jamie's eyes.

Once. Upon. A. Time.

Now they made her recoil.

So different from Dale's…

She shuddered. She didn't even want Dale and Jamie to be in the same thought process. Dale certainly didn't deserve that. He was a good man. Jamie was not.

"What am I going to do?" Petra wailed, dragging Lucie from her thoughts.

"What exactly happened?"

Jamie answered. "She went to find Harry because he'd been gone a while and she found him—"

"With that… *slut!* They were… doing it in the toilets. In the ladies' loo! I walked into the cubicle and there she was… straddling him as he sat on the toilet. Bouncing around, her bridesmaid dress pulled down to her waist and hiked up to her thighs. She… was… *screaming* with pleasure."

"Oh no." Lucie slid her arm around Petra's shoulders, trying to dismiss the graphic image from her mind. "What a thing to see! I'm so sorry."

"Not your fault. I knew… he was like that."

Lucie thought about what Tania had said to her. Could she have helped Petra avoid this, if only she'd told her? But would Petra have listened? "You did?"

Petra reached out and took Jamie's hand. Lucie flinched. She wanted to snatch her friend's hand right back.

"Jamie knows."

"You do?"

He hung his head. "It wasn't my place to say anything to Petra about it, but she caught him once before at a golf club dinner."

"With Tania?"

They both shook their heads.

"With another one of his tarts," Petra explained.

"When was this?"

Petra shrugged. "A few years back. But I suspect he's been doing it all along, and Tania's just one in a long line of them." She turned to Jamie and he blushed. "I'm right, aren't I?"

He swallowed hard. "Don't do this to yourself. What's happened today is bad enough."

"I know. But… you know what makes me really mad? He never made me scream with pleasure. Not once. Not in all the years we were together. I thought it was me… that he just didn't fancy me as much as I did him. Perhaps it was."

"Petra, don't try to analyse it all," Jamie said. "Sometimes we say and do things we later regret. Things we regret as soon as they're done."

"Harry didn't look like he was filled with regret!" Petra snapped.

"Maybe not. But perhaps he just cared a lot more about himself than you. He probably cares more about himself than he ever will about anyone else."

Petra released a long sigh and deflated on the sofa, letting her head rest against the backrest. "I can't believe I'm married, and this is my wedding night. What a letdown, eh?"

Lucie squeezed her shoulder. "You want me to try to find him. So you can talk?"

Petra shook her head. "Nothing to discuss with that creep. It's over. I've given him too many chances, and look what he did. Merry Christmas to me."

Lucie bit hard on the inside of her cheek. Merry Christmas indeed.

"Oh, Lucie, I'm so sorry. Isn't today the anniversary?"

Lucie nodded. "It's okay."

"How many years?" Petra took Lucie's hand.

"Twenty."

"Wow."

"I know. Christmas Eve has always been hard, but I don't know. This year, being in Manhattan, focusing on your wedding and seeing the sights and…"

"Being with Dale?"

Heat crawled up Lucie's neck. "Yes. It's all just helped me to deal with it. And at some point, I guess, we have to move on."

Petra nodded. "Sure do. And you have that wonderful fiancé to help you now. He's a good one, Lucie, I can tell."

Lucie avoided meeting Jamie's gaze, but she felt his eyes burning into her. She wasn't about to explain herself to him. He had no right to expect it of her. To expect *anything* of her, in fact.

The door opened and Joanna entered, bringing with her the unpleasant combination of cigarette smoke and floral perfume. She must have just gone outside to cater to her addiction, then doused herself in scent to try to cover it.

"Oh, Petra!" She held open her arms.

"Mummy!" Petra stood and accepted the hug.

"Come on, my angel, let's go to your room and get you a proper drink. Daddy will deal with everything downstairs. He's already talking to his lawyer… at the bar, I don't doubt. He'll make sure that cheater doesn't get away with this."

"I can't believe it, Mummy."

"I know, darling. But we'll sort it. Mummy's here."

Petra allowed her mother to lead her from the room.

Lucie sat still for a moment. Everything seemed to have taken on a fuzzy haze. Was all this really happening?

"At least it brought her mother to her side," Jamie said.

Lucie looked at him. He was right. "If this helps them to mend their relationship, then that will be a positive. But what an awful way for it to happen."

She stood up.

"Please don't go yet."

"What?"

"Now you're here, I'd really like to talk to you. About what happened."

"Between Petra and Harry?"

"No, Lucie. Between us."

"I… I don't think that's a good idea."

"Please, Lucie. Just hear me out. I promise you're safe with me."

She eyed him for a moment, yearning to flee, yet slowly accepting that if she heard him out, she might get some closure. If not, she wouldn't have lost anything. Besides, if she left now, she might always be wondering what he was going to say.

She sat back down, moving as far away from him as she could. "Go on then. Explain."

He nodded. "Thank you." He took a deep breath then released it slowly. "First of all, I want to say how sorry I am."

–

Dale kept looking at his watch. Lucie had been gone over an hour. What was an acceptable time to wait when a woman went to comfort her best friend? Perhaps it would be okay to go and find her now. He'd gathered from the others at their table that Harry had been caught with his pants down. Dale had never warmed to Harry, finding him a bit too full of himself, but for him to cheat on his new bride at his own wedding reception was something he hadn't expected. Harry was a successful banker, a man who'd glided through life, apparently without a care in the world. But unfortunately, that kind of ease sometimes eroded people's values. And now Harry had done this to his wife. Why had he bothered proposing to her if he didn't love her? He'd humiliated her in front of their families and friends, and for what? A quick bonk with a woman Dale thought actually looked a bit like Petra.

He shook his head. It was very sad, and he was grateful that his life had been simpler. He didn't need to be rich or to live the city life. He loved working with plants and tending to people's gardens rather than their finances.

Plants didn't cheat or lie. They didn't ask for much other than feeding and watering and some sunshine. People could be so very complicated. He was also grateful for his family; loud, noisy and jostling for attention as they were, he loved them all. He couldn't imagine any of them acting as Harry had. Hank would go ballistic if any of his sons treated a woman like that. Yes, he'd been taught morals, and he was glad of it.

He'd try to find Lucie then see if she wanted to go back to their hotel. Lots of the guests were leaving, realizing that the party was over and there was no point hanging around.

He checked that they hadn't left anything on the table or chairs, but Lucie hadn't brought a bag, as she'd been a bridesmaid, which meant that all her possessions – small purse, lipstick, fold-up brush and mobile – were in his jacket. He was effectively Lucie's makeup bag today, and he didn't mind at all. In fact, he quite liked that she had entrusted him with her things. And he'd liked the way she just slipped her hand into his jacket pocket for her lipstick or tapped his hand when she needed a tissue.

Dale said goodbye to the people at the table, then left the room through the exit Lucie had taken. He walked along the corridor and saw Petra and her mother going through double doors at the end.

"Petra!" he called and she turned to him. He made an effort not to grimace at the state she was in. Her face was extremely puffy, red and smudged. Her tiara hung at an awkward angle reminding him of the leaning tower of Pisa.

"I'm… uh… sorry about what happened. It must have been awful."

She nodded.

"Mummy's got you now, though." Joanna cooed as she stroked her daughter's messy hair. Dale watched as she wobbled on her impossibly high heels, clearly worse for drink.

"Well, if there's anything I can do…"

"Thank you. Are you looking for Lucie?" Petra asked.

"Yes. Do you know where she's gone?"

"In there." She pointed at a door.

"Thanks. Uh… see you soon." Dale gave a small wave then hurried back down the corridor. What did you say to someone in these circumstances? He had no idea at all. Lucie was far better at this stuff.

He pushed the door open and Lucie turned around. She was on a small sofa and at the other end of it, in his wheelchair, was Jamie.

"You okay, Luce?" They both stared at him as if he had two heads and Lucie seemed to surface from somewhere else, as if she'd been half-asleep, when he said her name.

"Oh… yes."

A wave of uncertainty washed over him. Why was she in this room, alone with her ex?

"I was looking for you."

"Sorry. I'm okay, though. We were just talking. Jamie was explaining a few things." Her voice was cold, not the Lucie he knew at all. Wheelchair or not, anger for this man burned in Dale's gut.

"Are you ready to go back to *our* hotel? The wedding party's over and everyone's leaving. No point hanging around here now."

"Yes. Of course. I'll be there in a minute."

"You want me to stay?" He eyeballed Jamie.

"No, it's fine. I won't be long." She flashed him a small smile, but her eyes were sad. Dale knew that look. It was Lucie's thoughtful face, the one she adopted when she was weighing things up.

"Okay. As long as you're sure."

Jamie hadn't taken his eyes off Dale's face, and he recognized the challenge there. For a moment, he considered accepting, fighting for Lucie and insisting she came with him, but then he remembered what had happened last night; how she'd pushed him away when they'd got closer than they had done in years. And now Jamie had reappeared. Still suave and monied, confident and arrogant. If Jamie was what Lucie wanted, then Dale had to concede. Didn't he? Or should he put up a fight and force her to leave with him now?

"Honestly, Dale. I'm all right. I'll see you soon." Her words were like an icepick being driven into his heart.

He wouldn't fight for what wasn't his in the first place, even though his heart and body were screaming at him to stay and claim her. Not to allow this creep to win her back. To try to make her see sense.

He stood there for a moment.

Waiting.

Willing Lucie to get up and leave with him. But she didn't; she seemed oblivious to his presence. Numb. As if

255

she didn't care about his feelings or hadn't even considered how he might be hurting right now, seeing her with this other man. And after all that had happened between them since they came to New York.

Something in him was crumbling to dust.

"I'll head on back then, Luce. See you... later."

As he closed the door behind him, slowly, leaving the woman he loved with her ex-boyfriend, he wasn't sure he'd see her again that night at all. Because it seemed as though she'd made her choice.

And Dale was the one leaving alone.

Chapter 15

Lucie slid the key-card into the door of the hotel suite. She slipped off her shoes by the door then padded into the room. It was dark except for the small lights on the tree that Dale had bought for her. He was such a sweetheart.

She grabbed a bottle of water from the mini-fridge and drank half of it, swilling it over her tender tongue, which had resumed its throbbing as the evening wore on. The water was cold and refreshing.

The clock on the elaborate mantelpiece said that it was 2:24 am. She hadn't meant to be out this late, but she'd been talking to Jamie for over two hours. There had been tears, recriminations and more tears. But it had been worth it. Then, as she'd been about to leave, she'd been called to The Plaza reception and asked to go up to see Petra. That had taken up another hour and a half, as she'd hugged her friend and reassured her and promised to go out for lots of girls' nights in the new year. Finally, Petra had fallen asleep in her huge canopied bed, and Lucie had left Joanna smoking on the balcony.

She couldn't believe how much she wanted to see Dale.

To feel his strong arms around her and his soft mouth against hers.

To tell him how she felt about him and to explain why she'd pulled away the night before.

To tell him everything about Jamie and what had happened all those years ago. She wanted to finally be free of the past so that she could move on: have a life, have a future, completely guilt free.

To be with Dale.

If he would have her.

She finished the water, then went into the bedroom. It was dark, but she could make out his sleeping form.

"Dale?" she whispered. "I'm back."

She waited.

No answer.

"Dale?"

He shifted a bit in his sleep but settled again.

Lucie stepped out of her dress and pulled on her pyjamas.

It had been a very long day and she was suddenly overwhelmed by exhaustion. She'd get some rest and they could talk in the morning. It could wait until then. They would both think more clearly when they had rested.

She climbed into bed and wriggled across to Dale, slipped her arm around him and snuggled into his broad back.

Then she slipped into blissful darkness.

–

Lucie woke up suddenly. She had that disconcerting feeling that someone had been watching her sleep.

She was right.

"Morning, Luce."

"Hey, you," she murmured. His head was on the pillow next to hers and he was gazing at her with surprise in his expression.

"What time did you come back?"

"Late. Or early. Gone two anyway."

She reached out and stroked his cheek but he flinched.

"What is it?"

He rolled onto his back. "This is all so confusing, Luce. I mean... I left you last night with your ex-boyfriend. It hurt me to do that. To know that you didn't want me there with you. Then I wake up and you're in bed with me. You know... which I'm glad about, because I worry about you, and it's great to know you're here safe and all that, but even so..." He rubbed his eyes. "With things being as they are between us, I don't know where I am right now."

"I know, Dale. And I'm sorry. Last night, after I spoke to Jamie, I was called to reception and told that Petra wanted to see me. I couldn't exactly refuse; she was in such a state earlier on."

"How is she?"

"Devastated, but she's stronger than she realizes. And at least the crisis has brought her parents to her side, even if her father is channelling his anger into the legal side of things rather than just going and giving Petra a big hug, which is what she'd no doubt prefer."

"I'm sure she'll be okay."

"I hope so." Lucie took a deep breath. "I was with Jamie for a while last night… but we just had things to discuss. Things about the past."

Dale stared at the ceiling.

"Dale?"

"Don't worry about it. You didn't want me there and it wasn't my place to be there. He's your ex… I'm…"

"My friend." She propped herself up on her elbow, then wriggled closer to him. "My very best friend and you mean the world to me."

Dale glanced at her. "Thanks." Spots of colour appeared on his cheeks.

"Do you want more from me, Dale? To make our fake relationship a real one?"

He frowned as he turned to her. "What?"

"Do you?" Her heart was beating so hard she felt dizzy. And suddenly brave. She had to ask. "Do you love me?"

"I… Luce, I don't understand. I thought last night that you and Jamie were… I don't know. It's just you stopped me… when we were in bed together the night before and sometimes I just feel like I'm a yo-yo. You're sure, then you're not sure, and I can't live like that."

"So let me explain once and for all, Dale. Let me tell you about my fears and my doubts, my sorrows and my secrets. Then you can decide if you do want me."

Please want me!

"Okay, Luce. But you have to be sure about what you want too."

"I know."

She leaned forwards and kissed him gently, breathing him in.

"Let's get some coffee and breakfast then we can talk it all through properly. It's about time."

-

Lucie ordered croissants and coffee. While Dale had showered, she'd browsed the TV channels, flicking between church ceremonies and festive cartoons.

Christmas Day had arrived, as it did every year. The days turned into weeks, into months and into years. How had twenty years passed since she'd last seen her mother? How had twelve years passed since she'd broken up with Jamie? How was she thirty-three?

She stood at the window, her face pressed against the cold glass, gazing at the winter wonderland below. It was early, so it was still quiet out, but a few tiny figures moved around in the park, their figures black against the bright, white snow. The glass kept misting up. Each time she'd wipe it, then it would fog up again. Was this what kept happening with her and Dale? They'd seem to clear things up, but they'd get all foggy again, as if something was there between them, like a glass wall. Here in New York, things that she had buried, feelings she'd once denied about Dale, all seemed to resurface. It was as if the Big Apple had shown them temptation and they'd bitten into it, falling harder and harder for each other, yet still not quite letting go. Lucie knew why she'd held back and she intended to explain that to Dale. She owed him a clear explanation.

But she wondered what Dale would say. What was it that held him back? Was it just Lucie pushing him away, or was there more to it?

Breakfast arrived, delivered by a cheerful porter who wished her a very merry Christmas. She thanked him, tipped him generously, then closed the door. It was Christmas Day. Lucie and Dale were finally alone, with no possibility of being disturbed. It was time to talk, and to be brutally honest, if they had any chance of a future together as more than just friends.

In the corner, the tree lights twinkled and the fairy on top smiled, her tiny hands outstretched as if in excitement or benediction, as if she had a special Christmas wish to grant and was delighted to have the opportunity to do so.

–

Lucie took the croissants and coffee into the bedroom and found Dale sat up on the bed fully clothed. He'd opened the curtains and the room was bright with morning light.

"Good morning."

He frowned. "We've already said that, haven't we?"

"Well I wanted to say it again. Good morning, Dale, and Merry Christmas."

"Merry Christmas to you too."

Lucie poured the coffee and passed one to Dale, then handed him a plate with two fat, freshly baked croissants on it. They drank their coffee and ate the buttery croissants as Christmas carols filtered through from the TV in the lounge. Dale usually spent Christmas mornings at his parents' house, and Lucie was invited every year. She'd accepted a few times, but it depended on how she was feeling in the build-up, and until last Christmas, she hadn't been there for a few years. Instead, she'd insisted on being alone on Christmas morning, on leaving the TV turned off and not listening to the radio. But it hadn't helped to drown out what day it was. Outside her flat, car doors had slammed as people left to visit relatives or arrived to do the same. Revellers had called out festive greetings, and car stereos had blared out festive tunes. It was as if the festive season was impossible to avoid, and try as she might, Lucie could not completely forget its existence.

Last year, Dale had turned up at hers at nine am, his hair messy and his pyjamas on under his coat. He'd begged her to go over his parents' house, because whatever she felt about Christmas, he just couldn't bear to think of her alone. He'd told her that he couldn't enjoy it all if she wasn't with him. There was no way she could refuse when he was so earnest about needing her. She'd put it down to him just being his usual kind self, but now she looked back at it, perhaps it had been more than that. Had she been walking around this whole time, so caught up in the loss of her mother, and with what had happened between her and Jamie, that she refused to see what was right in front of her? The chance of true happiness with her very best friend.

Breakfast done, Dale cleared away the plates and mugs and took them into the lounge. When he returned and passed Lucie, she caught his clean citrus scent and inhaled deeply. He was delicious, and she wanted to hold him. She ached to be in his arms, but that would just confuse things. They had to talk first. Before anything else could ever happen, they had to open their hearts completely.

"I hope Petra's okay this morning," Lucie said as she quickly checked her mobile.

"I'm sure she is. She'll either still be sleeping, or Joanna will be pouring champagne and valium down her throat to numb the pain."

"I still feel bad because I knew, Dale. Tania told me, and I could have said something sooner. If I'd warned her, she might not have gone through with it and she'd have been spared the humiliation."

He shook his head. "It wasn't your place to do so. Imagine if Tania had been wrong, or just lying and Harry really had loved Petra. Then you'd have been the bad guy, the stirrer ruining their happiness. It's their business, Lucie. Much as you care about Petra, you couldn't have ruined things for her. She had to find out for herself, to see things with her own eyes, as it were."

Lucie covered her face. "Oh, and she *did* see it for herself. How absolutely terrible!" When she let her hands fall, Dale was staring at her.

"She'll be better off now. Some men aren't meant to be husbands."

His words were dark and full of meaning. "You're referring to Jamie here too, I take it?"

He nodded. "He's not a good man, Lucie."

"I know. That's what I wanted to talk to you about."

"Go on." He turned slightly, so that his knees pointed towards her and he rested his right arm on the bed head. Lucie brought her knees up and hugged them. This was not going to be easy.

As she took a deep breath and prepared to speak, there was a knock at the door. She stared at Dale, but he shrugged and shook his head.

"I'd better check who that is," she said as she slid off the bed and walked through to the lounge. When she opened the door to the suite, there was a porter stood there, holding an enormous festive flower arrangement set in a deep red basket.

"Flowers for Mr Treharne and Miss Quigley."

"Oh! Thank you. Hold on." Lucie ran into the lounge, grabbed some cash from her purse, and returned to the door. "Merry Christmas!"

"Merry Christmas to you too!" He smiled then closed the door behind him.

Lucie took the flowers into the bedroom.

"That's what you call a flower arrangement, right?" Dale helped her put the basket on the ottoman at the foot of the bed. "Who's it from?"

Lucie took the card from an envelope that was tied to a silver twig. "It says: 'Merry Christmas Dale and Lucie. May this be the first of many that you enjoy as a couple. Lots of love, Mum and Dad XXX'."

"They must be missing us." He fingered a sprig of mistletoe.

"They probably are."

"I'll ring them later. Once we've talked."

"Yes. Good plan."

They went back to sit on the bed.

"Dale, I've never told anyone this before. I couldn't. Not even you. And not because I don't trust you, but because I was afraid of how you'd react... what you'd do."

He inclined his head slightly but his eyes had darkened.

"Well, you know more than anyone how Christmas has always been hard for me. I mean, after losing my mum on Christmas Eve, I just couldn't enjoy the festivities. When I was with Jamie at university, I fell for him hard. After... we... you and I... what happened... I just fell in love with him very quickly. It was that young, innocent infatuation and it carried me along for two intense years."

"This isn't easy to listen to, Luce." He picked at a nail, his Adam's apple bobbing hard.

"I know, and I'm sorry. I just want to explain it all to you, fully. So you can understand."

"Okay."

"So with things being as they were with my father and stepmother, I just felt rootless. Being with Jamie and living his glamorous lifestyle lifted me from it all for a while. I felt a part of something, almost as if I wasn't me. I believed that I belonged, that I could fit into his world."

"I can understand why you'd want that. It was when I missed you most, though."

"I know that now. And I'm sorry for neglecting you then, Dale. I never stopped thinking of you or wondering how you were. I guess I was just trying not to be me. Anyway, two years along and things were okay-ish between us. He wasn't exactly a model boyfriend but I was happy to accept the scraps he gave me, because I was young and vulnerable, needy for what he represented. I thought he loved me, and that was enough to keep things going. Until the Christmas after I graduated. When I went to stay with him in his family cottage in North Wales. It was just us and a few of his friends." The room darkened suddenly and small shadows appeared on the walls, floating softly downwards. "It's snowing again." She nodded at the window. "It was snowing that year too. Heavily. We had the most awful blizzard that Christmas Eve, it just came in from nowhere and went on for hours. Jamie and his friends had been drinking all day. I didn't have anything to drink until later on, but it seemed to affect me quickly. I hadn't eaten much and I was upset. It had only been eight years since I'd lost Mum and the grief was building."

"Luce, I'm not sure I like where this is going." His jaw was set, his knuckles white.

"Please keep calm and hear me out. I need to tell you now. I can't live with this secret any longer."

"It was dark really early because of the snow. Kind of like today. I was a bit upset because some sentimental film on TV had brought everything back. And Jamie was drunk. Really drunk. I asked him to stop drinking, but he refused. His friends were the same, all laughing and downing shots and boasting about women they'd shagged, or intended to shag. The atmosphere there changed. It became edgy. And I didn't like it. But I was trapped."

Dale got up then and walked to the window. He stared out across Central Park as Lucie watched, his shoulders tense, his hands clenching and unclenching. "Why didn't you tell me this before?"

"Why do you think? You would have gone after him. Hurt him and got yourself into trouble. I know you, Dale, and I know you couldn't have lived with it. It's different now, though."

He turned to her. "How is it? He ignored you when you were upset and he should have been punished for that."

Lucie shook her head and patted the coverlet. "Please sit back down."

He did but he kept one foot on the floor as if he needed to anchor himself in some way.

"In the end, I went to bed about nine o'clock. I thought they could drink themselves to sleep. I couldn't drop off at first. I was jumpy, afraid even, though I kept telling myself not to be silly; that this was my boyfriend and his friends and I wasn't in any danger. But at some point in the night, I drifted off. I only woke up when Maxwell, one of Jamie's friends, was standing over me."

"Oh Luce." Dale covered her hand with his. "I can't stand this."

Her throat was tight and her heart thundered at the memory. "He stank of booze. As he leant over me, it was so potent it made me gag. My head was fuzzy with sleep and from the alcohol I'd drunk. He climbed onto the bed and tried to pull my pyjama bottoms down. I was half asleep, Dale, and I tried to stop him."

"I'll find him and kill him."

"No. No." She shook her head. "He got angry because I wouldn't let him and he slapped me around the face. Then he tore my top open and grabbed me. It hurt and I was terrified." She paused, hating talking about that night because it was a blackness that she'd never wanted to recall. "He kept trying to pull my pyjamas down but I hung onto them for dear life. I couldn't fight him because I was afraid that if I let go, he'd get me naked."

"Bloody hell, Luce, this is awful." Dale's face had blanched.

"But suddenly, something snapped. I was filled with hot anger, fury like I'd never experienced before and I completely lost it. I screamed and reached around me until I grabbed onto something then I brought it down hard. I hit him again and again and again. Something gave beneath my blows and there was hot liquid gushing everywhere." She looked down and realized that Dale was holding both of her hands in his. Hers were lost there, tiny in his grasp, but all she felt when he held her was safe. She knew he'd never hurt her.

"So he didn't…"

"No. I knocked him clean out. I slid from under him, which was not easy considering that he was out cold. I dressed quickly, even putting my boots on. When I went into the bathroom, I locked the door and turned on the light. It was then that I saw the blood. So much blood. I cleaned my face, hair and hands, which wasn't easy because I was trembling so badly, then I went back into the bedroom. Cautiously. I saw what I'd grabbed. It was one of those fancy bronze paperweights in the shape of a bulldog. It was where I'd left it, on the pillow next to Maxwell. I picked it up again then nudged him a few times to check if he was alive. He was, but his nose was pretty smashed up and there was a wide cut over his right eye."

"I hope you left the loser there."

"I did. I went downstairs and found Jamie passed out under the table. I shook him until he woke up and told him what had happened. I was just worried Maxwell would die in his sleep or something. He'd been so drunk. Besides, I felt guilty."

"*You* felt guilty?" Dale's eyes widened.

"Of course. Don't all victims? I sat in the kitchen next to the knifeblock for the rest of the night, holding the bulldog as if it was some kind of talisman. I felt guilty, because I'd trusted Jamie and loved him and wanted to be something I wasn't. I felt guilty for getting drunk and crying over my mother again and for not realizing how badly things could go. I felt guilty for being weak, for what I'd done to you when I went away and because we never spoke again about what had happened between us. I felt guilty for hating my Mum. I felt guilty for everything, Dale. And that, apart from losing my mother, was my blackest Christmas ever."

"What happened then?"

"They all woke up in the morning with one hell of a hangover. Maxwell had a black eye and a broken nose. He was so full of remorse, said he was mortified at what he'd tried to do and asked me to forgive him. But I couldn't. And when Jamie begged me to forgive him, I couldn't do that either. He failed to protect me, let one of his friends think I was fair game."

"Why didn't you report it, Luce? Maxwell should have gone to jail for that, and Jamie should've been punished too."

"I'd let him believe I could be treated like that, like some kind of nothing, I guess, and I was embarrassed too. I couldn't bear to tell anyone about that night, so I just said that he'd broken my heart and let people read into that what they wanted."

"Oh, Lucie."

"I know. Do you think less of me?"

He tightened his hands around hers. "Of course not. I just hate that I wasn't there to protect you. I mean, you were assaulted, Luce. No man should get away with that. What if he did it to someone else?"

Tears stung her eyes as Dale voiced her thoughts. "Don't you think I've asked myself that a million times? It's gone round and round in my head. I should have reported him but I was so ashamed, Dale. I wondered if it was all my fault, if I'd done something to make Jamie's friends believe it was okay to do that to me. Did I look at Maxwell the wrong way, or encourage him with a smile or the wrong body language? I was consumed with guilt and anger and despair. So I came home."

"To me?"

"And you helped me. Even though you didn't know exactly what had happened, you helped me."

"I thought he'd cheated on you or something, though. Not let his friend attack you."

"I know. And I'm sorry. I should have been honest. But it was such a mess. And with time, with all my reading, and with work, I was able to try to put it behind me. I didn't see Jamie or any of his friends again so I put it out of my mind, apart from the odd thought that I always suppressed quickly. Until the wedding rehearsal dinner."

"He still needs to pay."

"But I think he has done. See, that's why he wanted to talk to me. I left him there that Christmas day. I took his car and drove to a hotel, and I stayed there all over Christmas. I cried, and I thought, and I cried some more. And I refused to answer his calls. I emailed him and told him where to find his car, then I came back to Tonbridge and rebuilt my life. In the meantime, he was destroying his own."

"The wheelchair?"

She nodded. "He told me that he threw himself into drinking, drugs and adrenaline sports. He went off around the world travelling and took big risks. He was consumed with guilt. Then one day, he fell while climbing. It broke his back, leaving him unable to walk. It was his way of punishing himself." She sighed and laced her fingers through Dale's. "Since then, he's been involved in charity work. It sounds so clichéd, I know, but I don't think he was completely bad. I wonder if anyone is, to be honest.

Are we actually black and white or do we have shades? I know that I shocked myself when I fought back. Something deep inside me, some primal instinct kicked in and I fought for my life. I could have killed that creep, Dale, if I hadn't stopped when I did."

"He deserved it."

"Perhaps. But it took me a while to come to terms with that. To know that I'm capable of such violence."

"You're strong. I told you that, and you were fighting for your life that night. If he'd actually hurt you, then I dread to think how things would have turned out."

"But he didn't. And I'm okay."

He nodded but his eyes glistened and Lucie could see that he had struggled hearing the truth. As she had always known he would.

"There's more."

"There is?"

"Best get it all out right?"

"I guess."

"Can I have a hug first?"

"Of course you can."

He moved further onto the bed with his back against the headboard and opened his arms. Lucie went to him, curling up against him, sliding her arms around him. As she listened to the steady beat of his heart, she knew that she'd done the right thing. She didn't want anything to come between her and Dale. She needed him to know her inside out. Because he deserved nothing less than everything she had to give.

Dale held Lucie tightly. His heart was thundering and he knew she could hear it, but she would understand. What she'd been through because of Jamie Davenport horrified him. Even though Jamie no longer had the use of his legs, Dale still wanted to go and punch him, to make him feel some of the terror that Lucie had suffered that Christmas. She was so brave about it all, her courage and ability to go on left him in awe.

"Dale?" She lifted her head.

"Yes."

"I'm ready to tell you the rest now."

"Okay." His stomach lurched. He didn't know how much more he could stand to hear.

"This isn't to do with Jamie though. This goes way back."

"Your mum?"

She nodded. "There are things I haven't told you about her. Reasons why I've always been so afraid of being hurt, of not being good enough. With Jamie, I believed I wasn't good enough, and that meant that I could cope with his indifference. But with you, Dale, I couldn't bear to feel that I wasn't what you wanted. We have such a good friendship that I've always been terrified of ruining it."

"I get that, Luce. After we… you know… then you went off to uni, I didn't know how to behave; what to do for the best. I fell hard for you that summer, and when it seemed like you'd rejected me, I almost went crazy. I missed you so much."

"I missed you too." Her eyes filled with tears and one escaped and trickled down her cheek. He reached out and smoothed it away with his thumb.

"My mother didn't just die that day, Dale."

"She didn't?"

"She was leaving us."

"Leaving you and your dad?"

"Yes. She left a note."

"She left you on Christmas Eve with just a note?"

"My dad and I were making mince pies but we ran out of flour, so we popped out to the shops before they closed. She must have had it all planned. Dad always insisted he'd bought enough flour with the weekly shop. Afterwards, he admitted that he suspected she'd thrown it out so we'd need to go shopping, thus clearing the way for her to go. When we got back, the house was silent. There was a brief note propped up by the kettle."

"And you never told anyone this before?"

She shook her head. "I was ashamed. I mean, if my own *mother* would run off and leave me behind, then I must be really unlovable, right?"

"That is so wrong, Lucie. But I understand where you're coming from. What did the note say?"

"That she was sorry. She never meant for it to happen, but she'd fallen out of love with my dad and in love with another man. Thinking about it now, it must have been even harder on Dad because she also said that she was pregnant. Imagine how he felt reading that, after they'd lost my brother and never conceived again – whether deliberate or not."

275

"Your poor father."

"He was devastated. But he couldn't fall apart. He had me to look after. It gets worse."

"It does?"

"Her boyfriend picked her up, but he'd been out drinking after work. It was Christmas Eve, so I guess he got caught up the festive spirit and just had one too many. Driving across town, he hit a patch of ice and crashed head on into a tree."

Dale watched her as she told the story. Her face was blank, as if she'd rehearsed this moment many times. "Lucie, have you thought about telling me this before?"

"Many times. I've practised the whole thing... the idea of confiding in you was so appealing. But as time went on, it just seemed harder to do. I suppressed it, pushed it right down deep inside and at times, I actually wondered if maybe I'd dreamt it all."

"I'm glad you're telling me now."

She smiled sadly. "Me too."

"So why'd she pick Christmas Eve? Couldn't she have waited until the new year? Seen out one last Christmas with you."

She shook her head. "Apparently not. Because she was pregnant and evidently overwhelmed by the urgency to leave. Dad told me that he thought she was just getting a bit fat. But no, she was carrying my half brother, or sister. Leaving me in order to build a new life with my sibling and her lover."

"I'm so sorry, Luce."

"It was easier to let everyone think she'd just been killed in a car accident. To tell people that she was killed as she left us was just too difficult. Dad and I agreed to keep it quiet."

"But, Luce, you were only thirteen. He should never have expected you to keep that a secret."

She shrugged. "I grew up quickly that day." She hung her head and rubbed the back of her neck. "As you know, my dad suffered. He became quite depressed and it took him a few years to even begin going out again. He went to work, came home, drank three beers, and went to bed. Like a robot. I never wanted that life for him. I was terrified of having that life myself. So when he did meet Thelma, I was happy for him."

"Even though she wasn't always too happy about you?" Dale gently stroked each finger of her hand in turn.

"No, she wasn't. My grumpy stepmother and the ugly sisters. My life is such a cliché." She sighed. "So there you have it."

"You've been through so much, Luce."

"More than some, less than others. But now you have a clear picture of why I hated Christmas."

He nodded. "Hated?"

"Until this year."

"Really?"

"Yes, Dale. You came all this way with me and have done so much to make it perfect."

"The wedding didn't exactly go smoothly."

"No, but that certainly wasn't your fault. Or mine."

"I guess not."

"But what about you, Dale? Do you dislike me, now you know that I smashed a man's face in with a bulldog ornament? Now you know that my mother didn't love me enough to stick around?"

Dale paused and took a deep breath. As he released it, he cupped her chin in his palms. "Lucie, I could never dislike you. I am sad that you've carried all of this round on your own for so long. Sad that you didn't tell me before, but I understand why. It's traumatic enough for a child to be abandoned by a parent, let alone to be attacked like that, and by their boyfriend's mate. I don't know how you've managed to hold it all together all this time."

"I do."

"You do?"

"I had you. Even when you didn't know all the gory details, you still knew some of it. And deep down, I suspect that you had an idea there might be more."

"I did wonder why your mum was in a car with another man, after it was reported in the papers, but I didn't want to ask and make your pain worse. Just in case you hadn't thought about it yourself. And as for Jamie… Well, I just thought he'd cheated on you and you'd caught him but were too embarrassed to say."

"You've been my rock."

"You've been mine too, Luce. I'm always happiest when I'm with you. When I'm not, I'm thinking about you."

"But this is risky, right?"

He nodded. "We have a lot to lose here. If we become more than friends, then we risk losing our friendship if things don't work out. Lucie... I need to tell you something too."

"You do?"

"I fell deeply in love with you after that day at my house, when we made love for the first time. I couldn't help myself. You were my... my first."

"I was?"

"Yes. Couldn't you tell?"

"I had a hunch, but we were young, I didn't expect you to be all that experienced."

He gave a small laugh. "It tore me apart when you went away."

"I'm so sorry."

"When you got together with Jamie, I was so mad at you. I didn't think he was good enough for you, but I wouldn't have thought anyone was. Not even me."

"Really?"

"You were so bright, so well read, so ambitious. You had plans, Luce, and I didn't want to hold you back by getting all clingy. So I backed off."

"If you'd just told me how you felt..."

"Would it have changed anything?"

She sighed. "I don't know. I was a different person back then. Life shapes us, eh?"

"It sure does."

They sat in silence for a while, staring at the wall where the shadows of snowflakes swirled. The television in the lounge now played some Christmas service, complete with readings and carols. Dale flexed his legs and fingers then turned to Lucie.

"The way I see it is that we have two choices. We give this a go. Which is my favourite option." He smiled. "Or we don't. We just stay friends."

"I like option one the best but… what if it doesn't work out?"

"Can you imagine that happening?"

"No." She grinned as she shuffled closer to him. "What I can't imagine is not waking up with you every day. I can't stand the thought of seeing you with another woman. And I couldn't bear not being able to kiss you now that I know how good it feels."

"I think," he said, as Lucie ran a hand over his arm, causing goosebumps to spring up on his skin, "that staying just friends will be far too tough on us now."

"Mainly because we'd have to break the news of our fake breakup to your parents." Lucie slipped her arms around his neck.

"Exactly. And that would be a trial to go through indeed. Mum would be devastated."

"She really would." Lucie slid onto his lap and moved her face closer to his so that their noses almost touched. "So I vote we don't do that. I don't want to break Glenda's heart."

"Deal. Now… How about we start this day over again?"

"Sounds like a good plan to me. Hold on!" She crawled down the bed to the flower arrangement and pulled out a sprig of mistletoe then held it over her head.

"Merry Christmas, Dale Treharne."

"Merry Christmas, Lucie Quigley."

Dale leaned forwards and kissed her softly.

And as the snow continued to fall outside, muffling the sounds of the world as it covered everything with a thick, white blanket, and the fairy on the tree smiled as her dress sparkled in the flashing lights, and the carollers on the television gathered to celebrate the festive occasion, Lucie snuggled up with the man she'd always loved, and finally understood why Christmas could be the best time of the year.

Epilogue

"I'd forgotten how beautiful it is here." Lucie held tightly onto Dale's arm as they walked into Central Park.

"Me too. It's absolutely perfect. I'm so happy that we've come back."

Snow had fallen heavily the night before and everything was white. The trees either side of the walkway were black against the steely sky and all sounds seemed muted, except for the tweets and warbles of those birds brave enough to remain in the park through the winter months.

"Wait up, you two!" Glenda called as she hurried behind them, dragging Hank in her wake.

"I can't believe that's the Dakota just across the road," Hank said, his eyes wide with excitement.

"We were like that last year, Dad. It's amazing seeing Manhattan for the first time."

"It's just as amazing seeing it for the second time," Lucie added.

Lucie breathed deeply of the icy air and a thrill ran through her. They'd saved hard for months to make a return trip to Manhattan, something that had been made easier by paying just one mortgage, as Dale had finished his house renovations in August and Lucie had moved in with him. She was still getting used to living somewhere so spacious after being at her flat, but at the end of every day she experienced a wave of excitement, knowing she'd soon be heading home to Dale.

Glenda and Hank had been keen to accompany them to New York ever since they'd been asked. It was a first for Glenda, being away from her family over the festive season, but since Lucie and Dale had returned from New York last December gushing about their trip, she had vowed to try new things, including travelling further afield. They'd arrived in the city two days ago and were staying at a very nice hotel just five minutes' walk from Central Park. It wasn't The Plaza, and it wasn't as luxurious as the hotel they'd stayed in the previous Christmas, but it was in a good location and had everything they needed. Its rate was reasonable, which meant that they'd be able to do some Christmas shopping too.

They stopped in Strawberry Fields in front of the Imagine mosaic. Just like last year, the ground around it was covered in snow, but someone had wiped the centre clean.

This time last year when they'd stood here, things had been so different. For starters, Petra had been about to get married, but after catching Harry in the toilets with Tania, she had decided to make some big changes in her life. Petra was currently backpacking around the world, courtesy of her employer, and the monthly emails she sent

Lucie suggested that she was having a fabulous time. As for Lucie, she was still working at St. Clotilde's, but she was also doing an Open University Masters in Creative Writing, which she was thoroughly enjoying. She wasn't sure yet what direction the qualification would take her in, but it was exciting knowing that there would be possibilities available to her.

"Imagine." Hank rubbed the toe of his boot over the edge of the mosaic. "I've always wanted to see this. Thanks for inviting us. I don't think we'd have got round to coming out here if you hadn't asked. Right, Glenda?"

She shook her head. "It was something we talked about years ago, but then with having the boys and being so busy, we accepted that we probably never would."

"Life is for living, Mum and Dad. I told you this."

"I did worry about leaving everyone over Christmas, but Helen said she'd be fine going to her parents' this year and, well… as for Ieuan, he's probably having a great time in the Maldives with Barry."

"Things change, Mum. They can't stay the same forever." Dale patted his mother's shoulder. "Anyway… I have something I need to attend to."

Lucie caught a look between Dale and his mother. Something was going on.

Dale walked to the centre of the mosaic and took a deep breath then released it slowly.

"Dale, what are you doing? You look like you're about to recite Shakespeare or something."

"No, my darling. Not quite." He pointed at the mosaic beneath his feet. "Lucie Quigley… Imagine a man and a woman who've been friends all their lives. Since they were very young children. Can you do that?"

Lucie chewed her bottom lip. People had stopped walking and were staring at Dale as if he was taking part in street theatre.

"Lucie! Answer him," Glenda said.

"Oh. Yes, Dale. I can imagine that."

"Okay then. Now imagine that they went all the way to Manhattan for a winter wedding one year and during that trip, they finally admitted how they felt about each other."

"I can do that," she said.

"Now... Imagine if one year later, the couple made a return trip to New York. And..." Dale dropped to his knees. "The man told his girlfriend how much he loved her, how much he'd always loved her, and asked her to be his wife." He reached into his coat pocket and brought out a small black box. "How'd you think that might go, Luce?"

Lucie looked into his big brown eyes. She felt light and floaty, as if she were made of gossamer and at any moment she'd be carried away on the breeze.

Dale opened the box and there, in the centre of a cream satin cushion was a ring. Lucie moved closer and gasped. "It's just like my pendant." She fingered the tiny silver book with an opal heart on its cover, that Dale had given her last Christmas.

"Yes, Lucie. I had it made especially to match."

"It's a silver band set with diamonds, and the heart is an opal," Glenda interrupted. "Isn't it beautiful?"

"Mum!" Dale frowned at Glenda. "Shhh!"

"Sorry!" Glenda placed a gloved finger over her lips.

"Lucie, I cannot *imagine* my life without you. Will you please be my wife?"

Lucie glanced at the crowd of people who'd gathered around the mosaic. Every pair of eyes flicked between her and Dale.

She crossed the space between them and held out her hand. "Yes, Dale. Of course I'll be your wife!"

He pulled off her glove, and slid the band onto her ring finger, then he stood up and Lucie fell into his arms.

As their lips met and Dale swung her off her feet, the crowd erupted into applause.

When they finally stopped kissing and Dale lowered Lucie to her feet, she held up her left hand and gazed at the ring. It shone as she moved her hand from side to side.

"I've never seen anything more beautiful, Dale."

"I have."

"Really?" She met his eyes.

"Of course. You – my bride-to-be!"

"Congratulations!" Glenda and Hank enveloped them both in a hug, and the crowd of onlookers began to disperse.

"Now then… how's about champagne at The Plaza?" Hank asked. "Our treat!"

"That sounds fabulous, Dad. We'll catch you up."

Hank and Glenda walked off.

Something cold landed on Lucie's nose. She looked up. Snowflakes floated down from the sky, white and feathered, cold and wet.

"I'm sure she knows," Dale whispered, as he pulled her close. "Wherever she is."

"I think she does," Lucie replied, her heart full of emotion. Dale knew her so well.

"Merry Christmas, Lucie Quigley."

"Merry Christmas, Dale Treharne. You know... I thought last year was my best Christmas ever! But I think this one even beats that."

"Really?" His eyes sparkled as he scanned her face.

"Really."

Then, hand in hand, they crunched through the snow, headed for The Plaza to celebrate their engagement and to enjoy a very merry Manhattan Christmas.